Praise for *Shy Girl*

"*Shy Girl* is worth reading for its lovely depictions of San Francisco, its gritty girl-on-girl encounters, and the way it weaves a multi-generational lesbian community throughout the story. This is Elizabeth Stark's first novel; I'll definitely be waiting with anticipation for her second."
—Lambda Book Report

"The indelible experience of first love and the haunting presence of secrets that cannot be shared are the central issues in Stark's probing, candid, often touching . . . debut novel." —Publishers Weekly

"[A] real triumph . . . Stark is clear in her 20-20 vision of relations between friends, parents and children." —Bay Area Reporter

"An entirely compelling novel, a gentle and ultimately heart-breaking page-turner that excavates the silences surrounding the lives of a pair of very intriguing young women."
—Bob Shacochis, author of *Swimming in the Volcano*

"Impressive . . . Elizabeth Stark looks with sensitivity and compassion at whether living with a lie is ever justified in the struggle to survive."
—San Francisco Chronicle

Shy Girl

ELIZABETH STARK

Seal Press
SEATTLE

First Seal Press edition, November 2000

Seal Press is located at 3131 Western Avenue, Suite 410, Seattle, Washington 98121. Visit our website at www.sealpress.com.

Cover design by Kathleen Kincaid

Library of Congress Cataloging-in-Publication Data
Stark, Elizabeth, 1970–
    Shy Girl / Elizabeth Stark—1st Seal Press ed.
       p. cm.
    ISBN 1-58005-047-6 (paper)
       1. Young Women—Fiction. 2. Lesbians—Fiction. I. Title.

PS3569.T335736 S49 2000
813'.54—dc21   00-064100

Printed in Canada

10   9   8   7   6   5   4   3   2   1

Distributed to the trade by Publishers Group West
In Canada: Publishers Group West Canada, Toronto, Ontario

For

Twyla, who showed me things I could only imagine
and things I could not imagine at all;
Ernesto, who doesn't need this book to be a legend

Shy Girl

ONE

There was a girl in Alta's bed when the phone rang, a girl all red-haired and fair-skinned and fleshy, which is to say, nothing like Shy. And that's just the way Alta wanted it. She was tired of trying to turn a vague resemblance into desire, tired of playing hide-and-seek between memories worn thin and a stranger's familiar face. They say things get easier in time and people forget. Yes, everything had changed, and for the better, but she remembered it all.

Alta smelled the girl on her hands even as she crossed the room. She thought it might be Renny, her best friend, calling, or one of any number of girls who had her phone number on business cards or lipstick-blotted scraps of cocktail napkin. She didn't care who was waiting at the other end. The girl was watching her and she liked it, liked her eyes from across the room, which was what she'd noticed about her last night before she'd brought her home. Pat, the bartender, had winked as they left. "People can always tell who Alta's gone home with," she'd said behind them, "because a shadow of her silhouette is burned into the wall."

"Hello?" Alta spoke as if she were saying it to the girl and as if it were the first thing she'd said to her. She was already replaying newness, one morning after one night, and she knew she'd never touch her again, not on purpose, after the girl left in an hour or so.

"Hello, Alta." Her mother.

"Hello," Alta echoed numbly, though it struck her as funny that if she could manage to call her Mother, the girl might think Mrs. C. phoned Alta as a matter of course on any random day. "To what do I owe this privilege? What's wrong?"

Mrs. C. ignored Alta's irony. "It's about Shy's mother, Mrs. Mallon."

The leaves outside kept bouncing in the wind, the cars moved by. Her mother spoke calmly, good-deed church voice taut over what sounded to Alta like triumph or at least a certainty about the order and rightness of events, a trait Mrs. C. called faith and Alta called rigor mortis. Mrs. Mallon was the one good thing from Alta's past that had made its way forward to her present.

"What happened? Is she okay?"

Alta held her breath the way Shy used to make her do when they'd pass through tunnels and under bridges, holding their feet off the ground, counting seconds in their heads. Those days when they still believed that they had mystic power over fate and that wishes could be held the way you hold your breath.

"I'm calling from the hospital, St. Luke's. They think it's some kind of stroke. At this point she can't talk or move, really."

Alta sat down on the edge of the chair by her desk. The girl wrapped the sheet under her arms and hugged her knees so Alta could see her freckled back, the curve of her spine.

"Everything okay?" she mouthed.

Alta shook her head and looked out the window. The day was so bright the few clouds glowed, and the dust on her windows was dappled by the shadows of bobbing leaves.

"She collapsed on her front lawn this morning. I came out and found her lying there. Lucky I was on my way to work, wasn't it? I had to call 911. They wanted to take her to Hamilton, but I convinced them St. Luke's was at least as close. They have to go by regulations, you know. I said she was Catholic, though if you ask me she wasn't much of one. Well, that's between her and God now, I'd say."

"What do you mean by that?"

"Hmm?"

"You mean she's dying?"

The girl got up and padded down the hall.

"I just mean she can't talk."

"I'm going to see her right now. St. Luke's is just off the frontage road, right?" Alta's father had died there when she was too little to know the way.

"Well, listen here, Alta. You'd best call Shy, because I don't have her number. She gave it to me when she was here for her dad's funeral, but I didn't hold on to it." Mr. Mallon had died three years before. Alta had been away at a special weeklong work retreat, and Shy'd left before she got back.

"You know I haven't seen her since long before that."

"Listen, Alta. They've been asking me all sorts of questions about her medical history, and, to be honest with you—and I told them this—I've lived next door to the woman for sixteen years and I don't even know her maiden name. Nothing. I can leave it in the hands of Father Hobin, but I don't see what more he can do. She's still in emergency, but they're going to have to move her up to intensive care, and they're going to need her insurance information, at the least. I know you go in and out of that house as you please, and Shy's number must be in there somewhere, don't you think? Dr. Gilbert has been very patient with my absence today, but I've got to get to work. He hardly knows how to function without me."

"I'll see what I can do." Suddenly, Alta was a child again, not trying hard enough, never pleasing her.

"Tell Shy I'd like to see her if she comes. She can stay here if she wants, but then that whole big house is empty next door, so she won't have need of a place, will she? But tell her to be sure to visit me."

"Of course she'll come—"

"Oh, and Alta, don't ride your motorcycle into the neighborhood. It draws a kind of attention to yourself that isn't right. I still have to live here, you know."

And then Alta was listening to the empty phone line.

The girl came back, naked, with a cup of coffee in her hands. "Careful—it's hot," she said.

"Aren't you an angel." Alta took a big sip, scorching her tongue and throat. She pulled the girl down on her knee. Suddenly bodies seemed to be electric conveyors of memory and mood, dangerous to touch. Alta had an uncomfortable urge to confide in the girl. She couldn't tell her about Shy and Mrs. Mallon. She had abandoned her childhood, except for Mrs. Mallon. She had trained herself in the hasty rhythms of this lovely city, its lusts and brawls and mini-tragedies stretched over a several-mile radius that extended into the Bay and then across that rusty brace at the mouth of the ocean and into its gray waters.

If she'd had time, she'd have drawn pictures for the girl of her life here, to remind herself that it was real, more real than Shy, more real than the past—it had to be, being the present, right? She brought home girls, elegant, playful, delicious girls, not for the sex, though she enjoyed that, too, but for the chance, half asleep afterward, to tell them the stories of her days, of her adventures, of her friends. She made them laugh, she held them as they fell asleep, yet, still, she had never told the real stories.

Tomorrow she would return to work, to her everyday routine of flesh and piercings, the present as she had created it, but Mrs. Mallon was the underpinning of all that was most important to her, and whatever Alta could do to fix everything, she would do.

"Would you like to go for a ride?" she asked the red-haired, eager girl. "I have some business I have to take care of, and I'd welcome company."

And of course, because Alta wanted her to, because Alta knew she would, for no other reason than that Alta was Alta, with heat in her hands, heat in her eyes, a way with women and words, the girl said, simply and without need of convincing, "Yes."

In California it's possible to ignore winter—a few weeks of rain, shut your eyes tight and it's done; the sun reappears, the sky is brighter, if possible, than it was. It's hotter across the bridge than in San Francisco. In the City the fog layers the cool over even the most unbearable heat. But go east, and the world is baked yellow, cracked dry. Alta's thirst when she lived there was immense. Shy and she would mix pitcher after pitcher of lemonade. They agreed exactly on the amount of sugar needed to cut the bitterness without dispelling it altogether.

San Francisco itself seemed to quench Alta's thirst, even as it stirred her hunger for things she'd only imagined and things she'd never imagined at all. The day sparkled across the waters on either side of them as they crossed the bridge—brilliant, harsh handfuls of light shot back from the rippled surface. Alta's Honda 450, with its straight black seat and what was left of the red trim, gleamed and grew hot. The girl held on to Alta lightly—at least it felt light to her because it was a purely physical hold. Just the thrill of the ride. The gravelly roll of roads buzzed in Alta's bones. She knew every inch of these roads, because she'd used them to put distance between herself and that place she'd once called home.

"Little place near San Francisco." That's what she used to tell people when they asked her where she had grown up. "Little place not far from here." In the last couple of years, people seemed to assume she'd sprung up full-grown in the City. Some people wonder about the kind of childhood that creates a person like Alta, but the wise ones wonder what kind of childhood didn't destroy her.

When she was very young her father would hold her hand while she was falling asleep. The skin of his palm felt reassuring and rough. She loved its warmth against the cool cotton of her pillowcase. After he died she had dolls and teddy bears, but none of them measured up to the sour-sweet smell of mothballs and beer and Old Spice, the low-down timbre of his voice that lulled her into a trance. She wanted to be just like him. When he died, the only space where she was just fine caved right in. Her cowboy outfit would disappear for weeks at a time, as if she might forget in the meanwhile who she was and what she wanted. Her Star Wars action figures were replaced with fuzzy toy mice in outfits of purple and black lace. The onslaught of dolls began. Nothing comforted her like her daddy's hand in hers until the first night she held Shy in her arms. Maybe Alta had learned the irrevocable lessons of loss and need before she ever met Shy. But her childhood was a fire that was trying to destroy everything that mattered to her about herself, and she buried herself in Shy so she wouldn't get smoke in her lungs, so she could keep on breathing every day.

Everything slowed as they went east: the speed of the traffic as if a cop were close by, the sound of the wind, the smiles, if they came at all. There were lies Alta told herself when she was riding; she liked to think that she was free, that she could turn on the road and head in any direction, go. The truth was, she couldn't go anywhere. Her face might as well have been printed on WANTED flyers in post offices for all the sanctuary she was given, even by those who had brought her into this world with no guarantees. Her life was full, plenty of girls and no shortage of business, but she crossed the boundaries of that world at risk. It was more than a mere disadvantage: her life was endangered every time.

"Mrs. Mallon, Mrs. Mallon," she chanted into the oncoming wind. She tried to imagine the woman who had become her friend lying in a hospital bed. But the Mrs. Mallon of her childhood had always seemed familiar with death, and it was she who came to Alta now. Her eyes were the darkest blue Alta had ever seen, clouded and full of sorrow. Alta thought of the meals Mrs. Mallon used to cook— strange dishes so different from the meatloaf and boiled vegetables of Mrs. C.'s kitchen—and the way they ate those meals in silence. Mrs. Mallon scared Alta in those days, but her rare, effortful smile encour-aged Alta to believe that the sweet and sour of her food were as much an unspoken message as Shy's closed-eyed sighs in the nights. At that time, Alta was forced to take what communication she could from the small gestures of the living—the way she would wake up in the night with Shy's body pressed against hers and once or twice Shy's shirt found bunched at the bottom of the blankets and all her skin under Alta's eager, careful hands; the way Shy looked at her occasionally when they were alone, her eyes staying on Alta's, not turning away, scarcely blinking, so that Alta sensed that Shy's longing for her might be as real as hers was for Shy.

Alta always thought memories pressed harder than the present. She didn't let many people matter to her now the way the people from her past had mattered: her father, Shy, Mrs. Mallon, her mother, her little cousins. They had all mattered before she even understood what that meant. Then they were gone; or rather, she was gone, but it amounted to the same thing.

Well, that was all the past, the pain and the comfort of it, she told herself, running one gloved hand behind her up the girl's thigh. She'd do what she could for Shy, who, even with all the anguish she'd caused, had made the years of her childhood and adolescence as bearable as they had been, and she'd see if she could do anything at all for Mrs. Mallon, who had reached through her own sorrow and shown Alta a way out. And then she'd leave again, as soon as she was finished, and be free of it—free of it all, if she could.

The first time Shy came over to play, all disheveled and tan, her family had just moved in next door and she had a rash from poison oak on her left arm. She and Alta sat on either side of the old, worn couch where Alta's father had slept the last months of his life, when he was too tired to move, even in the daytime. There were red bumps all over the skin from her wrist to her elbow. Alta couldn't look at them.

The girl had seemed more appealing when the moving van had first arrived, and Alta had watched her from her hall window until her mother had caught her and said, "Isn't it exciting that another little girl is moving in next door?"

The girl was nine and Alta was seven, though she was only one year ahead of Alta in school because her mother had started her late. The school, which was part of their church, had already told Mrs. C. about the Mallons' arrival. Alta hated when her mother said that: "another little girl"—words all full of her push for Alta to become

one, too. Her mother had always wanted a little girl, she used to tell
Alta, as if this were a sign of love. It took her longer than Alta's
father to accept that she hadn't exactly gotten what she wanted.
Alta began to dread this little girl's visit; she was such a pretty girl.
Even as a child, Shy was delicate and strong at the same time, a com-
bination Alta's mother longed for in her.

Then she was here. "Let's chase my cat," Alta suggested, turning
her eyes away from the rash. Old Spike sat in the window licking a
patchwork face. Slowly, they got up and tiptoed over toward the
unsuspecting creature. Shy was already several inches taller than
Alta. When they were halfway there, Spike raised an eye to them,
paw midair. They burst into giggles and ran toward the cat, who
plopped off the sill and scurried away. They followed, down the hall
and into the bedroom. The cat dove under Mrs. C.'s big bed. Shy and
Alta lay on their stomachs and watched. Spike settled low on
bristling haunches and eyed them. They waited. Alta noticed Shy's
lips parted for huffs of breath, then the bumps on her arm again.

"Here, Spike, come on girl," Alta called.

"He's a girl?"

Their eyes met and they giggled.

"Spike?" They rolled over, laughing.

Spike bolted. They followed. Up, out the door, down the hall.
They ran right into Mrs. C. Spike slipped around her ankles and
outside.

"What are you girls doing?"

She stared down at them—Shy all tall and skinny, and Alta with
her father's dark eyes and hair, even a bit of his tummy hanging over
her cowboy pants.

"Leave Kitty alone, you hear? She's an old cat now."

They were sent back to the couch. Alta stared at Shy's arm and
inched away from her.

"Is that catching?" Alta asked.

Shy shook her head. "Not anymore."

Alta moved farther away. She didn't want Shy to touch her toys.
She wondered if the next person who sat on her daddy's couch would

come away with those red bumps on their arm. Shy didn't say anything. After a while, Mrs. C. came over to them again.

"Don't you girls want to play?"

"I don't want her to touch me with that red stuff."

"Alta! That's not nice. Sasha's father told us it wasn't contagious anymore. Now go show her your toy mice."

Alta shook her head. She hated those mice.

"I'm going to count to three . . ."

"She can have them all."

"Sasha, I think you'd better go on home and come back another day. Alta is acting like a baby." Alta squinted her eyes at her mother and wished she could make her feel the burn in the look.

"Okay." Shy stood up and Mrs. C. walked her to the door.

"Welcome to the neighborhood," Mrs. C. said. "Tell your mother to drop by sometime." Every time a new family joined their parish, Mrs. C. pursued them. Alta knew her mother wanted to be friends with the new woman next door; she liked being a part of the parish community, though she was younger than a lot of the other church mothers, and a widow with only one child.

Alta heard the door close and her mother come back to the couch. "Stand up." Alta stood. Mrs. C. slapped her twice—hard, stinging smacks across her cheek. "No more rudeness from you, little miss." Alta swore then that she would be bigger than her mother one day, feeling in that moment that she could will this and—as indeed proved the case—it would be true.

Alta got off the freeway and neared the West Side, her old neighborhood. Alta wished she could take the girl somewhere else, sit her down and find out who she was, start to care if her eyes would follow Alta always, if she understood how Alta managed her days. The girl had layered eyes, a smile that came and stayed. Why couldn't Alta string these facts together and hold on to them, to her, to someone else besides Shy and their mothers and the past she had tried so hard to shrug off? Already the familiarity of the streets was sinking into her, the reddish-green bushes, the houses each so different from the next. If memories were more insistent than the physical world, it was because they crawled into things, took refuge in the structures of the present.

Shy and Alta had lived next door to each other on a side street in a jumbled area of town: part commerce, part warehouses, and in between, unexpectedly calm, more or less residential streets. As Alta approached them, the small changes jumped out at her. One house, formerly white, had been painted blue; a fence had been put up. A place soaks into you when you're young, a kid just walking around, not meaning to look, but seeing every leaf and every cracked foundation.

There was Jimmy Jimenez's house; and there Melissa Jefferies had had her infamous thirteenth-birthday party, when the kids broke into her father's liquor cabinet and got drunk on Irish Cream. Alta still couldn't even smell the stuff without feeling sick. There was the park where she had been the first girl allowed to play in the West Side Little League, and where years later she had told Shy she loved her and Shy had pretended not to hear.

When Alta turned onto her block, the reality of the street itself—the oil stains, the lawns full of crabgrass where there were lawns at all, the Dumpster across the street from their houses, and the stucco walls where her mother still lived—frightened her. She wished then that she didn't have the girl with her, much as the girl's legs, pressed against her on the bike, pinned Alta to the present. She didn't want the girl to see and get hold of any part of herself she had done her best to leave behind.

On all these quasi-residential streets, and theirs was no exception, the houses varied wildly. Her family home was an ugly stucco thing, one story. Shaped like a kid's picture of a house and that color green, too. The Mallons' house, flush up against theirs, was layered in dark, soft shingles, the kind whose wedges can turn to splinters, but which can also be carved with initials by the press of a thumbnail. s + A, she used to indent when she sat waiting on the steps. Did she think no one would notice or understand? Or did she want somebody to guess? The house had always seemed vast to her and kind of grand, the three wide steps to the front door almost royal. As she swung by it and turned in the driveway, it seemed considerably smaller. Alta didn't come back often—she tried, with no luck, to get Mrs. Mallon to meet her somewhere else—but every time she did return, her adult self was surprised that the sizes of the houses and streets fit her now.

After Mr. Mallon died, Alta had visited her mother; she had asked if she could come and see her. They hadn't seen each other on purpose in three years.

"I liked your hair long," Mrs. C. said when she first saw Alta, looking up for a moment at her shorn head, then glancing without pleasure at Alta's neatly creased black pants and the plaid shirt like one Mr. C. had owned.

Mrs. C. was decorating the living room, rehanging the pictures after her brother had painted the walls for her. Alta offered to help; Mrs. C. wouldn't let her. Alta sat, one hand on her motorcycle helmet, on the couch where she had lounged in front of the TV for so many years. Her old room was off the living room, and she noticed the door was ajar, but she stayed turned away from it just as her mother stayed turned away from her. Mrs. C. climbed up and down the three-rung stepladder, as if she'd forgotten Alta was in the room. Now and then she would glance at Alta as she turned to retrieve a picture. At first, moving around so much, she didn't seem any different to Alta.

"I forgot Saturday is the day to fix the house up," Alta said finally.

"I knew if I didn't hang the pictures as soon as the paint dried, they'd sit there for years."

Alta laughed a little, trying to force recognition into the laugh. "My apartment is the same way," she said, although in fact she had set everything in its place four years ago, and added to it meticulously from time to time.

"I'm so busy, working overtime for Dr. Gilbert, not to mention cooking dinner for the kids often as not." She worked in a dental office and helped out at church, and as far as Alta knew, since her husband died she had never even dated anyone.

Alta's uncle and his wife lived around the corner. They had two kids, boys who were cute now because they were young, and their lopsided teeth and close-together eyes still had puppyish appeal. When they'd been toddlers they'd followed her around, laughing and hanging on her legs, crying, "Alta, Alta." She hadn't seen them in years.

"How are the boys?"

"Coming on up." She chose a picture and leaned it on the ladder while she hammered a nail in. "They're good kids."

Alta stood and handed the picture to her. Her mother took it without saying anything, but handed Alta the hammer to hold. Alta hooked it over her wide leather belt so she could reach her hands to the bottom of the heavy frame in case it should fall. It was an over-colored copy of a painting of the Crucifixion.

Back in high school, Alta used to come home drunk and find her mother asleep on the couch below that picture, her face pale and blank in the green light of the television. If Alta was alone she would pull the afghan over her mother, turn the TV off. But if Shy was with her, they would tiptoe through, not wanting to risk waking her up. Shy liked to come to Alta's house, but something frightened Alta about having Shy in her own bed. In her house she wanted Shy too much, didn't wait as long for Shy to pretend to fall asleep; she would make Shy turn to her and she'd take her roughly, make her come fast, again and again. It was at Alta's house that she put her fingers inside Shy for the first time, lay pressed almost on top of her moving slowly in and out, wondering who had been there before her, feeling Shy rock against her hand. In her own house she required a lot to shut everything out; at Shy's house everything already was shut out.

"All right." Mrs. C. climbed down from the ladder and smoothed her slacks. She looked middle-aged, which surprised Alta. Her mother had always been the young widow, younger than the other mothers, younger especially than Mrs. Mallon. Her hair was the same almost-natural shade of deep blond, its curls just as tight around her head. But her skin was more papery now, her lips thinner and tighter. "Do you want a drink, something to eat?"

"No, thank you." She had never been this polite with her mother; they had never been polite at all. She took a breath. "I just want you to know that I'm happy with who I am. I have a good job and I work hard and there are girls who like me—"

"Happy?" Her mother shook her head, then turned to reposition the ladder and pick up another frame. "Could you hand me the hammer again?"

Alta jumped up and handed it to her. Mrs. C. wouldn't look at her.

"I'm a body piercer."

"Does this look straight to you?" Mrs. C.'s arms were stretched apart holding the frame up.

"I went through a special training and I was the top of my group. I make pretty good money, too."

"Alta." She put the picture down and started to hammer a nail into the wall. "Why did you want to see me?"

Alta looked up at Mrs. C.'s back. "You're my mother," she said.

Mrs. C. turned, the nail sticking out of the wall behind her. "Do you think that makes me proud?"

When Alta was little, when Mrs. C. still hoped they would be a pair—mother and daughter—Alta would beg her mother to tell her stories about her father.

"You look like him, you know?" she'd say. "He was so handsome when I met him. He tended bar over in Oakland and I didn't drink, but I went on a double date with a girlfriend of mine and the boys we were dating. Your father served us our drinks and danced with me on his break—though he wasn't supposed to do that. Jack—the boy I was dating—didn't know what happened. Three months later your father and I were married at St. Matthew's. He used to say I was the first girl who'd come to the bar who'd looked so out of place he knew he could marry me in church. Those were good times." She'd always end the stories like that: "Those were good times." And Alta could tell she meant it, too. Alta rehearsed saying it to herself. She tried to look at her mother the way her father must have seen her, tried to feel her heart exploding with warmth and love. She wondered how he could have died and left them alone.

"So this is where you grew up?" the girl asked lightly.

"Yeah, I guess so," Alta answered as she climbed off her motorcycle after the girl. "Next door." Alta barely turned her head, directing the girl instead toward the Mallon house. She saw that those lower shingles by the porch, the canvases of her adolescent ardor, were simply scratched and shabby pieces of wood clinging to the hollow house.

The girl followed her around back, by the bushes and walls between which Alta had found sanctuary as a child, and peered over at Alta's old house, toward the slab of cement that served as the porch, where Alta used to sit and wait for Shy to come out. Alta felt relieved that her mother was at work.

A splintered staircase doubled as a back deck. The key was hidden in an urn of pebbles by the rear door. Alta felt a wave of nausea pass over her. She hadn't been on this deck in years, and she felt like a ghost, a time traveler, someone—always—who didn't belong. Those times that she had tried so hard to put out of her mind came back to her so that she almost thought she saw Mrs. Mallon herself peering through the dusty glass again, as she might have if Alta had come last week or the week before, or even three days earlier; if she had come before her mother had called and asked her to.

She found the key beached in those rocks. She could hear the girl breathing softly behind her. The key slid stiffly into the doorknob and the lock popped out. The glass rattled in the door as she opened it.

The house surprised Alta. It was utterly absent of Mrs. Mallon. She might never have been there. There was the familiar white enamel sink and the rounded refrigerator, the slope of the floor and its brown painted boards. But nothing in the present animated the years the Mallons had spent there. The house seemed carefully tone-less. No blue plate of cigarette butts, no soiled towel hanging from the silverware drawer. Alta looked for the liquid soap Mr. Mallon had kept by the sink. Gone.

The house felt barren and unlived in, although Mrs. Mallon had been there only a few hours earlier. The dark hung around the edges of Alta's eyes after the glare of the sun outside. The girl, in her tight lime dress from the night before, seemed obscene in this strange house of the past, as if she were the loud moan of sex in a quiet church. But Alta was glad for that, too, glad to break with her brash-ness the spell of this place. Alta coughed into the darkness.

"Can we turn on the light?" the girl whispered. Poor thing—Alta knew why on a whim of desperation she had brought the girl with her, but why on earth had she come? Alta flipped the switch and took the girl's soft, plump hand in hers, this one-night sweetheart, and led her farther in, shivering against the empty house.

On the dining room table she saw it: the blue plate, a burned-out cigarette balancing on its edge. The phone, a brand-new one with extra-big buttons, was off the hook and an urgent, repetitive signal blared out. The girl came out from behind her and gently hung it up. The table moved slightly and the long ash of the cigarette softly crumbled to the wooden table. The vague lilac smell of Mrs. Mallon passed over Alta for a moment and suddenly there were ghosts everywhere. The girl couldn't see them—why should she? They were Alta's ghosts: Shy, laughing and so pretty and daring it was impossi-ble not to love her, her body urged toward movement, even in the stillness of this house; and Mrs. Mallon, trailing up the staircase, cig-arette in hand, her upswept hair pale and graying; Mr. Mallon, wait-ing quietly at the table, his fingers smoothing the place mat, on one of the good days when his wife was up out of bed and cooking, or—

when she wouldn't come down—scrubbing the house as if he could clean the misery out of it.

On impulse, Alta picked up the receiver and pressed redial. She thought she might hear her own machine, or Mrs. Koch's throaty greeting, but not the toneless "Hello?"

"Hello?" she said back, as if she had just answered the phone. Then, "Shy?"

"Hey, Alta." Not "hello" or even "hi," but "hey," as if Shy were standing on some lazy sun-filled corner Alta had just stepped around. As if she were barefoot and nineteen years old the way she'd been the last time Alta had seen her, six years ago now. As if she still knew who Alta was and had a right to. Alta almost hung up. She could run away as she always had, go back to the good life she had created in her place, and not let Shy shatter her again. But somehow without knowing anything at all, Alta had known Shy would one day be back in her life as suddenly as she'd split with Alta's two hundred dollars clutched in her nail-bitten hand. It wasn't just the money, either. It's the things people don't ask to borrow that you have to watch out they don't take for keeps.

"Alta?" Shy's voice faltered now, and the silence became Alta's.

Even with the light on, the house's dark colors and its stillness made it seem like a black-and-white photograph. The girl walked over and stood by the window. She looked like part of a negative print that had been colored in with pastel.

"Hello Shy," Alta said, and there was a warmth in her voice she would have banished. She carried the phone on Mrs. Mallon's long cord over to the window and, holding the receiver pressed between her shoulder and her ear, she ran her hand over the girl's ass, just as at work she'd take a piece of jewelry into her gloved palm or between her fingers to warm it against the shock of metal through skin.

She'd played this conversation so many times in her head. She'd always imagined an outpouring of explanation, emotion, perhaps even an apology.

"It's good to hear your voice," Shy said.

"How did you know it was me?"

"No one else calls me Shy."

"Where are you?"

She laughed gently. "Remember how you always said I'd be happier living underwater? I practically am, it rains so much here. Seattle." Shy loved to swim, was in water more than she was out of it, at least that's how it used to be.

"That's what I've heard." Suddenly Alta thought that if she could see Shy again, in person, she could show her a few things that would break her even breath. When she was fifteen she'd made love to her better than those groping boys in cars. And now she was eight years older.

"And how have you been, Alta?"

For a minute she sounded like the old Shy, the Shy who had been her best friend, her first lover, a girl who made her laugh and taught her she could love. Alta wished that she had been able to call Shy before, so that they could have the conversation her simple question implied.

"Shy, listen, I have some bad news. Your mother has had a stroke. She's in the hospital, and I haven't seen her yet, but she's alive and I'm going to visit her."

"Wait a minute." The sharpness in her voice was the only indication she'd understood. "Start at the beginning."

"Shy, this is the beginning. My mother called me this morning and said she'd found your mother collapsed on the front lawn. She called the ambulance, went with her to the hospital—if you can imagine a more comforting presence—and then called me. She said the number you gave her didn't work or something."

"Did you talk to my mother?"

"Shy, she can't talk. I had to let myself into your house and . . . well, it's kind of a long story. In fact, I need you to give me your number again. I'll explain everything when I see you."

"Oh my God. Alta, there's no way I can come right now."

"What?"

"It's a . . . it's another long story. There's just no way. I'm going to have to try to tell you where the insurance papers would be. My dad kept everything really organized."

"Shy, you have to come. They want to know things about her medical history."

"I don't know anything about her history. I mean . . . she was an orphan. The convent was destroyed during the war. I'm sure everything was lost, and even so, how could I get anything from Europe?"

"But what about after that? All her health problems?"

"Alta, that was her mind, not her body. She never, ever went to a doctor. She refused. My father said she could hardly stand to be in the hospital to have me. Can't they figure out what's going on right now? Aren't they doing tests? Do they have to have her biography to figure out how to help her?"

"Shy, even if they don't need all that information, you're her daughter. She needs you."

"I don't know what to do about that, Alta. I don't think there's anything I could do that you couldn't do better. I always make things worse for her, anyway. This kind of thing can go on for a long time, and if I did come I couldn't stay, so it would be better for me to wait and come later."

Alta didn't know what a long time was to Shy. Was six years a long time? "What kind of thing can go on, Shy?"

"Look, Alta, I can't just jump on a plane and be there. I can't. She's in a hospital. Maybe she'll get the care she needs. I don't know what to do for her, Alta. I never have, and right now I have to take care of myself."

"If it's a question of money . . ."

"No, it's just there are complications for me . . ."

"Complications?"

"Umm-hmn." She wasn't offering anything. When they were kids Alta had learned to read her so she wouldn't have to ask questions. Shy hated questions. Alta waited.

"It's a medical issue."

"What is?"

"Why I can't come."

"You mean you have a medical issue?" Shy didn't say anything. "Are you all right?"

"I'm okay. It just wouldn't be good for me to fly right now. Unless it's absolutely necessary. Unless, after you see her, you think it is. Absolutely necessary." Shy talked in riddles, and Alta wouldn't play the game and get caught trying to untwist them.

Alta said nothing, watched the girl shift from one foot to the other, her soft shoulder touching the window frame.

"Alta, I need you to go and see how bad things are. Please. I can trust you to act in my place and figure out what's best. I need it to be you." She used to say that to Alta. *I need it to be you.* In high school Alta would do anything for Shy. Boys used to come talk to Alta about Shy, even though Alta was younger, because Alta was her best friend. Alta would give Shy's phone number to the ones she liked, the ones who were her friends—they had played baseball together after school in the empty industrial streets—and tell them that blue was Shy's favorite color or that she loved to swim.

Her breath in Alta's ear sounded ragged now. It reminded Alta of the last time she had seen her, when her eyes were red and puffy and she refused to tell Alta why.

"Okay, Shy, where do you think I can find her insurance papers?"

A filing cabinet stood in the extra room, beside the tightly made single bed Mr. Mallon had slept in more often than not. The girl bounced as she sat on the bed, her feet pushing against the floor. Alta hated opening the drawers and wouldn't have looked further than the insurance file, which she found easily, kneeling before the cold metal cabinet. But the name on a folder caught her eye—SASHA MALLON—and when she glanced up the girl smiled unsuspectingly and Alta simply pulled it out with the other papers for the hospital and flipped it open.

An old rubber band enclosed a stack of letters addressed to Alice Mallon. Alta felt the weight of it for a moment and then gently lifted the band. It snapped, and the envelopes slid apart, their tops neatly frayed as if they had been cut open with a knife.

Mrs. C. had found and read Alta's diary several months before Shy left; Alta imagined her now, coming across it between her mattresses. It was evidence of a certain human curiosity, Mrs. C.'s urge to discover Alta's secrets. Maybe a mother's concern. Alta came home and Mrs. C. had her diary gripped in one hand, a box of tissues in the other, tears streaming, furious, down her face. She didn't have a free hand to pull a tissue out with.

"What is this?"

"I guess that's my journal."

"What you are doing is bad and wrong, Alta, you know that. I hope you've been praying for forgiveness."

Alta said nothing, let her go on.

"I can't believe . . . Shy?" Her voice dropped to a whisper. "I am going to have to have a talk with that mother of hers. This is unbelievable."

Then Alta realized: Mrs. C. couldn't believe it of Shy. She didn't want to believe it of Alta, but she must have had suspicions even before she saw Alta's scrawled descriptions: *Oh, Shy, I wish I could hold your hand at school. I wish I could make those boys shut up and go away. You looked so good in that dress I picked out for you, and you looked even better out of the dress. I couldn't wait to be alone with you, away from the world. I wish I could tell you how human you make me.*

And on another day: *Shy let me touch her everywhere last night. We got in late after an awful evening. Some guy tried to pick up Shy and made his friend distract me. And everyone looked at me like they felt sorry for me because even that ugly boy would only pay attention to me because he owed his friend a favor. And all the time I kept thinking, if only you knew. I don't want your ugly ass; I have the prettiest, liveliest girl in the room. She's mine. When we got home her mother was still awake in her room down the hall, so we had to be very quiet, but that made it more exciting in a way. I undressed her, like a lady in waiting, she said. I let her think about it however she wanted. When I pushed her panties down she had to press her face into my neck to keep from making any noise that might make Mrs. M. curious. It's a good thing I'm always quiet, because once I felt how wet she was, I forgot everything else but pleasing her. Which I tried to do in every way I could think of.*

"I want you to talk to a priest. You can't spend the night there anymore, or be alone with her."

Alta felt a numbing feeling settle over her. The offending little book tumbled from Mrs. C.'s hand to the floor. She yanked a tissue from the square box. She was going to take Shy away. She wiped under her eyes, looking toward the ceiling, and then crumpled the damp tissue in one hand.

"Listen, Mother. You're right."

Mrs. C. looked at Alta for a moment, her fist bunching and unbunching.

"It's not Shy. It's just me."

Her mother carefully uncrumpled the tissue, smoothed the wrinkles and folded it into a square. "But it says—"

"I made it up." Alta looked at her steadily. "It's what I wanted."

Mrs. C.'s eyes made little jolting motions as she looked everywhere in the room but at Alta. She sat down across from Alta. She wiped her face with the square of tissue. Her makeup smeared in a streak across her eyelid. "You wanted this?" She looked down at the journal as if it were a long way off.

Alta didn't want to make her mother so unhappy. She didn't even want to tell her that she wanted Shy more than anything. She felt anger ripple through her chest. She should have been more careful, should have carried her journal with her wherever she went.

Mrs. C. started to tear at the edges of the tissue. "How could you have written these things?"

Alta thought of Mrs. Mallon, how lonely she seemed, pacing around her room, staring out the window and smoking, or lying so still on her bed. Alta could feel her loneliness getting closer; what would Shy do if she knew what Alta's mother had read? Alta knew she'd be scared, that she'd give Alta up if she had to, if she even thought she had to.

"I made it up."

"Would you ever read someone's journal?" Alta asked Shy a week later, when she knew her mother hadn't said anything.

"You mean like a diary?" she said. "No, I'd never do that." But even then Alta had wondered whether that was a principled stand or merely Shy's lack of interest. Did she just not care?

Alta could pretend to Shy and to Renny and to any girl she brought home that she didn't care about why Shy had left. But Alta knew when she saw those letters, even before the elastic broke, that she would read them all.

"Did you find what you needed?" the girl asked brightly. For just a moment Alta was tempted to blast all those ghosts away and kneel now between the girl's full thighs. But she couldn't. Damn Shy.

For the sake of the nurses and nuns Alta would just as soon have had a girl on her arm as she walked through the hospital halls. She could almost forget, sometimes, how people looked at her if she went too far along Market Street in either direction. For weeks, she didn't go outside the Castro, the Mission, and South of Market, and she could almost forget. Here, though, the nuns bowed their heads and clipped along, but she received no benevolent smiles and a few cold, discreet stares. A priest avoided her eyes.

She had dropped the girl off at the train stop back to the City, touched her sweet face with the back of her hand, and watched her disappear.

The halls glared white. Last time Alta had consented to go to the hospital was when her daddy died. He'd been lying day and night on their couch, watching television and sleeping. When he felt strong enough, he'd tell Alta stories. At the hospital, he let her climb up on his bed to give him a hug, but he smelled different. No Old Spice, no mothballs, just the sharp, acrid scent of disinfectant and bedpans, the oil of dirty hair. Her throat swelled. She ran out of the room and down the hall to the cold cement steps outside. When her mother came out, she tried to hold Alta's hand, but Alta ran ahead, afraid of the tears burning the edges of her eyes. As it turned out, that was the last time she ever saw him. He never came out of there; much as she had missed him, she had refused to go back. After he died, she'd lie in bed at night after her mother had tucked her in, thinking about that last time she'd seen him, wishing she could go back and sit beside him, fill her lungs, even with the smell of his dying, just to ask him the questions her mother's closed face refused, and to hold his big hand and let him go.

"Can I help you?" a tiny nun asked from behind the reception counter.

"I'm here to see Mrs. Mallon. Her daughter"—she almost said Shy—"Sasha Mallon called, I believe. My name is Alta."

The nun shook her head and then, as an afterthought, typed a few words into a computer. She looked up, suddenly serious. "Alta Corral. Yes. We've just moved Mrs. Mallon to ICU. I'll need to ask you some questions, but first follow me."

Alta had loved the nuns in school, the nice ones. She'd loved the motherly kindness of them, the rustle of their habits, though by high school they didn't wear them anymore. Once at a straight friend's party, she'd met a nun and talked to her the whole time and brought her juice and a plate of crackers and cheese. The nun thanked her and called her "young man," and Alta let her think it, because straight people called her ma'am, when it didn't fit her any better.

The sister pointed through an open door, and for a moment Alta thought Mrs. Mallon must be on the other side of the curtain, for the woman who lay before her looked older than history. Her head was propped up on several starched white pillows. There was a tube going into her nose. Her arms lay useless by her sides; another tube taped along one of them disappeared into the sleeve at her elbow. Alta noticed the shadowy white scar she'd seen before on Mrs. Mallon's forearm; overhead, on a monitor, ran the jagged line of her heartbeat. The hospital room was crowded with equipment, a metal hospital lamp, plastic chairs. A pole on wheels held several IV bags.

Alta went and stood by the bed, not sure really of what to do, and not used to being so uncertain.

Finally, she took Mrs. Mallon's hand. It was warm and Alta realized with a start that she hadn't been thinking of Mrs. Mallon as alive. Her hand was very like Shy's—knobby and longish—though smaller. The thin gown rose and fell with her breath; her skin was gray. It was not that Alta didn't remember Mrs. Mallon's depressions, the days she spent in bed or smoking upstairs, looking out a window from a foot or two back. She could hush Shy's exuberance with a turn of her head or a tight look. But even before she'd saved Alta's life, she was kind to her. On certain days she'd rise early and cook—potato patties and delicious thin pancakes filled with sweet cheese. She'd send Shy and Alta to the store for sour cream and apples, and she'd stew her own applesauce. The house would fill with the sweet, wet smell of apples evaporating. Alta loved to watch her cook, moving quickly between sink and counter and stove. An occasional polished seed would float to the top of the bubbling pot and Mrs. Mallon would take a wooden ladle and spoon it out, bending close to the flame.

If Alta wasn't already over there, Shy would knock on her door on her way to the corner market and she'd escape her own house and enter Shy's bright, outside world. Those days, Shy was in a happy, forgiving mood. When they cut through the hidden part of the Sutters' backyard, Shy would hold Alta's hand.

Mrs. Mallon used to sit so still on the days she was unhappy that Alta could almost believe she might turn now in her listless way and say, "Alta, what are we going to do?"

Alta brushed Mrs. Mallon's hair back from her face. Mrs. Mallon normally kept it so neat, all wrapped up in a twist behind her head. Now it spread thinly across the stiff pillow, a few threads of blond shining in the paler gray. There was a narrow window high up on the wall, and through it Alta could see an incongruous bit of blue sky.

The day Alta woke up and knew Shy was not coming back, it was brilliantly sunny. She would have liked to sleep on—she was only seventeen, but she had stopped going to school and generally stayed awake late into the night and slept heavily in the mornings—but the sun stung her eyes through closed lids and her anguish awoke before her body did. She lay watching the translucent pink of her own eyelids, finally willing herself to open her eyes and face the damage. She knew then that she would have to live in the aftermath of Shy's great dramatic move. Shy had left—without saying goodbye, without telling Alta where she was going or why—and Alta had to live with the fallout.

Mrs. C. came to the door and tried to open it. Failing that, she conveyed the message through the door: Mrs. Mallon had called wanting to know if Alta knew anything about where Shy had gone. Alta said she didn't know.

After three days, Alta gathered all her courage, all her desperation, and went to Shy's back door. Mrs. Mallon was in the kitchen, wiry and gray, her bony face ashen. She jumped when Alta knocked, and scared them both. Alta was surprised to see her out of bed, as that was usually a good sign, and for a moment she imagined Shy had just returned. But the air was thick with misery, more pungent than the stale unhappiness that usually pervaded the place. Mrs. Mallon's frightened face quickly settled back into monotonous blankness. Alta had seen this face on Shy, when she was angry at Ryan and pretending not to be or when she didn't want to answer a question. Mrs. Mallon unlocked the back door.

"Have you heard from her? Do you have any idea?" Her voice had a slight accent. Shy used to tell Alta that her mother was from Paris.

She made up different stories about her mother, but most often she said Mrs. Mallon came from France.

Alta hesitated then shook her head. She didn't know what bound her then to secrecy. Certainly Shy had not said anything about not telling. Even that would have given too much away. Shy had come crying to Alta's room and borrowed the two hundred dollars she'd saved up doing roofing work for her uncle and piercing girls' ears at school. It wasn't that Alta knew much, but she told nothing, and in that way she was an accomplice to Shy's escape, as Mrs. Mallon would later be to hers. They depended on one another for survival, and even when they left, they helped each other go.

Suddenly Mrs. Mallon's eyes opened partway.

"Mrs. Mallon?" Alta said, the volume of her own voice surprising her. She wanted to call out Mrs. Mallon's Christian name, but at first, strangely, she couldn't remember it and when she did—Alice— it wouldn't come. Mrs. Mallon had never told Alta to call her Alice. She'd never referred to herself as Alice. She'd rarely referred to her- self at all. "Mrs. Mallon. Shy's in Seattle. I called her—"

"She can't understand," the nun interjected. Mrs. Mallon's lids slid shut. Still, when Alta was ready to talk about the medical situa- tion, they left the room.

"I really don't know anything about her medical history. I have these papers. Her daughter asked me to deliver them." Alta opened the file and the nun leafed through, taking out a couple of forms on bluish paper. She studied one for a long moment, and Alta saw that beneath it was Mrs. Mallon's baptismal certificate. She caught the year, out of the corner of her eye, and then full focus: 1952. She stared at it, trying to get her mind around why this would be. Her own mother had been baptized shortly after her birth in 1946. Alta had seen a photograph of the tiny baby that was her mother, swaddled in a long white baptismal gown; Mrs. C. had framed it next to a similar picture of Alta. Mrs. Mallon was considerably older than Mrs. C., at least fifteen years, Alta thought.

Mrs. Mallon and Alta had never mentioned Shy's disappearance after that first day. Alta's mother met her at the door when she came back from seeing Mrs. Mallon. She blocked Alta's retreat back to her little room.

"That's it, Alta. You never go to school anymore and you never go to church. You can't live in my house the way you are. You're queer," she said, bitterly, "and it's not my fault."

Alta slept in Shy's bed that night, slept in her dirty sheets. She ran her fingers over and over the pillowcase in front of her as she lay there awake. The cotton became smooth beneath her fingers.

Mrs. Mallon woke her up. "Alta," she said, "go to school. You have three months left, and Mr. Mallon has agreed that you can stay here until you have finished." She imagined Mr. Mallon would hardly notice her. He wasn't around often, and when he was, not much fazed him. Mrs. Mallon brushed by that and continued, "My father said education is the most important thing in life. No one can take it from you." Alta had never heard anything about Mrs. Mallon's family. "You'll have that diploma and go off to live in San Francisco. You'll like it there." She lit a cigarette and smiled. It was seven-thirty in the morning.

When Alta got back from school, Mrs. Mallon was sitting at the dining room table, a heap of butts on the blue plate in front of her, and a mug of half-finished coffee with a skin across the top.

"She called," Mrs. Mallon said, her eyes flat. "She's not coming back."

"Did you tell her no?" Alta turned a chair around, straddled it. "Did you say—"

"I tried. I'm old now. She's young. She wants to go. . . ." Mrs. Mallon opened her hand and the cigarette fell to the table, still smoldering. Alta picked it up and smudged it out against the others.

I'm young, Alta wanted to say. Where does Shy want to go? When is she coming back? But Mrs. Mallon didn't know. From the beginning, she refused to call the police. Mr. Mallon was terribly worried, but Shy's absence seemed to release them from any ties they'd once felt.

For the first several days Alta was there, Mr. Mallon all but disappeared, too, coming home late at night and sleeping on his narrow office bed, gone even before Mrs. Mallon gave up her tortured attempts at sleep and put the coffee on. He was one of those men who look boyish even as their hair turns gray. He kept his cut short, the way it had been when he was in the armed forces. He had green eyes whose tired sparkle slowly dwindled. There was nothing left in his eyes when he stopped looking at his wife. Alta knew he had loved her once. She remembered how gently he had looked at her, how fiercely he'd scrubbed the house when she stayed long hours and days in her room, how brightly he'd smiled when she emerged.

It was Mr. Mallon's curse to be drawn to such sorrow, much as it was Alta's own good fortune to find a woman who mourned beside her when there was nothing else she could do, and who sent Alta to a place where she could be happy when Alta's time of mourning ended and Mrs. Mallon's simply cycled on.

Alta's mother set herself the task of saving Mr. Mallon. Mrs. C. was a behind-the-scenes person, who drove Shy and Alta to malls to sell candy bars for charity and class prizes, gardened their frigid little yard, ran errands for Father Hobin and the other priests. Alta had watched her mother bob across Mr. Mallon's line of vision, trying to impress herself upon him, and she had noted her mother's failure. Some people are drawn to sorrow, and Mr. Mallon was certainly one, but Mrs. C.'s sorrow was brittle and shielded by self-righteousness.

Shy's departure revived an intensity in Mrs. Mallon, but it was too late and too inwardly focused to affect her hollow marriage. Alta thought at first that her despair matched Mrs. Mallon's, failing as she did to take into account the natural inflation seventeen years can bring to a first, crushing desertion that had left her unprotected in a dangerous world. Alta found herself audience to Mrs. Mallon, just as she had been audience to Mrs. Mallon's daughter.

"Alta," Mrs. Mallon said, "people disappear. People disappear," she repeated, drawing into herself again.

Just before Alta graduated, Mrs. Mallon got a card postmarked SEATTLE, WA. By then Alta didn't want to know the truth, didn't want the specifics of Shy's desertion, the parallel life she'd found or made in place of her. Alta felt each fact of Shy's existence would pin her more firmly away from her.

"Here you go." The nun had taken the papers she wanted and shuffled the rest, including the baptismal certificate, back in the folder, which she now returned to Alta.

"Where are the phones?"

The woman didn't look up as she pointed to a corridor. Alta remembered the worst part of bad news: the obligation to repeat it over and over.

"Alta!" Mrs. Koch's voice thrust across the phone line. She had her own agenda. "Alicia Mallon, she calls me each and every Saturday, but not this one. Do you know? I cannot reach her."

Gerda Koch was Mrs. Mallon's graduation present to Alta; at least that's how Alta always thought of it. Mrs. Mallon hadn't gone to the ceremonies because she disliked crowds, and Alta's mother hadn't gone because she disliked Alta, and so Alta hadn't gone. Mr. Mallon was traveling and no one else knew. Instead Mrs. Mallon and Alta had huddled away from the June day, a day Shy would have insisted on being out in, and Mrs. Mallon told Alta that she had done well. Mrs. Mallon was not an effusive person, even on her better days— and this was one of them. But Alta took what Mrs. Mallon had to offer: Alta couldn't expect more and so she was happier than Shy had been. And while her classmates were marching across the stage—Jesse who went on to college, and Ryan's little sister Melanie who everyone knew was pregnant, and the boys who had been Alta's buddies when they were young enough to play hard and fast for the fun of it, who became clerks, and mid-level businessmen, and junkies, and the girls who had liked Alta because she was funny and because she bought some of them sodas and because she made them feel thin and pretty in contrast—Mrs. Mallon picked up the kitchen phone and connected Alta to Gerda Koch in San Francisco. And Mrs. Koch hired Alta immediately, enthusiastically, sight unseen, to help out in what Alta learned was the older woman's perpetual remodeling and landscaping project. Mrs. Koch also got Alta the basement apartment in a run-down Victorian building, which the landlord, who was a friend of Mrs. Koch's, let Alta fix up and stay in cheap.

That first summer Alta had not gone crazy because Mrs. Koch's zealous enthusiasms gave her no time. Alta worked hard for her, and Mrs. Koch gave her errands to run, sending her out to Chavez Street to pick up paint samples or over to Cliff's Hardware in the Castro to buy window screens. Alta dipped into the chaos, noticing that as often as not the looks she received were curious, friendly, intrigued. Girls smiled openly at her. The thickest layer of her skin began to crack.

"Mrs. Koch," Alta said now, "Mrs. Mallon is in the hospital. She's had a stroke."

"Ach," she said, so quietly.

Alta grabbed a sandwich from the cafeteria and took it outside, into the glory of the day, to wait for Mrs. Koch. She put her back against the wall and stretched her legs along the concrete block by the front stairs. The doctors and nurses and nuns, the visitors, all glanced at her polished workman's boots, her thick white T-shirt and low-slung jeans, her tattoos, and then quickly turned away. Alta looked up to the distant hills, with their globs of dark green trees and scattered houses. The sun was just behind her head, moving down toward the City, where, this evening, it would drop into the ocean. Her scalp, under its thin veneer of hair, warmed deliciously.

The first evening after she'd moved to San Francisco, Gerda Koch said, "Stay for dinner, Alta!" Most of Mrs. Koch's sentences ended with such emphasis.

Pauline Beaufort lived in Mrs. Koch's house, too, and she was cooking, as it turned out she usually did. Mrs. Koch always did the dishes. They set the table with fine china and a thick linen cloth embroidered with a B.

"Beaufort linen," Pauline said, her voice ironic, but her hands careful. She cooked up a big meal of fried chicken, mashed potatoes, a salad with cornbread, and a bowl of sauerkraut, which Alta had never seen before.

"My father was German," Mrs. Koch told Alta. "But I, and my mother's whole family, we are Austrian!"

Over dinner, Mrs. Koch and Pauline talked and talked. Mrs. Mallon had said more over the time Alta had lived with her than she'd ever spoken when Alta had been around her as a child, but Mrs. Mallon had never become what anyone could call talkative. After the months of relative solitude and deep quiet Alta had spent with the Mallons, the lively banter between Pauline Beaufort and Gerda Koch roused her. Mrs. Koch told her all her plans for renovating the house. These schemes changed weekly, Alta would learn.

"Gerda's an artist," Pauline said. "My goodness, she used to do life-sized sculptures of naked women. So I let her have the run of the house, and think of it as creative expression."

"No more naked women for me." Mrs. Koch grinned. "Except for Paulie." She winked at Alta and held her hands up, palms forward. "Who could ask for more than the best?"

Alta stared at her, tried to look as though she'd never heard anyone say anything like what she thought she'd just heard. These two older women, closing in on eighty, with white hair, and fallen throats, faces full of wrinkles, flirted and teased each other with zealous mirth. The formidable Gerda Koch, who remained Mrs. Koch for Alta despite the fact that Koch was her maiden name, was unabashedly in love with Pauline Beaufort, and Pauline Beaufort loved her back, wholly and openly.

"She's the best of this country," Mrs. Koch said, her eyes on Pauline's fragile frame. Pauline rose to put the kettle on.

"Despite itself," she added in her Southern lilt.

"Where did you grow up?" Alta asked.

"Charleston," she said. "South Carolina. Home of Fort Sumter, the one the North never could capture."

"You came north."

"I consider this the West, Alta, but I did go to school in North Carolina, and then I taught in Tennessee."

"She taught the children in schools with no floors—"

"It was a little schoolhouse outside Knoxville, and it had a dirt floor." They finished each other's sentences and overlapped as if they were singing a round. "It was a very poor area at that time, during the Depression, you see. My family was rather . . . astonished. Of course, they never knew the full extent of it." She smiled as coyly as any Southern belle.

"And the mothers . . . " Mrs. Koch prompted.

"My mother's friends used to say, you're too pretty to be a spinster schoolteacher." Mrs. Koch and her companion laughed.

"But you never did marry?" Alta asked, knowing suddenly that this was very important to her.

"I never married a man," she agreed, tilting her head. "Tea?" The kettle had been steaming and shaking, and now it started a thin whistle.

"Thank you, Miss Pauline," Alta said. "I think I will."

"Ah. You've charmed her, Paulie."

After dinner they sat with their dishes pushed toward the center of the table, and Miss Pauline served tea.

"It can be hard to start a new life, Alta. I know. The old life is lost, and the new one is uncertain. Paulie and I want to help you, so San Francisco will be a home to you, as it has been to us. It is a good place for people like us, no?"

It was the first time in Alta's life that someone had said "people like us," understanding full well who Alta was and meaning her, too. Miss Pauline added three spoonfuls of sugar and stirred them into Alta's bitter tea.

Mrs. Koch pulled up in her olive-green Chevy and left it angled into the street. She headed toward Alta wearing one of her thick tweed suits, despite the heat.

"Alta!" Mrs. Koch hugged her in strong arms, and right away she felt safer with this sturdy old woman by her side. The nuns looked at them oddly as they made their way through the chilly halls of the hospital. Mrs. Koch walked resolutely, her gray hair pulled sharply from her face. The nun Alta had talked with before let them pass, though the nurse with her seemed reluctant. Mrs. Mallon had not moved, but the sight of her shocked Alta all over again. She looked older than Mrs. Koch, though that grand lady was her senior by over a decade.

Mrs. Koch thumped into the seat beside the bed and took Mrs. Mallon's hand in hers, rubbing vigorously. "Alicia," she said, bending closer as if Mrs. Mallon might respond. Then she murmured to her in a sweet staccato that Alta thought might be French. "Anh? Anh?" she kept asking. The smell of disinfectant rose up from the floors. Alta had never actually seen the two women together. Mrs. Koch rose and pressed her cheek to Alice Mallon's, her head on the pillow beside her friend's. They seemed for a moment to be staring together at something on the ceiling, something Alta couldn't have seen.

"I want to tell her it will be all right," Mrs. Koch told Alta, straightening up.

They stood side by side looking down at the emaciated figure on the bed. "I think she might be able to hear you," Alta ventured.

Mrs. Koch shook her head. "Hear me? Maybe. Listen to me? This would be the first time."

"We shall go to the house?" Mrs. Koch asked.

"What house?"

"Her house, Alicia's."

Alta hadn't thought Mrs. Koch would want to go there; it was after sunset, and Alta's mother would surely be home from work. But Mrs. Koch insisted that she go and she insisted that Alta be her guide. They left Alta's motorcycle near the hospital, and Alta directed Mrs. Koch along the familiar streets, discomfited to be going back so soon.

Mrs. Koch's big car glided through the half-light of the early evening.

"She liked you, Alta, your Mrs. Mallon."

"She was certainly more than kind to me."

"She admired your bravery. Hmm?" She turned and looked at Alta across her arms, which were outstretched to the large steering wheel.

"I wasn't brave then." Everything was still visible outside, but all the color was gone. "Or even now," Alta added, fighting the desire to scrunch down in the car seat and hide from her mother. "Did you know her a long time?"

"Since cavemen." She laughed.

"How did you meet?"

"Ach." She flicked one hand through the air. "Who remembers so long ago? You want to be an archaeologist, Alta? I am too old to be a useful specimen."

"Here it is. Pull into the driveway."

Mrs. Koch climbed out of the car with a big purse she pulled from the backseat. She seemed to know about the key in the rocks. She pointed to the clay pot and asked Alta to dig it out. Alta wondered what would happen if she rang her own doorbell. Alta's mother wouldn't look her in the eye. In church Mrs. C. prayed, confessed, repented. Her shame had followed Alta most of her life.

Mrs. Koch stood in the kitchen and then disappeared upstairs. Alta followed, but Mrs. Koch went into Mrs. Mallon's room and closed the door. What Alta had avoided when the girl was with her was Shy's bedroom. It had been Shy's bedroom when Alta'd lived in it and she was sure it was Shy's bedroom still, exactly as she'd left it. Now, because Alta feared it, she walked down the hall and opened the door. It was Shy's room in a way that this was not her house. Colorful where the rest was dark and muted, bright and curtainless where the other rooms seemed shrouded over. Six years ago Alta had surfaced out of her own childhood where she'd been left to drown and she'd surfaced here. At night she had stared out Shy's window and watched the pattern of headlights across the bridge. One stream headed into the city, the top one, smooth and light, capable, it seemed, of flying off into the dark orange of the night sky. The other line of lights flickered between the concrete layers, headed back. Every night for three months, Alta sat with tears in her throat. She held them there. If they came out, they came quietly, sneaking from the edges of her eyes. She pushed them off her cheeks. Over and over she asked herself, where had Shy gone? She had wondered where since the day Shy left. Seattle wasn't the answer to her question. She wondered still.

Shy and Alta had taken their last road trip together in spring of the year Shy left, at the beginning of a long, drought-induced heat wave. The hills dried to brown straw, and fire warnings went out. They drove northeast, right into the heat. Shy liked to plan their excursions on maps she'd get the gas station guys to give her for free. She'd trace a blue line up some old highway, or circle a town she'd suddenly decide she wanted to drive through. They got to use the Mallons' station wagon whenever Mr. Mallon was away. Shy drove; Alta hadn't learned how yet, and Shy had gotten her license the day before she turned sixteen, though they'd made her wait until the next day to pick it up. Shy and Alta found these adventures hilarious. Alta made Shy mixed tapes of oldies—from "Duke of Earl" to "Summertime"—and they'd sing along. Alta had always selected the songs to express what she couldn't herself, but Shy sang carelessly, happily. Still, when it was just the two of them, Shy's carefree jauntiness didn't bother Alta.

Shy's hand beat a rhythm out the window. They floated in the giant station wagon. That car embarrassed Shy, and Alta herself slouched down when they drove through the streets to get out of their town. But once they were away, the car kept them moving, and that was enough.

The heat churned in slow waves across the stillness of the day.

"My mom," Shy complained. "Did she take too much acid in the sixties or what?"

"Acid?"

"You're right; wrong drug. She's on permanent depressants or something."

The tape ended and the machine pushed against the empty plastic scroll. It was hard to know the right way to respond to Shy's occasional criticisms of Mrs. Mallon. Sympathy often made Shy turn sour, and Alta wasn't going to argue with her.

On they drove, and Alta handed her individual ice cubes from the tall cups they'd pick up at drive-thrus. She watched Shy pull the ice in and out of her mouth with her thin fingers, watched her slide them along the planes of her face, the slope of her neck, the shallow dip between her breasts. And back into her mouth.

"Learn how to drive!" Shy called out to some driver who got in her way. She overtook a long truck, speeding through patches of shade on the wrong side of the road.

"I spy something blue."

"The sky," Alta said.

Shy shook her head.

"That billboard."

"Questions. Ask questions."

"Where are we going?"

"That's it!" She let go of the wheel so that her ice-free hand could swing over to demand a high five.

Alta looked out the window.

"Get it?"

"No."

"We're going somewhere blue." Shy's knee steered them along, she slid the ice below the top of her blouse, and with her other hand she pointed to the line she'd drawn on the map. Alta dropped a piece of ice down the back of Shy's pants. She screamed.

"Get it out!"

"If you say so." Alta slid her hand into the waistband, felt the soft skin there, the track of icy water. Alta drew the ice up to her mouth and crunched it between her teeth.

"That's disgusting." Shy laughed.

It was their last drive together, but of course Alta didn't know that. They found a motel and Shy checked in while Alta stayed in the car, around the corner. Shy was already nineteen, and no one questioned her right to be anywhere she wanted. Except for the long, single braid down her back, Alta looked more like a fifteen-year-old boy, though by this time she was seventeen. Anyway, if Alta snuck in they got a cheaper rate.

Shy flopped on the bed, unbuttoned the top two buttons of her blouse.

"It's so hot."

Alta sat in a chair at the foot of the bed.

"Oh, look in the little fridge for an ice bucket."

Alta found a plastic container and Shy handed her a motel token from the pocket of her jeans. When Alta came back from the ice machine Shy's eyes were closed but the lights were still on. Two more buttons were undone. Alta stood looking for so long that Shy opened her eyes again.

"Put it here." She patted the bedside table. "Will you run it over my arms and face?" She grinned, then closed her eyes again. The ice sluiced off the cubes in slick trails of water over her skin—the heat was such that even Shy's body melted ice on contact. When Alta had covered Shy's arms and cheekbones, the delicate skin over her eyes and behind her ears, Shy helped Alta undress her, pushing at her pants and underwear, lifting so Alta could slide them off. Her lids stayed closed. She lay naked in that lighted room. Alta ran the ice across the ridge of her collarbone and into the slope of her throat. Slowly she moved it across her breasts, heard her breath riff and saw her nipples tighten. Alta took the ice between her lips. She held it, with a shiver, in her teeth. Her mouth became cold and almost numb, and when the ice disappeared she kept on, taking back the heat that rose in her. Shy's hands ran over Alta's shoulders and back as Alta bent over her. She never looked at Alta, but she cried out when she came, and held Alta tight. Alta shook against Shy's hands as pleasure shot through her body.

"Alta? Where have you gone?" Mrs. Koch peered at Alta through Shy's open door.

"Nowhere," Alta said.

"This is Sasha's room, yes?"

"Yes." Alta was startled to hear Mrs. Koch refer to Shy. She knew Mrs. Koch and Mrs. Mallon were fairly good friends, though of course Mrs. Mallon never came to San Francisco, and Alta didn't remember Mrs. Koch ever coming here.

"She will be coming?"

"I'm not sure."

"Well, I want you to bring her to see me."

"Does she know you?" After Alta said this, it seemed rude, but Mrs. Koch didn't notice.

"She wouldn't remember me."

"Yeah, well, she doesn't remember me, either." Alta laughed, but it sounded bitter. Mrs. Koch put one stiff hand on her arm.

"Not to talk about is not the same as not to remember, hmmn?"

Alta shrugged. Mrs. Koch led the way down the hall, and Alta noticed that the purse the older woman had brought in seemed to have something bulky in it now. Could she be taking something of Mrs. Mallon's? A memento? Surely she would never steal anything?

Alta said nothing and they left the house. Mrs. Koch dropped Alta off where she'd left her bike and watched as Alta climbed on and jump-kicked it to life. Alta waved and headed, in the dark now, back toward the center of the City. The low hills fell away behind her and the island marked the halfway point. She felt the world around her come into sharp focus again.

Alta had visited Mrs. Mallon the same day she and her mother had tried, and failed, to reconcile. It was the last time they'd talked about Shy.

"Do you tell her about me?" Alta had asked as casually as she could.

Alta saw Mrs. Mallon study her, and she realized that Mrs. Mallon was considering whether to lie, and that if she'd wanted to, she could have done it with ease. Alta looked back at her with the respect one ace liar gives another, and Mrs. Mallon told her the truth.

"She doesn't ask."

Alta wondered if they were talking about her being queer, or simply about the facts of her life in San Francisco.

"I want you to know—" Alta began.

But Mrs. Mallon held up her hand. "Never tell anyone more than they need to know." She paused. "Alta," she added, so warmly, her accent curling around the sounds, so that Alta believed Mrs. Mallon was letting her know that she knew more about Alta than Alta had ever said.

Alta couldn't believe she had seen Mrs. Mallon all hollowed out, and there was nothing she could do for her except try to get Shy here as fast as possible. Seven messages hailed her by the flashing red light of her machine and she listened to them as she made the bed. The voices of kind and eager girls played as she smoothed the blankets, containing the easy, careless passion of a one-night stand, the sort of night that is compelling enough at the time. There was a message from her best friend, Renny, inviting Alta to dinner that night. None of them was from Shy.

Alta didn't want to call Shy yet, wanted some feeling of advantage. She took the pale SASHA MALLON folder out of her bag, fingered the soft cardboard with its feel of being handled well and often.

"I don't know what to do," Alta had said, miserably, to Mrs. Mallon the night Mrs. Mallon told her Shy wasn't coming back.

Mrs. Mallon was quiet for a long time. She handed Alta the matchbook. Alta had to take the cigarette from Mrs. Mallon because her hands shook too much for Alta to light it. She lit it and gave it back.

"Some things happen and you just never imagined." Mrs. Mallon spoke softly, and with her accent, the meaning of her words took a moment to form. "Things no one imagines. No one worries. Sometimes you don't know enough to be afraid." She took a deep breath through her cigarette and a cloud of gray smoke covered her face. "I remember as a little girl . . . I remember falling asleep without dreams, I was so content. I remember a big, soft mattress and a thick woven sheet of cotton. So smooth. The sounds of voices from below. The good smells of breakfast and morning." She rolled the cigarette slowly back and forth between her fingers. Alta saw the porch light go on at her mother's house.

There seemed to be more Mrs. Mallon wanted to say. Despite the stories Shy had told Alta, about Paris and all that, it was hard to imagine Mrs. Mallon as a young girl. She stood up and, leaning over the table, stubbed out her cigarette in the plate of ashes. "What I mean to say, Alta, is this. All I ever wanted was to keep her with me. I could imagine losing her. I could imagine that one day she might leave. These are not the kinds of fears I could not imagine. I thought of them every day. Do you understand me? Every single day. All I wanted was to keep her with me." She lifted her hands, shaking, to her face, the fingertips reaching for the edges of her forehead, her cheeks. Then she smoothed her hair and held her hands tightly in her lap. "When you are a mother, all you want is to keep your children safe. Sometimes it is not possible. But you are like a mama lion trying." Alta thought of her own mother, who never made her way across the yard, though she must have known Alta was here. Mrs. Mallon stood up again. "Would you like a drink, Alta?"

Alta shook her head. The idea of getting drunk with Mrs. Mallon frightened her. Mrs. Mallon leaned under the kitchen counter to retrieve the brandy. Alta had seen both Mallons drink privately out of this store, but she never saw them share it. They never had a drink in the late afternoon or after dinner. Mrs. Mallon finished one shot standing by the counter and brought the second back to the table, where she took out a new cigarette. She put it in her mouth and Alta held the match inside her cupped hands.

"I had two miscarriages before Sasha was born." She looked at Alta. "I can't tell you how to bear her absence. Isn't that funny?" She sat down and smoked silently. Alta rocked back and forth on the legs of her chair, listening to the echo sound through the house. Mrs. Mallon finished her drink, tossing it back suddenly. She put it down and almost smiled. "At least we know she's safe."

But safe wasn't enough for Alta, and she lived her life less and less under its spell. If the answers to the last six years were anywhere in this short stack of envelopes now lying on her desk, she would find them.

The first letter, dated three years ago, a few months after the death of Mr. Mallon, was a postcard in an envelope, the message scrawled across both sections of the back:

I thought you'd want to see the water here, Mother. I remember one time you said you loved water, told me if anything happened, perhaps I could jump in the bay and keep on swimming. I think that was the only time you ever mentioned my swimming. It is all bridges and islands here. One fierce winter a floating bridge, which normally sits right on the water, broke loose and sunk below. This is not to worry you. I've come to a safe place. And very green. I can't come back now. I have a job as a receptionist in an advertising firm and it will take a while to earn vacation days. But thanks for offering plane fare. I hope you're feeling better.

Love,
Sasha

Her name in her own hand stilled Alta and swept in the days when Shy would pass her notes in the hallways of school, notes, between almost every class, that she'd doodled while the teachers droned on. Alta had missed her when she'd graduated and was torn from the routine of Alta's school days.

The next card was all black, with embossed gold lettering reading:

SEATTLE AT NIGHT.

Every place is the same when you close your eyes, Mama; that's another thing you never told me. You, who taught me everything I know about running away, and never told me what you ran from. And I forgot to notice that what you ran to didn't make you all that happy either, did it, Mama? So imagine me here, happy, as I imagine you there, content. Eyes closed, Shy.

A stack of letters saying, softly, no I will not return. The last several promised a visit, but each successive card or note put it off again. To a Mother's Day card with its preprinted message Shy had signed her name and scribbled, "I'd love to visit, but it will probably be a few months before I can." And later in the stack, "I'm trying to plan a trip to see you," but in the next card, "Plans to travel have fallen through for the moment." Mrs. Mallon had never let on to Alta that she was trying to get Shy to come back.

It seemed as though Shy's life was the landscape of Seattle. Besides excuses and accusations, that was all she wrote about. She had found her paradise of water. Shy loved water, the roaring ocean and the rushing creeks and ice-cold rivers, even lukewarm swimming pools at whose edges Alta would sit, trailing her fingers. Alta had followed

Shy to all the shores and banks and borders and watched her slip into the water and away. And Alta had waited and watched. She'd done it for years.

There was a time Alta thought she knew everything about Shy. Shy had whispered secrets in her ear at night in her narrow bed, secrets about Ryan and how she let him touch her, how his callused hands felt on her thighs, how her skin patterned itself to the bumpy vinyl of the seat of his truck. She'd cried in Alta's arms when she fought with her mother, who wouldn't let her dream about swimming at the Olympics in Europe. Alta tried to imagine Shy—that blur of girl passing through her yard—face-to-face with the adult Alta had become and rethinking all her departures, all her lies. Girls came and went now, but Alta couldn't shake Shy. Just like Catholicism. No matter how Alta questioned the Church, or even the existence of God, no other religion could take its place, no other belief could edge it out.

Boys had always liked Shy. She would have been popular with the girls, too, but until she was fourteen she was never allowed to go to parties. She didn't have parties either. On her birthday, Alta was invited for dinner and Mrs. Mallon baked a cake and cooked whatever Shy wanted. On her twelfth birthday—Alta was only ten—Shy met her out front as she approached with Shy's gift. Mrs. C. was an expert wrapper, and she'd curled the ribbon ends between the sharp edge of the scissors and her thumb.

"My mother makes me ask you," Shy said.

Alta stood looking at her, the box held tight in both her hands.

"She never lets me ask anyone else."

Alta kept her face, even her cheeks, frozen. She had learned a long time ago how never to cry.

"It's not because she thinks you're so special, either. It's because you live close by and she doesn't want me to make friends with anyone farther away. She never lets me do anything." Suddenly she was crying, her face still mean, the tears independently sliding down. Alta held the present out, and Shy took it.

"Happy birthday, Shy," Alta said as seriously as she could. She didn't know what else to say to help Shy.

"Why are you so nice to me, Alta?" The way Shy asked was a cross between an accusation and a plea. "You're the only person who really cares about me."

Alta wanted to tell her that they could run away together, that they didn't need anybody else. But later, Mrs. Mallon was in a good mood, and Mr. Mallon was there, solid and reassuring in his dinner chair. Alta could tell that Mrs. Mallon had just clipped his hair, and his thin face was closely shaved. Shy's tears seemed forgotten and her eyes shone as her mother carried the cake to the table. Mrs. Mallon's light accent tipped the melody against Mr. Mallon's deep American voice and Alta's own higher one. They sang "Happy Birthday," and Shy took the deep breath of a girl who could swim the length of an Olympic-size pool underwater and blew them into smoky darkness.

The next year Shy became a teenager. Mrs. Mallon was in bed, not feeling well.

"She was fine yesterday," Shy whispered to Alta as they went upstairs to say goodbye. Mr. Mallon was taking them out for ice cream sundaes.

Mrs. Mallon, lying in bed, frightened Alta. She didn't make much of a rise in the blankets, and her blond hair seemed wispy and dry spread out on the pillow. Shy and Alta stood in the doorway.

"Is she sick?" Alta whispered. Shy shook her head. Mrs. Mallon slowly turned her head toward them and reached out one arm. Her eyes were huge and dark blue, and even without makeup, she looked to Alta like some crazy, aging movie star.

"Sasha," she said, as Shy went over to the bedside.

"Are you okay, Mama?"

Mrs. Mallon stretched her arm up and touched Shy's hair. "You are so . . . grown up. What will we do when you are a young lady?"

Shy sat on the edge of the bed. Alta could see only her back and the side of her face. "I'm going to be a famous swimmer and travel all around the world."

Suddenly Mrs. Mallon lifted her hand and brought it against Shy's face. It was a movement with so little energy that for a moment Alta didn't realize she'd hit Shy, and as Mrs. Mallon's hand fell back toward the bed, two nails scratched hurt-looking red welts in Shy's cheek.

"Don't talk that way," Mrs. Mallon said fiercely and turned her face into her pillow.

"Mama."

Mrs. Mallon's thin body shook beneath the covers.

"Mama."

After a while Mrs. Mallon grew still, but she didn't turn around. The thought of ice cream, and the bright shop full of kids, and Mr. Mallon telling them to order whatever they wanted, made Alta feel sick. She suddenly grew aware of her own breathing, how loud it was, and she tried to let the air in and out silently, through her mouth. Finally, Shy stood up and came over to where Alta stood in the doorway.

"She fell asleep," she said and gently pushed Alta out.

Alta dialed the Seattle number Shy had given her that afternoon and listened to the phone ring hollowly up the fractal West Coast.

"Hello?" It was a man, his voice deep and rough. Alta hung up.

TWO

The walls inside Renny's house were covered in murals: there were blackbirds circling the living room, and a half-naked belly dancer gyrating above Renny's yard-sale couch. A forest of flowers grew from behind the shower curtain. Renny's housemate of the time, Liza, had painted them the summer after she graduated from college when she couldn't find a job and never left the house; her footprints were stained all the way from the front door down the long hallway to the kitchen, the shape of bright red bare feet along the hardwood floor.

Alta had been sleeping with Liza on and off a couple of summers ago, but something about her had reminded Alta too much of Shy. Liza had dark hair and animated eyebrows, but it was her laugh, too, and the solidity of her whims. Alta couldn't make up her mind whether to love her, and Alta told herself she was glad when Liza moved back to her parents' house in Rhode Island though there were times she'd thought of asking Renny for Liza's address. Alta used to imagine that Shy had somehow ended up in Liza's hometown, that both of them were wandering, leaving blazing trails of color and lust behind them in some soggy steepled township.

The wild walls of Renny's apartment gave Alta the kind of glad courage the city itself did. She could explain anything to Renny here among these blackbirds and belly dancers.

Marcie, Renny's girlfriend, answered the door. She was a chubby, voluptuous blonde with a penchant for bright red lipstick. She gave Alta a warm hug and left a bright kiss mark on her cheek.

"Hey, gorgeous," Alta said.

"Shabbat Shalom."

"Yeah, right. That, too."

"Come on up. Everyone's gone home, but there's leftovers if you're hungry." She pulled Alta up the stairs.

"I'm used to leftovers."

"You're the one who comes four hours after we start," Marcie scolded over her shoulder.

"You start too early."

Marcie laughed. "Just when the sun goes down."

Alta followed Marcie to the kitchen, where the table was covered in dirty plates and empty glasses with the red film of wine settling to the bottom. Two candles in tall silver candlesticks were just about burned out.

Renny had her head stuck in the fridge. Marcie pinched her ass.

"Hey now."

"It wasn't me. It was Alta." Marcie put on her wide-eyed innocent face.

Alta shrugged. "Sorry, babe, but you're not my type."

"Think you're mine?" Renny gave Marcie a big kiss and handed Alta the beer bottle she had in the hand that emerged over Marcie's shoulder. Renny was with Alta on this: beer only from the bottle—never a can, never a glass. "Unless you'd prefer Manischevitz."

Alta made a face. "Is that the candied grape juice I had at that . . . dinner for Passover?"

"You prefer the blood of Christ?" Marcie asked.

"I prefer beer."

"So how're you doing, kid?" Renny took a swig of the beer she'd gotten for herself.

Alta rocked her hand back and forth. So-so.

"Hey," Renny inclined her head. "Let's go stargaze." She turned to Marcie. "Do not clean up. I'm going to do it. Okay?"

Marcie pulled Renny's baseball cap down over her eyes. "Go butch-bond," she said.

Alta and Renny made their way onto the landing outside the kitchen and stared down into the dirt floor of Renny's backyard two flights below.

"So what's up?" Renny asked after Alta had let some beer slide down her throat.

Alta shrugged. "I talked to Shy."

"Shy!" The bottom of Renny's bottle hit the wooden railing. "The girl-next-door Shy?"

"No. A different girl named Shy."

"All right there, no sarcasm needed. What's she say?" Renny flipped her cap off, and her blond hair tumbled into her face. Then she caught it back again as she replaced the cap.

"I just went to visit her mother in the hospital. She's in bad shape. She's dying."

"Mrs. Mallon?"

Alta sighed. "It's so unreal. I hadn't called her in, like, a month."

"That's not so long."

"You don't understand. This woman had . . . has no one. Her husband's dead. Shy's off doing whatever the fuck she's doing." Alta took a mouthful of beer and swallowed. "I used to be so scared of Mrs. Mallon when I was little. She seemed strange. She never really left the house, and she'd sort of lurk around watching me and Shy. Sitting completely still, watching. Or she'd pace. She was kind of glamorous in this haggard, forgotten-movie-star way. I used to imagine she was hiding out from her fans, like Greta Garbo, you know?"

"Yeah, except I think Garbo hid in a mansion."

"Maybe Mrs. Mallon was more clever." Alta balanced her bottle on the railing. "I had to go get some papers from her house."

"Next door to where you grew up?"

"Yeah—scary territory."

"Shit, Alta, your life just doesn't quit. Where is Shy? Did you see her?"

Alta shook her head. "She's in Seattle of all places and she has some kind of health problem preventing her from flying."

"She's sick, too?"

"Oh, God, I don't think there's anything seriously wrong with her. I don't know what's up with her."

"Tell me more."

Alta shrugged and took a long swallow of cold beer, draining the bottle.

Some few hundred miles up the green coast, Shy was living out her life. This is what Alta had heard of that place. The sea was gray up there and relentless. It was a place for Shy to relocate, start again. The sea got colder as you headed north—you traded blue for gray in the sky and yellow for green in the grass. People thought California was a stretch of surfers and hippies from Mexico to Oregon, but Alta knew the little towns built in the crux of highways and freeway junctions, the flat farmland—artichokes and strawberries, the hills of wineries full of sunsets and grape-sweet air, the industrial spreads, and the small-town minds that run up and down the coast and inland. Alta had grown up in this state, the other California. Yes, there are redwoods and the salt air of the ocean and days when the sea is furious and the land so fertile that the sea is a mere coda. But there are people just as mean and scared as any and worse, because they're mean in the face of that land, with the breath of that sea.

Alta left Marcie and Renny and walked home through streets crowded with queer couples holding hands, men cruising each other from the doorways of bars, teenagers sitting on top of the metal newspaper boxes on the corners. What made the strangers of San Francisco Alta's family was the kindness in their unfamiliar faces, the curiosity in their eyes. Her hometown was peopled with faces she knew: even the ones she'd never seen before were familiar in their contempt. The queer folk of the City were people with bodies—full or thin-lined, aged or unwrinkled—and hands that were eager for hips, asses, breasts, lips. They watched for each other. They knew they were watching, knew they were watched. In this way they encouraged each other to exist, applauded the daily performance of self.

Shy, Alta whispered into the silence of her apartment when she got home that night. She saw the shape of her head reflected in the floor. She polished the floors every month. Alta liked the clean tap of girl-feet against all that shine.

Seeing Renny and Marcie had centered her. She picked up the phone again, more prepared this time for the man than for the immediate breeze of Shy's voice in her ear.

"Shy?"

"Hey, Alta, did you see her?"

"Shy, you have to come."

There was a pause. Mrs. Mallon had never let on to Alta how much she hoped Shy would come back, even to visit. But Shy had known. The letters made that clear. Don't do this, Shy, Alta thought. Just pull it together and get here.

"What did the doctor say?"

"Well, I talked to a nun and she was vague. They always are. They don't talk death, they talk about time left and, basically, she doesn't have any."

"Well, what could I do, even if I were there?"

"Yeah, I guess goodbyes have never been all that important to you."

"What's that supposed to mean?" Her voice was still soft, but decidedly less calm.

"Look, Shy, I don't know what's going on in your life and, frankly, that's your business. But you asked me to go see your mother and tell you what I thought. And what I think is: she's dying, and whether it's convenient or not, you'd better get down here just as fast as you can."

Shy was silent so long, Alta thought she'd hung up. Alta couldn't even hear her breathe. But she waited. She'd spent a lot of time waiting for Shy, years and years, and if there was one thing she'd learned well it was patience. When Shy broke the silence her voice was calm again, but chilly and distinct.

"You know how she is. Every time I say something, she winces. Just my presence makes her terribly nervous. I've tried to engage her in my life—or even hers. She gave up, Alta, a long time ago."

It was strange how differently Shy saw her mother. Mrs. Mallon had looked out for Alta, let her into her home, and when it was time for her to go, she'd gotten Alta her first job in the City—an accomplishment for a woman who rarely left her house. Mrs. Mallon was funny, too, though Alta only came to know this side of her in the months after Shy left.

"Alta," she'd say in her accented voice on the days that the town closed in on her. She'd look at Alta wryly, her cigarette burning in one hand against the wooden counter. "It's living at the edge of the Bay, hmm? These people think it's the very edge of the whole world. Very important." Then she'd wink. "Go on." She'd blow the smoke from her mouth audibly upward, her nose wrinkling. "Cross it." And they'd laugh together, as if they were two outcasts who could step away from the place they lived and shrink it all to points on a map. It was she who made Alta think her survival was merely a question of escape.

"What did she give up, Shy?"

"I don't know." Her voice was still cold.

"Do you think that might matter?"

"I don't know." Her words came sharper, faster.

"What are you giving up, Shy, not to know?"

"I can't come right now, Alta."

"Well, then, there's nothing else I can do for you, except wish you luck and say I hope you can live with yourself. Oh, and goodbye." Alta held the phone and waited for the line to go dead. They'd never said goodbye, never formally parted, and Alta hoped that if she got nothing more from Shy, she could comfort herself with finally having it said.

"Alta—"

Alta stayed quiet.

"How did you get my number? You said it was a long story . . ."

"Not really. I went to her house and picked up the phone and pressed redial. And there you were."

"You think it's my fault."

"What are you talking about?"

"You really think she's dying?"

"I'm not a doctor, Shy, and I'm not God, but you're her family. You've made a lot of choices I wouldn't have made, but there're just so many years and events you can miss out on before you've just missed it altogether."

"Missed what?"

"Life."

"Or death."

Alta didn't say anything. It crossed her mind that in some unfathomable way life and death were events in each other's circus, but her penny wisdom would be worth to Shy what she was willing to pay for it.

"Will you pick me up at the airport tomorrow?"

Alta smiled at her own reflection in the window. "That depends. How many bags will you have?"

"What? Just one. Why?"

"Let me know what time and I'll be there."

In her empty apartment Alta berated herself. She was always there for Shy, always waiting. But if Shy thought everything would be the same, she was wrong. Alta knew then, in the moment after Shy promised to call before she left, that she didn't want to hear Shy's explanations. Whatever answers Shy had to offer—and there must be some—would be wholly inadequate. Alta's life had progressed, too. No longer was she a suburban tomboy awkwardly retaining her boyishness past adolescence, in love with her next-door neighbor.

She'd had women more beautiful than Shy chase her shamelessly. Women who woke up in the morning and could still look her in the eye, fix her a cup of coffee, kiss her on street corners and dance floors.

Alta had fallen in love with her life. She could trace it to the moment itself, one late-August afternoon, two years after she had come to San Francisco. She was still working for Mrs. Koch, and she was discovering the bars that would let her in even though she was underage. She had just gotten hired at Stigmata, and Indian summer was blowing into the City. Alta saw the motorcycle, a Honda 450, parked on a slight incline, by a lamppost covered in flyers, and as she stood reading the FOR SALE sign, everything around her—the people's bare shoulders and legs, the soap bubbles blowing out of the Bath Shop across the way and drifting through the bright sky, the rainbow flags that dotted the street, even the dirty sidewalk with its stains and circles of chewed bubble gum—encouraged her to live. Maybe other people, straight people in a straight world, get this feeling all their lives. Maybe Shy had had it always, a sense of belonging utterly to the pulse of the moment and the wide-open day, a sense of filling a place in the world that would be empty without you. But that summer afternoon was the first time since her father died that Alta had felt that way.

Alta saw her first butch in a San Francisco bar she'd lied her way into a couple of months after she moved in with Mr. and Mrs. Mallon. With her flat, unwavering eyes, the tough set of her chin, the butch was far more than a mirror to Alta. She was a crystal ball, a promise that a future was possible. She didn't even smile at Alta. Alta wouldn't have wanted her to.

The femmes Alta came to know envied the girl she'd slept with in high school—they would have liked to find themselves underneath her eager sixteen-year-old hands. They imagined a mythical queer adolescence. Alta never told them it was a living hell.

Shy was sixteen and Alta fourteen the day Alta stopped in the middle of one of their uproarious tickling matches and stared down at Shy.

"What?" Shy said, still thrashing like a pinned fish beneath her. "What?" She burst out laughing, as if expecting Alta to join her, but Alta couldn't. She let go and climbed off Shy and the bed. Shy grabbed her leg, still playing, but Alta shook her off and went home.

That evening Alta avoided dinner and a repeat of that morning's fight with her mother about getting her hair styled, this time with an audience. Her uncle had moved the television into the dining area between the kitchen and the living room, so that it felt like they were all always together when everyone was over. Her mother didn't like how Alta wore her hair, pulled back starkly in a single braid straight down her back. Alta could reach behind herself and grab it.

Even when the phone rang, Alta stayed in her room, though she could hear the chair scrape and her mother sigh. Mrs. C. always shook her head when Shy called from next door, a habit they'd gotten into after Shy started high school—but she liked Shy, so she didn't bother Alta about it too much.

"Alta!" Mrs. C. called, and Alta stumbled out and took the receiver without saying a word to her mother. She'd stopped wearing dresses even to church, and her mother vacillated between not letting her attend and trying to force her into a dress, trying to get her to change her hair. Between fights a moody silence served as peace.

"Alta," Shy said, her voice an antidote to Mrs. C.'s. "Come over."

It must have been a weekend night, because Alta remembered asking if Ryan wasn't taking her out.

"Oh, he has to help his dad fix the car or something. Come over."

"In a while," Alta said reluctantly.

Mr. Mallon was watching the news by himself in the living room when Alta got there. She could hear the television even through the glass door.

"Come on in," he said in his quiet, slow way. "Sasha's upstairs. She said you'd be by." He left Alta to secure the door behind her and poured himself a mug of hot tea from a pan on the stove. It hissed and steamed. Alta left him to his methodical, concentrated solitude.

The hallway upstairs was dark, and though Alta knew it well, she felt her way along nervously.

"Shy," she said outside Shy's bedroom, which was at the other end of the hall from Mrs. Mallon's. Alta stood hearing her own breath and seeing the dark shift. "Shy."

She opened the door and peered in. Shy was sprawled, the sheet pulled up to her bare shoulders. Alta could see the angle of one bent leg, one straight, under the sheet. Shy's hair was undone over the pillow.

Alta knelt down. "Shy? Are you fooling?"

When they were little, they used to pretend to fall asleep over at their friend Jesse's house, and he would say, "I know you're fooling 'cause people don't move around in their sleep." Then Shy would sit up furious and explain that that wasn't true; did Jesse always wake up exactly as he had fallen asleep? Jesse would insist that he always did, and Alta would rise up from next to Shy, and the strange warmth and calm of their faked sleep, their bodies side by side.

Now she put her hand out and brushed the hair from Shy's neck. Shy sighed, but did not move. Alta took her hand back. Her eyes settled into the darkness more, and there was light coming through Shy's window from a street lamp above and from Alta's front hall below. Alta could see Shy's nipples against the sheet, and the shape of her breasts.

"Shy." Whispering. Alta took off her shoes and lay down on her side at the edge of the bed and stared at Shy. Very lightly she ran the tips of her fingers along Shy's collarbone and down to the top of the sheet. At the other end of the hall, Mrs. Mallon's door opened and she turned on the hall light. The brightness shot in through the door Alta had left half open.

"Close my door," Shy whispered, her eyes still closed, her head thrown back, so that the moment after she'd said it Alta felt she could not be sure she had. Alta got up and closed it, trying not to see Mrs. Mallon standing in the shock of light at the end of the hall. Shy turned, as if in sleep, toward Alta, her body moving so that there was more room on the bed. In her jeans and T-shirt Alta climbed under the sheet and for the first time found herself next to Shy's naked body, her sleepless dreaming body, a body Alta came to know better than her own.

Now that Shy was coming, Alta had to prepare for her. In the morning Alta stared—mean—into the bathroom mirror. Shy used to stand half-naked in front of her reflection and Alta would watch her and tell her again and again that she was perfect. What a tease she was. Alta smiled, tossed her chin. "Hey," Alta said aloud, her voice dry from the night's silence. She tried to picture Shy swinging off the plane, six years older. Alta brushed her teeth, hard.

She headed into her shower. The water was hot and she let it burn and redden her skin for a while. Finally she added a bit of cold and shampooed her quarter inch of hair. The best sign of whom Alta was fond of at the moment was whom she allowed to shave her head. Alta had to trust somebody to go over the curves carefully, to watch for the patches of hair the razor missed, scattered long and thin as weeds across her scalp. Liza was the one who'd shaved it all off the first time. Scraps of black fell, itchy, on Alta's shoulders and the floor by the chair where she sat. The buzz of the electric razor was as hypnotic as that of a tattoo needle.

The day after she graduated, Mrs. Mallon had watched her pack. Mr. Mallon was away on business, as he was almost all the time after Shy left.

"Alta." Mrs. Mallon stubbed out her cigarette in a little ashtray she carried in her palm. "You always wear your hair braided, never down."

Alta looked in Shy's mirror. Her schoolgirl self had almost vanished except for the dark braid straight down her back. "I'm going to cut it off soon," Alta said, meaning short, shorter than she thought Mrs. Mallon could imagine.

"Would you like me to do it?" She pulled another cigarette out of the pocket of her long sweater, not lighting it but flicking it between her fingers. The smell of dried tobacco floated up from it.

"I don't want a bob or anything like that."

Mrs. Mallon shook her head.

"I want a boy's haircut."

"Like Ryan," she said, nodding.

At loose ends in anticipation of Shy's arrival, Alta filled her kitchen with Shy's favorite foods. She bought ice cream and corn on the cob and a whole crate of lemons, which she had to balance and tie carefully to her bike. She bought flowers, too, bright ones that smelled pungent and wet as cut grass. Her bike on the way home seemed to Alta like a carnival float, a fusion of fruit, vegetables, and blooms.

She spent a couple of hours tightening up the engine, polishing the chrome, scrubbing the rust off the backs of the mirrors. She went over her leather jacket with black polish, too, and cleaned the entire apartment. She put new CDs into her player. There was so much she had found in the past years that she wanted to share with Shy. Songs, and new food, and proud, brave women, the oasis of her own apartment.

She leaned outside, sprayed cleanser onto the windows and rubbed them with newspaper, the way her mother used to do. In their unspoken ways, they'd hated each other, Shy's mother and Alta's. Lonely women looking across a fence at opposite lives. The C.s', crowded with relatives visiting, kids running around, Alta's mother in and out all the time, working and visiting and cleaning and shopping; the Mallons' house big and empty, the stillness of Mrs. Mallon's life, her husband's quiet, bland manner, his extended absences, his constant scrubbing and dusting and sweeping.

Thinking of Mr. Mallon's continuous, futile cleaning, Alta laughed at herself for believing she could be equipped for Shy, have all the props. Some superstitious part of her believed that she could be too prepared, that if she were truly ready for Shy, Shy might not show up at all.

Mrs. C. stopped trying with Mrs. Mallon once she realized they couldn't have the kind of church friendship she had with other women. People are not kind to difference, and Mrs. Mallon's accent was hard for the neighbors and schoolyard mothers to understand.

"I swear, the girl's as unlike her mother as a child could be," Mrs. C. would say, her face tight with disapproval. She used to give Shy snacks after school and ask her about her boyfriends. It was she who hemmed Shy's prom dress—the one Alta had picked out for her—on the afternoon before Shy went off with Ryan, tuxedoed Ryan in his big truck. The same dress Alta peeled off of Shy's sweaty body when she came home to Alta at three-thirty that morning. Such a dark green velvet it was almost black. Alta had picked it for her eyes, and the shine of her nut-brown skin.

Mrs. Mallon was nice enough to Alta, though they didn't talk much until Alta moved in later. But though as a child Alta was a little afraid of her friend's mother, she took Mrs. Mallon's silence as a refuge; she liked how Mrs. Mallon stayed out of their way; she liked how Mrs. Mallon smiled at them when Shy was turned in the other direction, and said nothing as Shy chattered on. Mrs. Mallon never made them be quiet or leave the room.

Mrs. Mallon came to school only once in all the years Shy and Alta were there. It was during an assembly, held in the church because it was the only place all the students fit at one time. Miss Johnson came up to the pulpit and whispered something to Sister Martha, their principal.

"Sasha Mallon, please gather your things and meet your mother by the doors," Sister Martha said, looking sharply out over the students. Alta's heart had jumped a little to hear Shy's name echo through the church. Everyone turned around. Mrs. Mallon stood in the archway at the back of church. She'd seemed odd to Alta before, but only as something separate from Alta and her family, the people she was familiar with. The Mallons' house was so strange to Alta, so different, that Mrs. Mallon fit in with it, though she never seemed very relaxed. But here in the church she looked so thin and pale, her skirt and sweater hanging loosely, her black shoes cloddish and old-fashioned. She looked scared, for some reason, staring straight ahead, not at Sister Martha, but at the altar at the front of the church.

Alta tried to meet Shy's eyes as she walked alone up the aisle, but Shy looked nowhere in particular: not at her mother, not into the rows of children from which Alta tried to telegraph sympathy to her. If Shy wanted to disassociate herself from the shadow in the door, it didn't work. As she walked directly past her mother and out into the sun, her high chin and steadfast nowhere gaze looked like nothing so much as Mrs. Mallon herself.

Later Alta asked Shy why she'd had to go home. Shy shrugged.

"What happened?" Alta asked more insistently.

"She got worried, that's all. My father was away on business. She worries a lot."

Then Shy turned her attention to the paper dolls she used to design and draw herself on the stiff paper Mr. Mallon brought home to her. But Alta knew Shy meant something Alta couldn't understand. *Alta's* mother worried, made her wear sweaters when it was a little bit chilly, insisted on checking her homework, hissed at her to go to sleep when she tossed and turned late at night listening to the sounds of television in the living room. Mrs. Mallon didn't care about those things, at least not regularly. She insisted Shy go to church and to school, and she let her go to swimming practice. Mostly she wanted her to stay close to home—which is maybe why Shy played with Alta all the time—but as long as Shy was nearby, it seemed to Alta that Mrs. Mallon didn't care or even notice much what she did.

As Alta got older, she understood that the quiet she felt in Shy's house was the result of Mrs. Mallon's pervasive depression. But she also came to realize that Mrs. Mallon, in her distant, hovering way, actually watched Shy all the time, was never far when they were around. She kept her door ajar while they played, and if her gaze was hollow, her ear was trained. Alta didn't know exactly how she'd come to know this, except that she had learned to track who watched Shy and who might observe the special attention Alta gave her, and no one was more aware of Shy than Mrs. Mallon, not even Alta.

Shy had left a message while Alta was out at the store.

"Maybe you work weekends," she said. It was the first time she'd mentioned Alta or her life since Alta had called her—was it only yesterday morning? In fact, Alta did have to work the next day. "I arrive this afternoon," she said, her voice sounding tired, defeated. If she was defeated, Alta was the victor, and Alta remembered again how unpleasant winning could be. Still, Alta wouldn't lose, couldn't afford the kindness of that now. She wrote down Shy's flight number, her arrival time.

Shy was really coming back. The fact of this charged through Alta's body like heat. She remembered the way Shy used to flip her hair back from her face, and how she'd wear her bathing suit underneath her school uniform, the blue straps showing through the starched white cotton. Alta remembered how much Shy had loved Alta's busy house. They'd fight over where to play. Shy was nine when Alta met her, sixteen when she first held her as a lover, nineteen when she went away.

Alta saw Shy as if she were in front of her, older and more certain, one hand on her hip, laughing. She imagined touching Shy's arm, and the iciness of her skin causing shocks of electricity to flash. Alta forced herself to focus on the beautiful dresser Mrs. Koch had found for her at a yard sale, the life-sized poster of one woman going down on another that Renny had given her for her birthday last year, the dome of her motorcycle helmet. What if Shy simply didn't arrive? Alta tried to imagine that Shy might not come. If she didn't, Alta thought, she would probably leave her apartment and never come back. The neighbors would notice the stench of rotting vegetables and withered flowers. The landlady would bust down the door and find the pile of shriveled lemons, the floor awash with petals.

Even at the airport, Alta wanted to turn back. She worried that in her anger she would want to shove Shy against the airport wall, shake her, demand answers. As she strode toward Shy's gate against the inevitable feeling that something was closing in, something was bursting open, Alta told herself this was curiosity—a last favor to Shy, a favor to her mother, really; a chance to dispel tired mysteries, to finish what had been over long ago. A young family came walking toward Alta. The small child's voice carried across the flat gray carpet.

"Daddy, is that a man or a woman?"

The father, dressed almost the same as Alta was, in a thick white T-shirt and jeans, looked over at her. He took his little girl's hand. "Well, if that's a woman, it's one damn ugly woman."

The mother shifted her suitcase and giggled.

Alta thrust her hands in her pockets, the chain from her wallet slapping against her leg as she kept up her stride. Ugly to people like that was everything that didn't fit, could not be contained. A lot of the world was those people.

Passengers were already appearing from the accordion tunnel attached to the plane. Alta had timed it so she wouldn't have to wait. She figured she'd been waiting for this moment long enough without having to hang around an airport wondering if the plane would land all right. She saw the top of Shy's dark head first, through business suits and jackets. She knew she'd recognize her; how could she not? She'd studied her face so often growing up. And there she was, utterly familiar, the same almond eyes and full, wide smile, that creamy, almost olive skin, the broad cheekbones and thin nose. Still, Shy surprised her. Under an otherwise well-fitted flowered dress, her belly ballooned out from her body.

That unmistakable curve made everything she'd imagined—anger and lust, love and sorrow—somehow impossible and immediate at the same time. "You'll never have children," Alta's mother had warned her. But Alta could imagine raising a child with someone; she liked the idea of having a pregnant wife. Shy's body suggested something Alta'd been told she could never have. She appealed to Alta even more. But her belly marked another layer of the distance between them.

"Hey," Alta said, smiling more than she wanted to. Shy's face had filled out—though with pregnancy or adulthood, Alta couldn't tell. Shy smiled, and her one dimple stuck in her cheek.

"Hey, yourself."

They didn't touch. They stared at each other. When Alta had first started going over to the City, she used to ask the girls who stared at her what they saw. "Hot," they'd say, Alta's eyes boring into them, her face expressionless, "tough." Alta wasn't the kid Shy had left, but if anyone should have known what Alta could become, it was Shy. Her eyes were surprised, though, and she looked at Alta the way she'd looked at boys she was crushed out on: Ryan in the beginning, and José for a little while before him. Alta knew she had become everything Shy had always wanted. If only Shy had been able to acknowledge that Alta was what she wanted all along.

"Shit, girl . . ."

"Yeah . . ."

Alta noticed the same gorgeous humor in the way Shy's cheekbones underlined her dark, bright eyes. People were staring at them as they walked past. A man took a woman into his arms and kissed her intensely for a long time, but the other passengers streamed politely past them. Shy looked around nervously.

"God, you look really different."

Alta smiled at her again, and for a moment Shy might have been a girl she'd just met. "Not just me, hmm?"

"It's been a long time," she said as if it hadn't.

"How was the plane ride?"

Shy shrugged. "There are only two emotions in a plane: boredom and terror."

Alta looked at her. "Says?"

"I can't remember who said it."

"I take it back; you are exactly the same."

Shy looked at Alta seriously. "I'm not, though, Alta. I'm not—"

"I guess you want to see your mother right away," Alta interrupted her, unprepared for Shy's confessions.

Shy nodded. "We'll talk later."

Alta took her suitcase from her, careful to avoid brushing her long fingers. Still, she remembered the cool of her skin as vividly as if she were feeling it, the shivers Shy's touch sent through her. "Any other bags?"

Shy shook her head. "Just like I promised."

The word "promise" stung, and Alta started walking. Shy kept up with her easily. Alta snuck glances at her belly, her face. She still had a touch of foreignness, something she'd absorbed from her mother. Otherwise she was willfully American: optimistic, self-centered, brashly pretty. Her eyebrows were broad arches, her mouth full and expressive. She caught Alta's eye and her look threw Alta like no one else's could.

"You used to go to school with more stuff than this," Alta said. "I didn't think you'd be able to do it."

"I love a challenge."

"Yeah?" This time, Alta looked at her deliberately, and held her eyes.

"Besides, I don't have many clothes that fit me now."

"My bike's out here," Alta said as they headed for the parking levels. "I think we'll all fit. I didn't know there'd be two of you."

"Yeah. Almost." Shy rolled her eyes and laughed.

Alta noticed that Shy had no wedding ring. She found herself wanting to say more, but nothing seemed casual, and anyway casual would not have been appropriate either.

As they left the oasis of the airport building and moved into the sizzling heat of the day, silence overtook them. All the questions burned in Alta's throat. They reached her motorcycle planted on the shiny plain of cement amid rows of cars. Shy's hands moved beneath her rounded belly, cupping it protectively. The flowered linen gathered at her hands. Alta focused on attaching the suitcase to the silver rack behind the seat, using bungee cords she had brought.

Once she had the bike running, she twisted around to help Shy climb on behind her. Shy stood, heartbreakingly delicate against the dark cement wall and vast pale sky. But she gamely fit the helmet over her long hair and straddled the bike, her hard belly pressing against Alta's back, her hands bunching the leather of Alta's jacket as she held on. Alta squinted into the sun ahead of her as they started down the circular ramp. After a moment Alta felt a second pressure, higher on her back, as Shy lay the side of her helmet-clad head against her.

They swept out onto the freeway, and Alta felt Shy's weight on the bike. It's not body, but character that throws the weight in one direction or another, centers it in the chest or the pit of the stomach or the grip of the legs. Shy leaned so far forward, Alta wondered where she'd balance without her belly; before, where had she put her certainty?

The industrial hills of South San Francisco rose up before them; ragged white letters spelling out the City's name stood against the hillsides. Flat gray water spread from the edge of the freeway to the right. Alta took them over the bridge, all silver and sun, and into the sprawling suburbs that considered themselves towns, cities, even small, liberal countries that founded sister cities in China and voted in city council meetings on foreign policy decisions while their gay staff members remained closeted and almost all the politicians were white. From the height of the bridge, the buildings looked like a cluster of large, irregular objects that for a time one year served as the focal point of activity in the yard at school. What can they have been, those giant three-dimensional puzzle pieces painted kid-bright colors, their jagged edges full of invention? Shy and Alta had scrambled over them, their uniforms flashes of blue-and-red plaid. For the kids, they were spaceships, safety zones, moon rocks, bear caves, home base, the Grand Canyon. Alta used to dream that she and Shy were playing on them alone, in the dark. Sometimes they were jumping together over the gaps, peering down at the sand below. Sometimes they were running around and between the objects, laughing. Sometimes they were playing hide-and-seek and Shy was lost. "Shy," Alta would call, and the smooth surfaces would echo back her name.

When they reached the hospital, Alta went with Shy to the semicircular counter. A wrinkled nun and a younger woman in a white nurse's outfit stood behind it. The nurse was on the phone.

"What can I do for you?" the nun asked Shy.

"My mother." Shy swallowed. "My mother is here. Alice Mallon. I just flew in from Seattle."

"I'm glad you could make it, my dear. I'm Sister Ann." She took Shy's arm, and they walked down the hall. Alta followed, feeling awkward and invisible.

"Any change?" Shy asked.

Sister Ann shook her head. She stopped at Mrs. Mallon's door. Shy glanced at Alta and then walked in slowly.

"Mother?" Shy sounded formal and uncertain. She stood close, her belly pressed close to the faint lines of Mrs. Mallon's body under the hospital blankets. "Mother," she said again, sharply, leaning so far over Alta was afraid she might lose her balance. "I didn't know it would do this to you. I just wanted . . . I'm sorry. It's my fault. It's my fault." Shy's despair echoed back across all the years Alta had known her. It was the part that always got pushed behind the beauty and the daring. Alta went to her side and cautiously—as if she were a fuse and Shy a bomb—put a hand on Shy's shoulder. It had been six and a half years since they'd touched, not counting the leather and metal on the motorcycle, but the body remembers what the mind tries to forget.

"I don't know what to do," Shy said.

Alta looked at the floor, her shoes, and then back. She slid her hand to Shy's back, gently pulling her in. Shy glanced at the nun, hesitating.

"I'll leave you now," Sister Ann said, her mouth tightening. "The doctor should be by within the hour." She turned and closed the door behind her.

Then Shy came to her, eyes squinting as if in an effort to push back the pain that might give her away. Alta recognized that, like swimming, this was something Shy had gotten better at through years of practice. Alta wrapped her arms around her. Shy's belly pressed sideways into Alta, and she buried her face in Alta's shoulder. Alta remembered the smell of her: chlorine and the perfume she wore. She still smelled like vanilla, but the swimming pool essence was gone. Alta could see Mrs. Mallon over her shoulder, the frail shadow of a woman connected to the world only by thin tubes and by the girl in Alta's arms who was about to bear a child of her own. She brushed the strands of hair from Shy's face.

"I knew it would be like this to see her." Alta could hear her voice, muffled against her shoulder. "I can't stand it. I can't stand it that there's nothing I can do." And then her words no longer made sense; they turned liquid with her sobs. Alta held her, tight. She hadn't held on to someone with that urgency in longer than she could remember.

When Shy had recovered somewhat, they separated. Though Alta did not want to let her go, she did so easily, showing no reluctance. Shy, for her part, untangled herself quickly and stepped backward.

"You all right?" Alta asked.

Shy took Mrs. Mallon's wrinkled hand. "I came to visit you, Mama." Mrs. Mallon's eyes were closed, and her body was utterly still except for her soft breathing. Alta watched her open mouth, the gentle rise and fall of her chest, the will of her body to breathe and go on.

There was a tap on the door, and the doctor came in holding a peach-colored binder with the name MALLON block-printed in marker along the spine. He wore a white lab coat open loosely over casually expensive clothing, and his head shone bald above a fringe of hair.

"Hi, I'm Dr. Jeffreys. Are you Mrs. Mallon's family?"

"I'm her daughter," Shy said. Alta said nothing as they shook hands.

"Shall we step outside?" Dr. Jeffreys directed them into the nurses' station. He consulted the notes in the binder. "We don't have a lot of history on her."

"I'm afraid I don't know much," Shy said apologetically, and Alta remembered the tone that always came over Shy when she spoke of her mother to strangers.

"Nothing recent? Heart trouble? High blood pressure?"

"I don't ever remember her going to the doctor, Doctor. She was never a very healthy person, but no one was ever sure what was wrong with her."

"How do things look for her?" Alta asked.

Dr. Jeffreys glanced at Alta and then turned back to Shy, answering her as if she had spoken the question. "She could be fine, or she could be permanently damaged. We'll know in another day or so."

"You don't know?" Shy said.

"Do you know much about strokes?" the doctor asked.

Shy shook her head. Alta didn't bother.

"A stroke is caused by bleeding or blockage in the brain, which cuts off the oxygen supply. If the blockage is momentary or partial, the patient can recover fully in a matter of days. If the blockage lasts long enough, it causes brain tissue to die, and the damage is irreversible."

"How do you tell which it is?"

He shrugged. "You wait. If she walks out of here in the next two days . . ."

"If not?"

"She's suffered paralysis on her left side and partially on her right, as well as speech loss," he replied, consulting his notes again. "It says here she's sixty-three."

"That's what I guessed," Alta said. Shy massaged her temples, each hand framing her tired face.

"Can she hear us when we talk to her?" Shy whispered, coughing to clear her throat.

"She may be able to understand everything that's going on around her, but, of course, since she can't respond, it's hard to say." He glanced at his watch. "I'll be back by in the morning to check on her. Don't worry. Our nurses will take good care of her. And make sure you get some rest yourself, Mrs. . . ."

"Sasha," Shy jumped in, holding her hand out. "Thank you, doctor." He shook her hand, nodded at Alta, and ducked out through the controlled bustle of the nurses' station.

"We'd better leave," Shy said.

"Okay. I'll bring you to my place," Alta said. Shy threw her a cold look and walked toward the elevators. Alta glanced back at Mrs. Mallon and followed.

The fading day outside was still bright, and Alta felt as if they had stepped out of a great darkness and not the neon-lit whiteness of the hospital. The natural light fell on Shy and all her coldness vanished for a moment.

"Let's go to my house," Shy said.

Alta shrugged. "I thought you'd probably want to stay with me. I have some food, stuff like that."

"Aren't you over in San Francisco?" She said it as if it were an unreasonable place to be.

Alta nodded slowly. She held Shy's gaze and raised an eyebrow. "San Francisco," Alta said, charging Shy's alien abstraction with the heat of prayer. The very syllables formed a shield of comfort around her.

"Well, I'd like to see your place sometime," Shy said, vague as ever, "but right now I have to go home."

She wiped the hair from her face and pushed the helmet over her head. She'd been gone so long, neither of her parents would be there, she was almost a mother herself. Presumably the man who'd answered the phone had some connection to the baby and played a role in her life. But—"home"—Alta knew exactly where she meant.

Alta cut the engine in the Mallons' driveway and kicked the stand down with her boot. Shy's weight lifted off behind her, and before she could help Shy she was standing beside the bike, helmet under her arm. The block was quiet, a shady, oddly chilly quiet. Neither of them seemed to want to go into the house, though Alta felt the same external compression that she always felt with Shy, unless they were completely private. It was as though neither of them was certain she could exert enough personal force to keep the outside from crashing in on them. The end of their last Tahoe trip had played out fears they'd held for years. Even now, Alta pushed the thought back, still keeping a silent pact she'd made with Shy the moment the disastrous event had happened.

Alta cleared her throat. "Shy-girl," she said.

"What?"

Alta looked and said, "Nothing."

"Always nothing." Shy handed Alta her helmet to strap back onto the bike.

"Well, then, tell me something I don't know." In her first year of high school Shy used to say this all the time, sarcastically, but now Alta asked it reluctantly, and the echo came to her after the words were out.

"What?"

Alta thought to say, "Are you in love? Married?" but reminded herself it was better not to know, so she said, "When will the baby be born?"

"At the end of October. Two and a half months." Shy's eyes got all wide and bright and she smiled. "Erik and I have been—"

"Halloween?" Alta asked.

"Maybe."

"A Halloween baby."

"It'd be better to have some other birthday."

"That's true. Remember the first Halloween when I was a cowboy and you were a ballerina?"

"Princess," she said, "I was a princess." They'd stood in this very driveway waiting for Mr. Mallon to come out of the house. Shy wore a flowing pink dress and a glittering crown. She was excited that her mother was letting her trick-or-treat, and she twirled to make her skirts flare out. Alta could scan this scene more clearly than she could remember whom she'd brought home the weekend before.

"The car's gone," Shy said now.

"She got rid of it after your father died."

"She never did learn to drive."

Shy went to the front porch, which is what the Mallons did after church and on formal occasions. She had a key with her.

"You know, I've never been here alone. She was always home." She pushed the key stiffly into the deadbolt, more like a real estate agent, or a naughty child, than an adult daughter returning to her childhood home. Shy always seemed less comfortable in her own house than anywhere else. Especially outside. That's where Alta thought of her. Mostly in water, but also barefoot on patches of brown earth and the hot sidewalks. She avoided her house; they both knew this, though they had never talked about it.

Shy pushed the heavy oak door. It stuck, and Alta banged it hard with the flat palm of her hand just above the doorknob. It swung open.

"I lived here for a while," Alta told her and went in. Alta was relieved to be off the porch, since it was a Saturday, and her mother wouldn't be at work.

"What?" Shy said. "When?"

"After you split town."

Shy didn't respond.

The front hall was tiled in mud-brown ceramic squares. Alta used to wait for Shy in that entryway, staring at her scuffed Vans against those dark tiles. The house was all beige and washed-out, faded browns. Shy loved blue, all blues. For a while, when she was fifteen, her whole wardrobe was blue. Even now, she seemed a bit of sky coming in through a crack in the ceiling.

"Alta." She exhaled audibly and spoke quickly and matter-of-factly. "Didn't it seem like she was keeping guard? She never left this place." She looked at Alta challengingly, her head high.

"I think she was pretty depressed."

"Depressed? Depressed is like they don't have your size left in the clothing sale. Depressed is like you planned to go to the beach and it's overcast. She was . . . a black hole."

"Did you ever try to talk to her about it?"

"Did you?"

"We talked a lot after you left."

"And?"

"And, well, not that much. She's not really an open book, your mother."

"I don't even think I considered asking her until after I left. I just accepted it to some degree. We all acted like it was normal, the way she was. You get used to things when you live with them your whole life." She started up the entry stairs, flipping on every light as they went.

I never got used to you, Alta thought. All these years she thought she'd frozen Shy in time, but Shy had kept going. Alta thought change was *her* weapon, her surprise tactic. But what was her shorn head and new confidence to Shy's pregnant body?

Shy placed one finger over her lips as she used to when they'd come back too late from a party. They laughed out loud, but the noise echoed painfully through the house.

Alta followed Shy at a short distance as she circled the downstairs. Shy kept looking into the kitchen, but she walked into every other room before she finally went in there.

"What are you thinking?" Alta asked her, remembering too late how Shy hated to be asked that. But either she'd changed or she was upset enough just to answer Alta.

"There are all these unspoken rules here. Things I'm not supposed to do or touch. Ways to keep the peace. I don't even know how I learned them. Just—you know, one time I broke a glass, I must have been about seven or eight, before we moved. And she just lost it. She had her back to me and she whirled around and started screaming. 'No. No.' Over and over. And she put my hands in the kitchen sink, pulling my arms up over my head so I could reach, and she washed them for a long time, looking for cuts." Shy spread her hands out on the countertop. "I hadn't cut myself. I kept saying, 'I'm okay, I'm okay.' And he'd just say—my father—he'd just say, 'She's worried about you.' And she'd nod and say, 'I'm worried about my little girl.' After one of those episodes, she'd go to bed for days." Shy looked up at Alta. "I know she's dying, Alta. I wish I were the kind of daughter who offered comfort to her. I just never saw anything that offered comfort to her. Everything I ever tried was a big mistake. I just can't tiptoe around her anymore. I have a life I have to get—to get back to."

Suddenly Alta felt she'd taken on more than she'd bargained for. She found herself unable to ask Shy about things she'd wondered for years: why had Shy left? why had she never tried to contact Alta? what did she think of the years when they were lovers and best friends? Alta wanted to know her and she wanted to leave her behind. She didn't want to pick up where they'd left off, to be Shy's sounding board, confidante, someone easily dismissed. Alta wanted to free herself from the past Shy, not get entangled with this complicated stranger.

"Are you going to be okay here?" Alta asked, standing across from Shy in the kitchen as she'd stood across from Mrs. Mallon six years ago, as unable then to tell her just how deeply she shared her loss. Shy's eyes went dull, distant. They slid down to the chain that hung from Alta's back pocket where she hooked her wallet to her belt loop. She blinked abruptly and looked up at Alta's face.

"I'll be okay," she said. "I always am."

Alta adjusted her jacket. "Well, I guess I'd better go."

"Alta." Shy stared straight into her eyes. When she used to do this, Alta felt Shy could see inside her. It scared the hell out of her.

"Don't go yet. Let me cook you dinner. Bet you didn't know I could cook."

"No." Alta tried to smile at Shy. Shy needed Alta now, much more than she wanted her. A dangerous ratio.

"No which? You can't stay, or you didn't know I could cook?" Her teasing tone came back, the sly angles on her eyebrows and cheekbones and glances, the twist of her mouth.

"I didn't know you could cook."

"Erik says I'm the best."

"Erik?" Alta said coldly.

"The baby's father." Shy cradled her belly again.

Alta shrugged. "I have a date tonight." This was true, but it was a backup date, a safety valve. A sweet girl—there when Alta wanted her, and she didn't ask too many questions.

"A date?" Shy seemed surprised. Alta nodded. Shy switched gears, talking fast. "I don't have long here. As soon as I see what I can do for my mother I have to get back and prepare for the baby's arrival." She said this matter-of-factly, yet Alta suspected Shy knew that to Alta "back" meant the void Shy had disappeared into long ago.

"You aren't going to visit your mother again tonight?"

Shy shook her head, that was all.

They walked down to the corner store. Shy had offered to run out without Alta, to pick up the things she'd need, but Alta had sensed Shy's fear of being seen with her, Shy's inability to deal with whatever equation strangers might make of them.

"I'll walk over with you," Alta said. "I don't mind."

Shy shrugged and flipped the key over in her hand.

There was a guy behind the register who didn't know either of them. Shy wandered around squeezing fruit and piling potatoes and onions into her cart.

Up front the rows of candy bars reminded Alta of Shy's old favorite. "Hey, do you have Now & Laters?" she asked. The guy didn't look up. The hum of the produce cases became noticeably loud. He said nothing until he gave Shy her total and took her money.

Shy cleared her throat uncertainly. "Do you have Now & Laters?"

"Everything we have is on display," the guy told her, handing her change and a receipt. Alta took the bag and walked out. For a moment, she thought the bag would slip out of her hands and hit the ground, and they'd be forced back to that parking lot outside of Tahoe, kneeling together on the loose gravel that dug its way into their knees as they salvaged their broken flower pots, the weedy roots already drying in the hot sun, the dirt crumbling around them. She wondered if Shy was remembering, too, but when Shy caught up to Alta, she just shook her head.

"I don't think he heard you," she said.

Shy fed Alta just as she'd promised, the strange, delicious dishes Mrs. Mallon had cooked. What were they called? Alta asked. Shy shrugged.

"One of my mother's concoctions. I think she made them up. I used to watch her."

"When's the last time you saw her?"

"When my father passed away."

"Well. That's good. I mean that you, you know, came back."

"I saw your mom. She didn't seem to know where you were, and it made me feel sad to press her."

"That's funny, because I remember when *your* mother didn't have a good idea of where *you* were."

"That must have been a long time ago."

"I guess so."

"Look, Alta, do you really want to dredge up the past? Because we can get into it if you really want to . . ." She pushed her plate away.

"I don't care. It's so long ago . . ."

"Exactly."

Alta took their plates and carried them into the kitchen. As she scraped leftover scraps into the can below the sink, she noticed Mrs.

Mallon's trash at the bottom—a few tissues, some half-burned matches, an orange peel. Mrs. Mallon loved fresh fruit, craved it. Alta used to bring tangerines and baskets of strawberries home to her after school.

"Whatever made you come to live here?" Shy called from the next room. Alta straightened up and looked at her over the counter, where a half wall left the dining area visible.

"My mother kicked me out right after you left."

"She kicked you out?"

"Queer daughter got to be too much for her to handle. Admittedly, I was pretty sulky, too. Stopped going to school, never went to church—"

"You used to love church." Shy stood up and pushed open a couple of windows. "This place reeks. She always did smoke like a chimney."

Alta started washing the dishes. How often had she stood in front of that sink with her hands plunged into darkening, soapy water, thinking of Shy? Same plates, same kitchen. If only Mrs. Mallon were upstairs, staring out her window.

"How long did you stay here?"

"About three months. Until I graduated." Alta scratched her cheek with the side of her arm, bubbles hanging off her fingertips. "We kept each other company. We were both pretty . . ."

"What?" Shy came over and leaned against the other side of the counter.

Alta looked at the pan she was scrubbing. "Sad. Lonely."

There was silence. When Alta looked up, Shy was still there in front of her, studying her.

"What?" Alta said.

"You have soap bubbles on your face." Shy reached out and brushed Alta's temple. "There. Now you're perfect." She smiled and Alta laughed. "She let you move in? Where'd you stay?"

"In your room."

Shy picked up a glass and put it down again.

"Is that okay?"

Shy shrugged. "I don't care."

"It's because of her that I finished school. I would have dropped out. Hell, I practically had."

"She made you go?"

"No one makes me do anything, Shy. But she encouraged me. She said how important education was in her family, about her father and all that."

A struggle fought its way across Shy's face, a flash of what Alta used to see right before Shy would wipe all expression off her face and turn her body over to Alta. "Her father?" she said softly. "What did she say about him?"

Alta thought about it. "That was the only thing. That he said education was important, couldn't be taken away."

"She didn't go to college."

"Really? She was always talking about books."

"Well, she did nothing but read all day, when she did anything at all."

"She was a good friend." Alta dried her hands on the dish towel that hung on the refrigerator door.

At the end of the evening, Shy settled Alta on the living room couch with blankets and pillows Mrs. Mallon probably never used. Alta positioned herself away from the window that faced her mother's house. Even the lights that cast shadows around the room disturbed her more than she cared to admit.

Some of the nights she'd spent with Shy had been broken by Mrs. Mallon's cries. "She has nightmares," Shy'd whispered, pulling a pillow over their heads. Alta had forgotten these episodes, though, when she moved in. Blocked them perhaps, or not given them significance; accepted them as typical of the Mallon world. A few days after she moved in, Mr. Mallon went away on a business trip. That night Alta woke to hoarse cries, shattering crowlike calls broken by terribly human sobbing. Alta went and stood by the closed bedroom door, rubbing her hands up and down across the wood.

"Mrs. Mallon?" she whispered. "Mrs. Mallon, are you okay?" Mrs. Mallon began yelling—words Alta couldn't make out. Then silence, Alta's own labored breathing, her own fear. Suddenly the door opened: Mrs. Mallon, in a nightgown. She jumped when she saw Alta and began to shiver violently. Alta thought perhaps she had been sleepwalking.

"Come back to bed," Alta said, taking Mrs. Mallon's skinny arm and turning her around. She tucked her under the heaps of covers and then stood looking down. Mrs. Mallon's eyes bounded around Alta's face for a long time, then slowed, and then she closed them. Still Alta stayed watching her. Her eyes opened again, and they gleamed, sunken, in her face.

"Alta," she said, "go back to bed." She held her hand up. "It's better. It's best. I'm fine."

Alta nodded.

"It was . . . a bad dream, a nightmare." Her English seemed more faltering than usual. "I am sorry—" She shook her head. "I am silly and noisy. Please try to keep your sleep. Go." Her eyes followed Alta out.

After that, when Alta heard the screams, she lay in bed and tried to force herself to sleep.

Alta had always had a hard time falling asleep alone. If Shy had replaced the gruff comfort of her father's presence, Alta had replaced Shy with a series of beautiful strangers. She slept best spooned around the lovely body of a sleeping femme.

But tonight she had said to Shy, "Sure, I'll stay on the couch. I don't have to work until the afternoon." Maybe if she hadn't said that, Shy would have brought her to her bed. She doubted it. She certainly wasn't going to let Shy know she needed her now. Alta put her arms awkwardly around a corduroy couch cushion and lulled herself toward sleep, trying not to think about Shy. The last picture that floated through her head was the flat surface of Shy's stomach, watery tracks of ice crisscrossed over it, and her own tongue longing to dip into the tiny pond of Shy's belly button.

Alta drifted in and out of sleep, and it was hard to tell what she was remembering and what she was restlessly dreaming.

Ping. She opened her eyes. *Ping.* She followed the strange noise out to the balcony. Shy was dropping small pebbles from a window box down into the rain gutter below. They hit with an eerie, metallic ring.

"What're you doing?" Alta asked.

Shy wore a long flannel robe. Alta guessed it was blue, though she couldn't make out colors in the black moonless night. She could just trace the straight line of Shy's nose and the rise of her cheek behind it, and her shadowy hair falling around her shoulders.

"Did you know that bats see by bouncing sound off objects?" Shy dropped another pebble.

"Really?" Alta leaned over the railing.

"Well, I think so. I read it somewhere." Shy was always full of facts and quotations. Her odd bits of knowledge gave Alta a sense that there were unseen layers to the world.

"Do you remember when I taught you to whistle?" Alta's voice sounded constrained. Even in the dark, she knew exactly where Shy was, exactly how far away.

"No, I taught *you* to whistle, the summer before I started middle school."

Alta could see the faint silhouette of Shy's head turn toward her.

"No," Alta said. "It was the year your parents wouldn't sign you up for swimming at the Y, and you moped around all summer, standing absolutely still with the sprinklers going full blast and you right in the middle with your eyes closed. I taught you to whistle, and at first you didn't want to learn."

Shy laughed. "I remember showing you how to pucker your lips and you said people would think I was teaching you how to kiss. We laughed so hard I had to run behind that azalea bush in your back-yard to pee."

They'd known "azalea" because one year, after a child's lifetime of flowerless leafiness, that bush had bloomed. Alta's mother had picked one of the delicate, bunchy pink flowers and stood in her front yard holding it as if it were some kind of offering. Patrick Mallon had pulled up in his car, and Mrs. C. had called out, "My azalea bloomed."

Mr. Mallon came over to the property line. "Well, Joan. Isn't that pretty."

"Pretty things do grow here, Patrick," Alta's mother said. Shy and Alta giggled.

"Sure they do, Joan." He smiled and walked toward his house. Alta looked up, and Mrs. Mallon was in her window, one hand holding the opposite elbow and the other holding a cigarette. Her own mother seemed silly to Alta, with her permed hair and thin lips. Her mother felt sorry for Mr. Mallon. She'd said so. But Alta thought Mrs. Mallon was the most beautiful older woman she'd ever seen. She looked like Shy, only pale and blonde where Shy was dark.

Shy hurled another pebble. It thudded against dirt.

"You missed." Alta looked up at the stars in their chalky cloud. There were more stars visible here than in the City, but to her the lights of the City were their own dense galaxy.

"Here, hold your hand out." Shy's fingers touched Alta's arm and felt their way down. She poured a handful of gravel into Alta's palm.

The sharp pieces dug into Alta's skin as her fingers closed around them almost automatically. She picked one up between thumb and forefinger, then closed her eyes and leaned through the darkness. She thought of Shy squatting behind the leafy bush, a stream of warm yellow splattering the dirt below her. She dropped the pebble from her hand, giving it a mild toss. *Ping*, it clinked through the grating.

Alta ran her tongue over her lips and pursed them. She pierced the hot air with the notes of a song Sister Martha had taught them one May: "Mary, we crown you with blossoms today." She hit that minor tone and each of the careful pauses Sister Martha had taught them with endless practice. "Queen of the Angels, Queen of the May."

Shy joined in, her whistle clear and strong. They each held the last note, stretching it out as long as they could until it became a tuneless monotone. They sounded like an emergency broadcast signal. *This is a test. This is only a test.* Shy ran out of breath first and stopped. Alta changed pitch and threw in the final three notes again as her last bit of breath trickled out.

"Show off," Shy said. But she was laughing.

Shy poured her entire hand of gravel off the balcony and into the trough. It crashed down like muddy rain.

"Shy, I can hold my breath long enough to make a woman come with my mouth. You didn't stand a chance."

When Alta woke up in the morning, Shy was standing by the couch in her robe, watching her. Alta sat up quickly, surprised that she had stayed asleep while someone else was awake.

"You always look so—*solid* when you're sleeping," Shy said.

"Oh, you've watched me sleep before?" Alta ran her hands over her shaved head to clear off any lint. "I don't remember ever sleeping around you."

"What are you talking about? We slept together all the time. I mean . . ." Shy flushed.

"I was always awake long after you fell asleep."

"No. I'd wake up in the middle of the night and you'd be sleeping." Shy leaned against the banister, the thrust of her belly against the blue flannel as suggestive as breasts straining against a low-cut top. "I watched you because you seemed so . . . real. My mother always looked as if she might vanish or disintegrate. She'd lie absolutely still, but when I tiptoed around the bed to study her face, her eyes would be wide open, staring. Sometimes I thought she was dead." Shy met Alta's eyes, intense and worried. She rubbed a hand over her face and settled it back on the curve of her stomach.

"Let's have breakfast," she said abruptly.

Alta stood up. "Moving pretty fast there, Your Shyness." She scuffed the top of Shy's head, mussing her thick hair. "May I listen to the baby?"

Shy lifted her hands. Alta slid onto her knees and placed her cheek against the stretch of Shy's dress. Her belly was hard, much harder than Alta expected, and her belly button pushed softly against Alta's cheek. She wanted to just stay with her face glued to Shy's body, to master the mysteries of it. But she knew she mustn't. She stood up.

"Kid says, 'Nice to meet you, Alta, my mom's told me a lot about you.' Kid can read your mind, you know." Alta smiled.

"Come on, I'll make you breakfast."

"Woman, you are a born femme." Alta laughed. "Because food charms a butch more than beauty. It's harder to come by."

"The combination must be unbeatable."

"It is, Shy, it is."

They moved into the kitchen. With the morning light coming in the windows and last night's dishes piled in the drainer, the room seemed almost lived in. Shy retrieved some of the potatoes from the bag of groceries Alta had carried home for her from the store.

"What would you like me to do?" Alta asked.

"Just talk to me." Shy rinsed the potatoes in a large colander she dug out from under the sink. She knew where everything was; indeed, nothing had changed. For a moment Alta wondered if the cereal and the plates and everything were in the same place next door, at her mother's house. She focused back on Shy's confident hands as she cut each eye out.

"Have you ever looked at your parents' papers?"

Shy pulled a metal cheese grater out from one of the drawers and shook her head. "I can't go there, Alta," she said, meeting Alta's eyes for a moment. "I thought you took care of all that." She began shredding potatoes against the grater in quick, jerky movements. Alta looked away as Shy's knuckles approached the sharp-edged holes.

"There are things that don't make sense to me. Maybe you should just look around, go through their papers and stuff."

"Why does anything need to make sense, Alta?"

"What is wrong with you, Shy? You used to want everything, all at once."

Shy sighed wearily. "I still feel like I'm not supposed to touch them. There were all these invisible barriers around our separate lives, and to cross them meant risking . . ." She stopped grating for a moment. "I don't know." She cracked a couple of eggs over the shredded raw potatoes.

After a moment of silence, she looked up again. "What do you think happens when someone dies?"

"They have a funeral," Alta said dryly.

"I mean it, Alta, what do you believe?"

"I believe in surviving as well as I can, and when that is no longer possible, then dying."

"Are you scared?" Shy smiled when she said "scared." Her eyes looked into Alta's again.

"Sure," Alta said. "All the time."

"What scares you most?"

Alta thought to say, "You," but, after all, it wasn't true.

"Hmm? What scares you most of all?"

"Ignorance," Alta said finally. "The things people want to believe that just aren't true."

"That scares you the most?" Shy squinted at her. "Why?"

"Because plenty of people want to believe I don't exist, or shouldn't."

"You think about that all the time, don't you? About being different, wanting women or whatever . . ."

"Yes," Alta said. "I think about it all the time."

They were silent for several minutes.

"Are there relatives of your mother's you should talk to? Do you have an aunt or anything?" Alta asked.

"She never mentioned anyone."

"What do you mean?"

"I never met anyone. She never talked about anyone. I think she sort of cut them out of her life." She pressed her lips together. "When I was little I used to think sometimes that I was adopted."

"What does that have to do with meeting your mother's family?"

"I don't know. We just weren't like your family, all right?"

Alta could never get away from her family. There were always stray relatives staying with them until they got on their feet. On holidays they'd have huge barbecues with all the cousins. When Alta got older, she'd bring Shy with her, and Shy would serve Alta her plate, just as Alta's aunts served their husbands. No one ever said anything. Alta'd just sit down in one of those fraying lawn chairs and talk and drink beer, or play darts with the older boy cousins, while the women inside the house made potato salad and punch. Everyone could see that Shy was much prettier than all Alta's cousins' pimply girlfriends. Alta knew they knew it and that was part of her pride, how she could survive the way they looked at her, their stupid questions about boyfriends, the way their pauses assumed she couldn't get someone to love her because she was ugly. And all the time, Shy was crawling into Alta's bed nights saying, "Alta, if you were a man, I'd marry you," waiting for Alta's hands to do what nothing of Ryan's could ever do.

One year Alta's cousin Peter with the oversized Adam's apple asked her for Shy's phone number. Alta ignored him, stared at the barbecue pit and took a swig of beer from her bottle. Alta'd just beat his ass at darts, and when she knew she could look at his ugly face without ripping him apart, she said quietly, "Don't take it past darts—it won't get any prettier."

That was near the end anyway. Shy left later that year, and even if Mrs. C. hadn't kicked her out, Alta never would have gone to the family barbecues without Shy to act as buffer. Instead, Alta watched them from Shy's bedroom window and felt for the first time how lonely Shy must have been in her big, empty house, hearing all that laughter and noise coming up from below.

. . .

Shy brought a heaping plate of crisp potato patties out onto the back deck, and they ate their way through them with applesauce and sour cream. As Shy lounged in a lawn chair, Alta leaned back against the deck rail. The sun was already blazing through the pale sky.

"There's a lot more earth in Seattle," Shy said. "I mean it's green there. Green and gray."

"I'll take cement and a clear sky myself," Alta said.

"I don't see how you stayed here." Shy wrinkled her nose.

"Actually I hardly ever come over here."

"It's always so hot." Shy peeled her robe away from her sweaty mound of stomach.

"I swear you bring this heat, Shy. It was damned hot when you left."

"Left?" Shy seemed puzzled, as if she'd forgotten that she'd left, or maybe that she'd ever been here before.

"You know, when you ran away or whatever."

Shy said nothing. She didn't deny having run away. She reached for her water glass and took a deep sip. Water pearled on her hands, transparent against her faintly olive skin. She had said she was thirsty all the time now. Alta remembered her always in water anyway, her hair dripping wet, onto her shoulders. Alta waited as Shy swallowed her mouthful of water. Belly and all, Alta kept expecting to see Shy in her St. Monica's plaid, or one of the series of bathing suits she liked to change into after school.

"I'm taking you out tonight," Alta said finally, authoritatively, the way she spoke to other women.

"I'm very pregnant."

"Yes." Alta nodded. "Be ready at eight."

She shook her head. "I have to visit her."

"Visiting hours will be long over by the time we go out."

"I never go out anymore. Besides, I hardly brought any clothes."

"What about your old clothes?"

Shy used to wear bohemian layers of loose cotton, silk camisoles, knit sweaters. Her long, straight skirts shaped themselves around her narrow hips.

"My high school stuff wouldn't fit, and anyway I got rid of it all when my father died." She dipped her fingers into her glass and trickled water across her collarbones and down between her breasts.

Alta looked away, over at the sewer grating. "Anything black is fine for the clubs."

Shy shrugged, sucking on her fingertips. "They don't make a lot of maternity dresses in black."

Alta bent over and retied her bootlace.

The phone rang shrilly into their silence, and Shy heaved herself up and went to it.

"Hello?" Alta could hear Shy's neutral voice, speaking to no one, to everyone, the way she sounded in public. Alta had sat through hundreds of hours of Shy's phone conversations with boys during their high school years. While Shy talked Alta used to rub her bony feet or straighten her room, hanging her silky dresses, her uniforms, the stiff, starched shirts. Alta had studied the nuances of Shy's voice, come to learn when trouble had arrived, and another boy had surfaced as a potential rival.

At first Shy murmured. "Hospital . . . tired from flight." Then Alta heard her apologize. "You're right," she said—rare words for Shy. Then "I don't know," her favorite phrase, one only Shy could assert as a definite opinion. "I don't know," again, sharply. And Alta knew it was the man—Erik.

"As soon as I can," Alta heard. A pause, and Alta imagined Shy winding the spiraled cord around her hand. "I have to try, Erik. And I have to go now."

Alta turned back to the yard, saw their scattered pebbles in and around the cement trough. "The baby's kicking." She heard Shy laugh softly: she held her forehead against her fist, staring down into the dirt and cement below.

Alta needed to get Shy out of this house and into Alta's world. She straightened up and looked at Shy as she came back. Every time

Alta turned away and then saw her again, Shy surprised her: that pregnant belly, those grown-up eyes.

"Look, Shy," Alta said. "Wear anything you want. Just come."

She'd ridden plenty of girls on her bike, but none of them left the emptiness that Shy did. Alta didn't let any one person ride more than a few times. A motorcycle becomes a part of you, and having someone on the back can get too comfortable. When she's gone you feel it like an amputated limb. Alta'd had Shy to keep the other girls at bay, to remind her of the price you pay for getting used to a person. Alta'd kept Shy out of her system with a burning rage.

She headed away from Shy's house toward the City, feeling the wind on her back. She would be feeling Shy there soon enough, and she'd do things Shy had never imagined when she'd rolled away from Alta's hands in the dark of their teenage years, still breathing hard, never speaking.

Shy had come back to Alta's yard a couple of weeks after their first meeting. It was hot: the onset of summer. She wore a yellow bathing suit covered in delicate red flowers. Alta was fascinated by the red flowers; they fell like freckles on her body.

"I'm not usually so shy," Shy had said, her big eyes widening humorously. "Look." She held her arm in Alta's direction. "My poison oak is all gone." The skin was smooth and faintly pink—perfect.

"Wow. Do you get that a lot?"

"Nah. There was poison oak in the park by my old house, but I'm not going back there." They stood with the fence between them. "Do you have sprinklers?"

"We have this thing." Alta kicked the spouted hose attachment that was lying in the rough grass.

"Let's turn it on." Shy scrambled over the fence. Alta watched, amazed.

"There's a gate over there."

Shy shrugged, standing in front of Alta. "Go turn it on. Okay?"

Alta turned it on and stood by the corner of the house, watching Shy dance through the spray.

"Come on."

Alta shook her head.

"Don't you like water?"

"Not that much." Alta couldn't swim. She had refused even to try on a bathing suit.

"Want to hold the hose? You can spray me."

"Okay." Cautiously, Alta approached the spurting water from behind, leaning back. Shy burst out laughing, and Alta realized she was grimacing.

"It's just water. Here." She unscrewed the attachment. Water leapt about in great arcs. Alta ran over to the bushes.

"Here." Shy handed Alta the hose, with water pointed away from her.

"Okay, shy girl. Watch out." Alta turned the hose on her. Shy laughed hysterically.

The skyline of San Francisco appeared as Alta emerged from the tunnel at the midpoint of the bridge. For once the air was transparent, though thick with heat. The heavy, graceful columns of the bridge sloped gloriously above her head and before her. The wind beat hard and Alta pushed into it, loving the battle with its salty harshness. Alta paid a second toll to the homeless man at the foot of the freeway, and he God-blessed her and she thought: the prophets are in the streets where they belong and not in any dark cathedral.

She almost went straight to work and then on to the bar in clothes that smelled like sweaty dreams of Shy. Closed-eyed thoughts of Shy had gotten her through more than one boring fuck. But her basic desire for cleanliness won out. Alta took a shower; her appetite for heat reawakened the instant she shed her clothes. It felt so good to stand under the scorching billows of steam and piss-hot streams of water.

She put on a garage-mechanic-blue short-sleeved button-down that was hanging in her closet and a pair of new jeans she'd broken in with repeated washings. She ran one hand over the shiny almost-black new growth of hair on her head and was ready to go.

She worked afternoons, and piercing flesh was routine to her. Trees grew out of small squares in the concrete on the street where she worked, trees that took their only encouragement directly from the sun. Outside Stigmata Tattoo and Piercing Parlor a tiny Christ figure was nailed to one of these scraggly trees. Little holes had been bored into the metal mold of his miniature hands, and the doer of the deed had put penny nails through them and hung him there. Neighborhood teenagers, punks, and hippies tucked wishes on scraps of paper behind Jesus' lowered head, caught between the crown of thorns and the gray branches of the tree. Alta made it her job to take them down and read them. They were never signed, or, if they were, no phone numbers were given. Wishes don't work that way.

Alta pulled two new crumpled notes from Jesus' head. "Tracy plus Robbie," one said cryptically. "Please don't let my little brother die," the other read. Alta would burn them together in a tiled box in her piercing room below a poster of the Virgin, huge and colorful. Her clients looked up into Our Lady's eyes while she drove needles through their flesh. Holy Mary, Mother of God, pray for us sinners now and at the hour of our death, amen.

The door to Stigmata jingled when Alta pushed it open. Harriet had strung a line of rusted cowbells along the top a couple of months ago. They rang like industrial wind chimes with people coming and going. They announced the bodily changes produced in people there, anticipated them, a reminder that metal could produce, along with heat and holes, a lot of sound. Harriet stood behind the front desk in a fuchsia mini-dress and matching fingernails. She winked at Alta through cat-eye glasses, her Cleopatra haircut swinging.

"Have a good day off?" Harriet leaned her elbows down on the appointment book. Harriet was what Alta called a San Francisco straight girl, which meant she flirted with everyone, and, if the moment was right, she might do anything. But Harriet had given it the right amount of thought and experimentation, and she was ultimately straight, had this faggy-looking boyfriend they all called Lanky.

"All my days are good ones and—"

"All your women hot. I know, I know."

Alta swung into her "office," regaining her equilibrium with the routine of her day. Harriet had laid out her sterilized tools. She had two eyebrow piercings, one belly button, five ear holes, and a clitoral piercing lined up. She put a match to the scrap-wishes she'd taken from the tree, holding them between her fingers as the flame grew up the paper. All she had of Shy were the bits of lined school paper on which Shy had written notes to her. She had held on to these as if they were the IOU Shy had not given her for the money, for herself. Alta hadn't wanted to think she could be left with nothing. Now that she knew, she tried to let nothing be enough. On the other side of the door, she heard the phone ring and Harriet's cheery answer. It all seemed far away. Shy seemed imaginary and nothing else seemed real, either.

For years Alta had contented herself with the nights of her adolescence when Shy had turned to her, answering in secret a desire Alta could barely articulate for herself. At least in those days she'd been so grateful for the access Shy permitted her that she hadn't complained. Alta needed more this time, more than the silent agreement of Shy's body with hers, more than one night in darkness.

Alta dropped the last burning edge of white into the tiled box and it curled into black.

After work, Alta could have called any one of those girls she kept on file in her Rolodex. But she felt up to a challenge, wanted the collective murk and mirth of the bar, the multiple eyes, the other butches circling the pool table, the glance of long hair against leather, the anonymous press of bodies in a crowd. Well, that last would have to wait. The bar wasn't very full this early.

Alta chatted with Pat, the bartender, until a disheveled beauty with dyed black hair and a pale face cruised through the door. Then Alta watched her and sipped a beer, and after a while the edges of the beauty's body started to glow. She ran her hands over the bare flesh of her own arms as if she were cold, but she wasn't.

The beauty watched the pool game, leaning against the railing of the stairs and sliding the nail of her thumb under her other nails, one at a time. Soon she swung her head around. When she saw Alta she smiled and then looked down at the nails on her hand. A pronounced shiver ran over the femme's body, and Alta watched it shake through, the kind of ice-cold you feel when you accidentally touch a lit stove.

The game ended—Alta wasn't paying attention to the shots—and the femme sauntered over to the bar, her short dress swinging and her athletic legs strong beneath her. Never underestimate the strength in a woman's legs. Any woman's legs can best any man's arms if it comes to a fight. She raised her red Shirley Temple to Alta, just slightly, and Alta, just as slightly, raised her eyebrow at her. Sometimes Alta would go to them, but there were days when she wanted her pick to come to her, and this was a day like that. The femme brought her drink to Alta's end of the bar, and Pat smiled at Alta and turned to shining glasses with a rag.

"Lara." She opened her mouth for that first wide *a*, and her tongue flicked and disappeared.

"Alta." They shook hands.

They looked at each other and Alta thought, I could go for a few slow hours in bed with her.

"You drink Shirley Temples," Alta said.

Lara nodded. "I like sweet things." She smiled with her mouth open, and her tongue made another appearance.

"Well, what are you doing over here, then?"

Lara took a long sip of her drink. Alta thought of Shy and her interminable glasses of water. She reached a hand up to Lara's face, pulled her hair back with her fingers. She smelled pungently of amber and grenadine. Alta stood up and Lara sat down on the bar stool behind her. She still hadn't responded. She looked a lot less cocky now, but Alta liked that, too. Then again, she opened her legs and Alta pressed between them. Her body was warm and her hair long and Alta's hands ran marathons. Alta delighted in the beauty's vulnerable availability, the certainty of her half-finished drink forgotten, the buttery-toast taste of her beneath the cool sweetness of ginger ale and syrup on her lips. She wanted her alone in her bed, spread out for her, before she went back to the challenge of Shy.

Alta pulled back a little and Lara leaned into her.

"Let's go."

She looked at Alta wide-eyed for a moment, then tossed one shoulder and smiled wryly, her mouth closed this time. "All right," she agreed.

"That wasn't too hard." Alta pulled a five out of her wallet and left it on the bar.

"You're very convincing," the femme said, sassy again.

Alta arrived at Shy's, shored up against the effect Shy had on her, and eager to have her belly-centered weight on the back of her bike, excited to bring Shy across to the sparkling, queer city night. She knew she looked good, too, in a navy blue button-down with a couple of the top buttons fastened and a crisp white T-shirt showing below. A chain hung from her belt to the wallet in the pocket of her jeans. She'd rubbed Vaseline on her tattoos so they shone—the Virgin of Guadalupe on one arm and Cat Woman on the other.

But when Alta knocked on the Mallons' front door, there was no answer. She tried the handle, because she was standing on the front porch in full view of her mother's house. The door opened.

"Hey, Shy," Alta called out.

As she turned the corner coming up the stairs, Alta saw Shy's hair first, thick and black, fanning out and spilling over the top step. Alta moved faster than she had in a long time. There wasn't much that made her run. Shy lay spread on her back in a short black dress, her belly rising and falling on the horizon of her body. Her eyes were open. Alta remembered then how Shy used to flop down wherever she felt like it, though she never felt like it for long.

"Shy, honey, what's wrong?" Alta bent down, stroking her hair, brushing her bangs back from her soggy face.

"That's not my name," she said hoarsely, wiping her nose against the back of her hand.

"I know," Alta said. "It's the nickname I gave you, the first time you leapt over my fence in your bathing suit and introduced yourself to me."

Shy half smiled, and Alta watched her face upside down. "That was the second time."

"Was it?"

"I just got back from the hospital. It's so strange how she's there and not there. I miss her so much, and at the same time I feel like I don't even know her." She wiped the film of tears off her face. "How could you be friends with my mother while I hardly even knew her? Why was she there for you and not for me?"

Alta brushed a strand of hair off Shy's face. After all this time, Alta was still used to Shy's anger and the sorrow behind it. "I didn't want anything from her, Shy. I didn't want her to go to the PTA or pick me up from swim meet. I didn't want her to cook dinner unless she happened to feel like it, and—"

"You didn't want her to tell you she loved you, or that she was proud of you, or that you were special, not like all the other kids. You didn't care if she got up happy or sad or if she got up at all. And she didn't have a heart attack if you were one minute late coming home, did she? Or if you didn't call when you said you would? Or if you called and asked to stay with someone she didn't know very well, someone who didn't live next door."

"Mothers are like that, Shy."

"Oh, yeah? Did your mother shake so violently that her teeth clattered if you came in late? Did you know that, Alta? I'd get home and she'd be sitting, hunched over on the steps, watching the front door. If you were with me, she'd run up the stairs and into her room. But if I was alone, she'd stay there, shaking and clicking her teeth, while I walked by her on the stairway. She wouldn't even look at me."

"Shy." Alta closed her eyes. She took Shy's hands. "I'm sorry you had to go through that. I really am."

"It's not your fault." As quickly as Shy had unleashed her feelings, she reined them in. "Help me up."

Shy struggled onto her elbows. Alta braced one hand below Shy's back, and Shy arched up, belly leading, until she was sitting on the top step. She used to be able to go into a backbend from a standing position. She'd do it all the time. Alta would be talking to her in her yard and suddenly Shy would lift her hands over her head and sink down into a bridge, her ribs a sharp line above her tight stomach. Now her adult body undid this motion, reversed it, and she struggled to her feet.

She smiled ironically, her cheeks tight. "You were right, Alta."

"Those are words I like to hear."

"I mean, I had to come . . ."

"Yes, well, I didn't know about your condition." Alta reached one hand to where Shy's dress bucked along the full curve and smoothed it down, feeling again the unexpected hardness of the flesh there. Shy closed her eyes and Alta rested her fingertips, warming to hot, against her.

"But Erik's right, too. There's nothing I can do for her," Shy said, opening her eyes again. Alta's hand fell away. "I'd better wash my face."

Shy headed down the hall and Alta followed, leaning against the door as Shy blasted water into the porcelain basin, giving Shy an edge of burning in her gaze, though Shy didn't seem to notice particularly. She buried her face in handfuls of water. Alta took a deep breath. She was trying so hard for a calculated distance: close enough to ensnare Shy with warmth, far enough to avoid the trap herself.

Shy surfaced from the sink, droplets rolling down the angled planes of her face. She stared into the mirror. "Should I wear makeup?"

"Tonight or in general?" Alta leaned against the wall behind her.

"Just tonight," Shy said sharply. She stared at Alta defiantly. Her face looked very young despite the outfit she'd managed to create, which was pretty fitted for a maternity dress. Looking closer, Alta could see that Shy must have taken the dress in at the hem and in the back.

"Lots of girls do. Eyeliner or whatever. Not that pancake stuff you smear on your skin, though. I don't like it."

"Didn't 'girls' go out of use in the civilized world around the time we were girls?" Shy collected drops of water off her jawline with two fingers.

"It's back in. Riot Grrrls. Guerilla Girls."

Shy looked at Alta with a blank mirror-face as she walked past her into her room. There was the bedside table Alta had spray-painted baby blue for Shy in high school. Some of the grass from the Mallons' lawn had gotten sprayed with the paint, too, and Shy had pointed out the blue grass to Alta every day for a week afterward.

Shy pulled an eyeliner pencil from beneath her clothes, and then a tube of mascara. Shy lay each of these on the bedspread and kept digging. Alta wanted to wrap her arms around Shy, cradle her newly full breasts, reach up under her dress. Shy turned and caught Alta's look. She sat heavily on the bed.

"I'm not a good girl, Alta."

"I know, Shy, I know."

She looked up at Alta. "I know you know." They stayed that way for a moment. Then Shy heaved herself up from the bed. "How do I look?" She presented herself, one hand on the wall, the other skirting the edges of her body, her hair. Her eyes jumped around Alta's face, as if she could find deeper truths hidden there that Alta wouldn't say. Her thick black eyebrows arched high over her deep eyes. Her hair fell around her shoulders.

"You're beautiful, Shy. Don't you know that by now?"

Her eyes lowered. She turned her head, laughing. "I don't get bored hearing it."

Alta could tell no one paid attention to Shy the way she had. Alta counted on that with most women: hardly anyone listened to them talk. And Shy's pregnancy could only have abetted this. Now the men who used to vie for her favors would just smile nervously, hold doors open, and turn away. Alta knew how carelessly Shy's body had been handled. It had started with Ryan, but Alta could see it hadn't stopped there. Shy had loved people's eyes on her, wanted to be watched, to be seen. Now, it was a rare glance that saucily demanded full attention. She used to walk around with a book on her head. "Look, Alta," she'd call out, her chin balanced high, her small breasts pushed forward, her spine a taut rope of certainty. Now all her body sunk toward her pregnant stomach, and even that was tight and compact.

"Are you going to take me out or what?"

Alta relished Shy's mean edge, even as she sought to press it back on her, relished the rebellion that had reminded Alta of other places that Shy—even more than Alta—had no idea existed. Alta smiled at her. "Are you ready to go out?"

"As soon as I've done my makeup." Shy took off for the bathroom, turning to say, "By the way, I never use pancake. It clogs the pores." No one ever accused that girl of moving slowly from one thing to the next. It was staying in one place that she feared.

They were in the driveway before Shy stopped and asked, "So where are you taking me?"

"My good friend Renny's having a birthday. Should be a fun party, and I need to make an appearance." Alta held out the helmet for Shy.

"You know I won't drink." Her hands flitted over her extended stomach.

"All right." Alta gave Shy the smile that had persuaded more than one uncertain woman her way. "I won't drink either, how's that?"

"Really?" Her eyebrows bunched.

"Hell, Shy, half the women there won't touch the stuff." Alta thrust the helmet out again, and Shy took it.

"You sure do swear a lot now, Alta." In the old days Alta wouldn't say *hell* or *damn* or take God's name in vain.

"Times change," Alta said and looked Shy right in the eye until Shy bent her head and put her helmet on.

The darkened streets of their hometown had turned gray with the night. Alta's bike seemed to roar against all that quiet. Once they were heading into the City, Alta felt buoyed up. Clouds of fog reflected rows of bridge lights. Alta loved that bridge. She'd heard that most people who jump off it face the City, and she supposed that if you're going to fly, that would be the way to go. Shy's hands pressed into Alta's sides. The City, lights covering the velvet hills, opened up before them. Alta wanted Shy this once—maybe always—to see the world looking over Alta's shoulder. Alta would remember the press of Shy's hard belly through leather on her back, Shy's bony hands holding tight. Alta knew how a memory became part of her skin and heat; that encouragement, which she took from everything, was not soft smiles and baubly words, but steaming chunks of life—the hard asphalt rolling blurred and molten beneath her wheels, the tears she wanted to lick off Shy's face while she gripped Shy's hair close to the scalp—things that give courage by their opaque reality.

She pulled behind a huge truck, waiting for a Greyhound bus to pass on her left. In her side mirror, she caught sight of Shy holding on to the back of her leather jacket. The bus passed, and Alta revved the engine and changed lanes. The play of headlights on the wide lanes of concrete suspended before her grounded her in the present. So Shy Mallon, her one and only girl next door, was about to enter Alta's real world.

The City was a home Alta had found too late. How she would have loved it in her tomboy years, walking up those steep hills with smiling girls moving fast all around, and leather-men nodding at her with respect, with their gray mustaches and their denimed asses showing through chaps. She had cruised in their bars and liked the hot smell of sweat in leather. The sidewalks splattered with unknown stains; cans of garbage plundered like treasure chests; blue mailboxes standing like sentries; bar balconies packed with girls, girls standing and girls on stools; stinking ashtrays, Persian carpets, hardwood floors, candy-house Victorians, and billboards. Long movie lines jammed the sidewalks. When she'd first gotten here she would walk up and down those lines, pretending she was looking for someone she'd planned to meet, just so she could see the muscles and pierced lips, noses, eyebrows, the leather caps and shaved heads, the bright cherry lipstick and dark eyeliner, the shiny dresses and see-through shirts of netting, stockings and garter belts and short-short skirts. And the absolute acceptance of all those eyes looking back.

Alta parked her motorcycle down the hill from Renny's, and they had to hike up. Walking with Shy in this city, Alta knew everyone thought they were lovers. What Alta liked about San Francisco was its assumptions, even when they were wrong.

Two young things in long velvet dresses let them in the door, took their coats, and ushered them up the staircase. The so-called lesbian community is a damned small place to move around in, especially if you've slept with half of it. The first person Alta recognized when she reached the top of the staircase was Lara, off at the end of the hall with a bright orange drink in her hand. She laughed with her mouth wide open, just the way she came. When she tossed that head of long black hair, her eyes caught Alta's, and she beelined for her, pushing her way through leather and lace. As she reached Alta, she finally noticed Shy with her wide eyes and face set blank.

"Is this the wife?" Lara's tongue danced around on the stage of her full lips.

Alta raised one eyebrow. "She's somebody's wife, but not mine."

"My name is Sasha, and I'm nobody's wife, actually." Shy dropped her left hand away from her belly and thrust her right hand at Lara.

"Charmed." Lara took Shy's hand and gave her a femme-on-femme kind of sexy smile. She ran her tongue along the ridged bottom of her two front teeth, and God knows that restless tongue could do more for Shy than Alta would ever let it do for her.

Renny came blustering down the hall, flushed and drunk.

"Damn, Alta," she said, looking right at Shy, "you find the sexiest women. And pregnant! I love it!" Renny's mucky blond hair flopped moppishly over one eye, and she grinned. A flush climbed into Shy's cheeks, but she smiled.

"Renny, this is Shy."

Renny raised an eyebrow clear to the middle of her forehead.

"Let me clear these animals out of the way so you can sit down," she said. Renny tucked Shy's hand in her tuxedo-shirted elbow and led her into the living room, boldly chastising her guests. "Give the lady a seat, slackers!"

Shep, a boyish young butch whose given name was something like Annette, stood hurriedly and then bowed. "Excuse me, m'lady." She squeezed her leatherman's cap in both hands. "Volunteer boy scouts at your service, Alta."

"Hey, Shep." Alta bent over Shy, who had been zealously tucked into the couch corner by Renny. "Are you okay, Shy?"

She smiled defiantly. "Never say chivalry is dead."

"That's my girl."

"Seattle's not a backwater, Alta. It's not like you can show me something I've never seen," she muttered, her head angled up at Alta.

Alta touched her chin.

"No?" she said.

• • •

Amanda twisted a lock of butterscotch hair between two fingers. "I wanted to get my belly button pierced, but someone told me I don't have enough of a shelf." She leaned against the smooth white tile of the fireplace, one tightly covered hip seductively out.

"It really depends," Alta said. "I'd have to look at it to tell you."

"Would you mind? Or do you hate to think about this? Is it like asking you to work at a party?" She wrinkled her freckled nose. Above her short skirt, she wore a skimpy daisy-covered baby T-shirt that left her belly button easily visible.

"I don't mind it now and then. I sometimes do public demos, as a matter of fact."

Amanda was pretty short, say five-two, so she had to look up into Alta's face, and Alta liked that. She had a sudden desire to kiss Amanda, there by the mantel, just to push her head back and arch over her, to feel Amanda's arms reach up around her neck.

"Keeping busy, Alta?" Renny said as she rushed by, jolting Alta from Amanda's curves. Alta looked around the patches of bare flesh and swaths of black leather for Shy. Shy was seated on the soft gray couch surrounded by half a dozen butches with shameless grins belying their standoffish slouches. The whole group laughed at something Shy said. Max, the tattoo artist at the shop where Alta worked, brought Shy a cup of the nonalcoholic punch. Shy caught Alta watching her and winked. Alta realized how little she'd seen of the old Shy, the girl who bounded over fences and dived into rushing rivers every chance she got, and how happy it made her to rediscover that skinny girl who loved all things blue—and sometimes Alta— laughing out of the voluptuous body of this lovely woman. Alta remembered her wet and laughing, her hair plastered back from her face, water trickling down her cheekbones, the hairs of her eyebrows all pushed up. Now her raw sensuality had divided. She was more sophisticated with an edge of hysteria. Alta wondered what the skin stretching over her womb looked like, how it felt.

"Excuse me, I'm going to have to get back to you about your belly button." Alta handed Amanda her business card and Amanda smiled graciously. Alta made her way over to Shy.

"Hey, Alta," said Max. "Now we know your secret." A flash of heat gurgled up in Alta's stomach, and she studied Max's pale blue eyes as impassively as she could. "None of my childhood friends looked this good," Max said. Everyone laughed, and Alta shrugged.

"Yeah, the beautiful ones flocked to me early." Alta looked down at Shy. "Enjoying yourself?"

"I'm being well taken care of," she said, smiling.

"Oh, I bet." Everyone laughed again. "But if you'll all forgive me, I'd like to show Shy something now besides the butch charmers."

"I don't know if I can forgive you," Shep said, grinning nervously.

Alta put one hand firmly on Shep's shoulder. "One thing you'd better learn as soon as you can, Shep. Women come and go, and if you can't keep them, you've got to be able to watch them leave." The group laughed, and Alta offered Shy her hand. Several of the others gave helpful pushes from behind.

"See you later." Shy waved.

"Bye," everyone chorused after her. "Watch out for Alta," someone called. "Come back soon." Alta led Shy through the crowds, stopping to say hello to people as little as she could manage. It was important to look utterly determined and to keep going if you wanted to get from one place to the next at a party like this one. Alta held Shy's hand firmly, relishing her ever-cool skin in the heat of her grasp. Finally they made it through the kitchen and out the back door to the stairs. Alta stopped to let the dark and relative silence of the night settle over them after the buzz of the party. It wasn't any cooler outside, though.

"Wow." Shy put her hands on the rail and took a deep breath. "Renny sure has a lot of friends."

"You stick around one place long enough and that happens," Alta said. Shy didn't look at her or say anything, and Alta relented. "Come on, I want to show you something wonderful."

They climbed the wooden staircase to the roof. No one else was there. Renny's place was at the top of a steep San Francisco hill, and the City spread out below them, waves of light with bridges like tentacles reaching across the deep black water. On the sidewalk people walked by, a group of teenagers, a couple of drag queens, and fragments of conversation and high-pitched laughter reached up to them. A low murmur of city noise—far-off traffic, voices—lapped over them as gently as silence. Two people left the party, zooming off on a motorcycle. Shy and Alta stood next to each other, and Alta was filled with that lust and love that she'd felt in high school. Nothing about then was better than now, except that she never felt lost in the rush of those feelings. These high school feelings were still about power, but they were the underbelly, a place she hadn't looked in a long, long time.

"I love your motorcycle," Shy said with an almost drunken solemnity. She turned and leaned back on the gravelly tar wall that rimmed the roof, and threw her head back. "Remember Ryan's truck? I hated that crowded seat, the stick shift always pressing into me. In a way your motorcycle is bigger than any car, because the sky is the roof."

Alta laughed. The orangy glow of the City lit Shy's face.

"I've always had a fear of small spaces. I bet you didn't know that, did you?" Shy turned just her head, still craned to the sky, and looked at Alta.

"Well, I knew you didn't like to be indoors much."

"Yeah, especially not at my house." Shy shook her head and turned back to the sky. "But it's more than just wanting to be outside. It's like . . ." She hit one palm with the side of her fist, making a gentle slapping noise of skin against skin. "It's like my body. I love being pregnant." She looked at Alta fiercely. "I feel like I finally take up enough room. I was just tired of being able to squeeze onto someone's lap in a crowded car, or being the person to share a bench at a full table when everyone else got chairs."

"That's one hell of a reason to get pregnant."

Shy smoothed her dress down over her belly, shook her head. "It is such an intense thing, having a baby. I remember when I first started to feel it move. It tickled. Really! It was the strangest thing to have something moving around inside me. I talk to it, too. I don't even know what I say. Just whatever. I know you were joking this morning, but I have told it about you, and about my mother and father, and even about your mother—"

"Don't frighten the little one."

"Why do you joke about her, Alta? You used to love her so much."

"Did I?"

The shadows on Shy's face seemed darker against the orange light. Alta couldn't think what she was talking about.

"When we were little she'd fix you those great lunches you were so proud of, and she always came to school events, and she was so young. She was like the perfect mom."

"Well, maybe she would have been for a different daughter."

"Maybe."

"But that's the Russian roulette of having a baby, isn't it, Shy? You can't decide they didn't send you what you wanted."

"I want this baby, Alta. Whatever it is. You know, for the first time in my life, I don't feel alone. Don't laugh." Shy watched Alta carefully.

"It used to seem like you were never alone," Alta said quietly.

"When?"

"In high school and before." Alta scanned the sky casually. Shy didn't say anything, and suddenly Alta felt frustrated by the unspoken agreement they seemed to have to keep some things that way: unspoken. "What about your mother, Shy?"

"Do you think we should go?"

"I think we should talk about what's up with her."

"I guess she's . . ." Shy pressed her lips tightly together.

"Hey, hey, that's not what I meant. I mean, she seems to be a lady with a lot of secrets, and I feel like we're just going to have to let her slip away if we don't try to figure her out."

"You really think you can figure people out, don't you, Alta? You keep wanting pat answers where there isn't even room for questions. Listen to me. I've tried with her, and it's only made things worse."

"Do you know about her baptismal certificate?"

"What are you talking about?" she said quickly, her eyes shifting away from Alta's.

"It was in with her other papers. It says she was baptized in the fifties. That doesn't make sense, Shy. Nothing about her makes sense, and I think we have to ask ourselves—"

"The fifties?" She shrugged, an oddly casual gesture, except that she looked like a freezing child huddled against the cold.

"Listen, Shy—"

"I don't want you to call me Shy anymore." She turned and peered over the edge of the roof.

"Sorry." Alta met Shy's hostility with her own brand of gentlemanly calm. "It's an old habit."

"That's what we are, Alta, isn't it? An old, old habit, something we should know better than to take up again, like nail-biting or teeth-grinding."

"If that's the way you see it . . ." Alta shrugged. What did Shy mean, "take up again"? Could she be thinking . . . ? No. Shy pushed past Alta and walked toward the stairs. A siren blared in the distance. Shy turned around.

"I shouldn't really be here. I mean, my mother . . . Look, I wasn't going to tell you this, but you know how you said I was the last person she called, and that's how you got my number?"

"Yeah."

"I think that was right before she had the stroke." Shy shook her head back and forth in a tight, frantic motion. "I asked her questions, the kind of questions you want to ask. God, Alta, do you think I never wondered? So you had your few months of grief-bonding with her. She was my mother. But I learned what's important from her, and this was one thing she was absolutely clear about: it would wreck her for me to push. And goddamn it, Alta, it did."

"Shy, it wasn't you. Look at how she was your whole life, ever since I knew you."

"She had good days, Alta, you're always talking about them. Well, they were the ones when she forgot about the past. If these are her last days, let's do what she wanted. That's the only thing I can think of to do for the few days I have left to give to her."

"Few days?"

She paced around the roof. "I'm supposed to go back in a few days."

"Says who?" Alta asked, still standing by the wall.

"Well, that's what my ticket says, for one." She stopped pacing.

"And for another?"

"Erik doesn't want me to be gone so long, what with the baby due so soon and all." She looked smaller than she might have liked, in that short black dress in the middle of the roof.

"We'd better get back." Alta walked toward her. Shy just stayed where she was. Alta got really close, and Shy remained firmly planted. "Promise me something?" Alta asked.

Shy looked at her. "All right."

Alta touched her cheek. "Are you cold?" Shy shook her head impatiently.

Alta meant to say something warm and comforting, and then, because they were standing so close in the hot night, Alta thought she might kiss her. Shy stepped backward. Always about to leave.

"Say goodbye this time," Alta said.

Shy's mouth opened and then closed. She pushed her hair back with one hand. "It was better I left like that. The way I did."

"Better? Damn it, Shy!" Alta hadn't meant to yell. "Is that what you tell yourself? Is that how you live with—"

"Don't yell at me." She spoke quietly, but her voice was hard. "Take me home." She started down the stairs.

"Fine." Alta followed her. She felt suddenly that if she didn't know Shy, she didn't know anybody, and the noise of the party, even as they got closer, seemed very far away. She didn't want to take Shy back to the Mallons' house. She wanted to comfort her, to leave her behind forever, to make her laugh, to rip her in two.

Shy opened the door to the kitchen and almost knocked Marcie over. Marcie, in bright red lipstick and a matching sequined dress, carried a cake full of lit candles.

"Just in time," she stage-whispered. "Follow me." Shy and Alta were swept along with the crowd. In front of Marcie someone was flipping off the lights, and the cake glowed like a beacon.

A disjointed, awkwardly melodious chorus of "Happy Birthday" burst out as the cake entourage reached the living room. Renny, eyes shining through her bangs, blew enthusiastically, and a cheer went up. Alta turned to go look for their coats.

"Alta." Renny came after her. "Where have you been?"

"Don't you have to cut your cake?"

"That's why it'll be waiting for me. I'm the birthday girl. So what's up?"

"Here's the thing about Shy. You can only get so close and no closer. I mean, sometimes we talk and it's good, it's real. And then she shuts down. I just haven't had to scale walls in a long time."

"Think it's good for you? Ego getting too big?"

"It's not that kind of thing. This isn't hard to get. It's just hard."

"Are we going?" Shy came up behind Alta.

Alta looked at her levelly. "I thought we would."

Shy followed Alta out. They walked slowly down that steep hill.

"So you have no regrets?" Alta said scornfully.

"I'm thirsty."

Alta turned her bike around on the hill, and Shy climbed on with some difficulty. Alta gunned the engine and headed away from Renny's, not really sure where she should go. She took an unfamiliar route in the direction of nothing in particular and ended up below the freeway. The lights of a 7-Eleven lit an otherwise empty industrial block, and Alta stopped there.

Shy had to climb off the bike so Alta could park it, and she followed close to Alta as they went into the store. Alta found a bottle of mineral water for Shy and put it on the patchy counter. Shy chose a roll of butterscotch Lifesavers. As Alta reached into her wallet, the clerk muttered something under the neon hum of the store.

"What'd you say?"

A cardboard cutout of a soda can vibrated with Alta's words. She saw Shy's hands grip the counter.

"Nothing." He was a young, pimply boy with a broad jaw and oversized limbs.

"You're wasting a lot of noise saying nothing."

The boy's eyes darted around the store, to the camera in the corner, the rows of juice and beer behind glass, the aisles of pudding and aspirin. He pressed a couple of keys on the register. It rang cheerfully.

"A dollar fifty-seven." His Adam's apple bobbed in his throat.

"I know what you said, and I know what I am. There's no shame in that word, so don't mumble. Let's hear it."

"Are you crazy?" The boy wrinkled up his pasty face.

"Alta . . ." Shy tugged at the edge of Alta's jacket.

"Be quiet, Shy." Alta jerked her chin at the boy. "I'm waiting."

"Crazy dyke." The boy's voice cracked.

Alta reached up and grabbed his shirt and dragged him down to her face. "You got the dyke part right. Say it again."

"Dyke," he said tightly.

"I'll take that as an apology." Alta let go of him with a shove. "Let's go." She threw two dollars down and walked toward the door. Shy reached for the roll of Lifesavers on the counter, and a fake, uncertain smile crossed her face. The nightmarish image of her going into labor right then flashed. Her hands shook, and Alta made her own perfectly still. The boy's mouth hung open. They walked out, the kick-ass bulldagger dyke holding the door for the lovely expectant mother.

"God, Alta." Shy stood by Alta's window. She pulled the desk chair over and sat down. "I'm still shaking." She held one hand up. Her bony fingers quivered slightly.

"If I let it slide, then it's inside me. Let him feel it."

Shy shook her head. "I don't even know what happened."

Alta thought of Tahoe, the orange bedspread and the ice, and later the parking lot and the broken shards of terra-cotta. "Yes, you do."

Shy looked out through the glass.

"I can't tell if some of these people are men or women," she said, her head against the pane.

"Does that scare you?" Alta hung up her jacket and Shy's, which she'd tossed over the back of a chair.

"Scare me?"

"How are you going to know who you are supposed to be attracted to?" Alta sat in her most comfortable chair, a fine granddaddy-type armchair. Shy twisted around to face her.

"I know who I'm supposed to be attracted to."

Alta stood up. "Would you like something to drink?"

Shy tilted her head. "Maybe water."

Shy followed Alta down the hall to her narrow kitchen. Alta poured her a glass of water from the pitcher in the fridge. Shy looked happy just to have it in her hands.

"Thanks." Shy rolled the glass across her forehead. "The heat is intense. It's so gray in Seattle most of the time. I only swim in the summer."

"Really? I can't imagine you staying away from water for months at a time." Alta leaned back against her counter.

"Yeah, well . . . I take long showers." They laughed together, and Alta liked the sound of that. "Actually . . ." Shy looked down into her water glass.

"What?"

"No, nothing." She shook her head.

"Tell me."

"Well . . . I could go for a shower right now."

"Be my guest."

"I guess I am." Shy smiled at Alta. "This is a beautiful place, Alta." She took a sip of water.

"Thanks." Alta wanted to touch her, to feel her as solid and genuine. Give her something to really smile about. And then she wanted to get angry at her. Shake her. Say, "What the hell happened to you?" Say, "You disappeared, you took two hundred dollars and walked out of my bedroom saying 'see you.'" Make her live those months when all she'd wanted was for Shy to call her or write or just saunter back in her room, her narrow hips rolling and twisting in that sassy way she walked.

Shy started to look a little worried. She opened her eyes really wide, and her brows rose.

"Lost in thought?" Shy asked.

Alta shrugged and kept looking at her.

"So could I take a shower?"

"Anything you want." Alta said each word slowly, seriously, giving Shy every chance to interpret the words as she wished. Then she smiled. "There are clean towels in the bathroom. Down the hall on the left."

Shy's face relaxed. She put her water down on the counter. "I guess I'll go do that, then."

Alta nodded.

When she heard the bathroom door click shut, Alta headed into the living room to leaf through her mail. Suddenly she heard a shriek.

"Why is the water so hot?" Shy yelled from the bathroom.

Alta rushed down the hall, calling out ahead of her, "You know I like hot showers!"

Alta pushed the door open and there stood Shy. Her breasts were full and heavy, the nipples cocoa-brown. The skin stretched taut over the great curve of her belly. A thin brown line rose from her dark pubic hair and up toward her protruding belly button. Alta looked quickly up to her face. Shy's hair was pulled back sharply, twisted and barretted on top of her head.

"Sorry," Alta said. "Turn the knob more toward the center." Shy just stood there in her bare pregnant body, an adult body Alta had never seen or touched. "Here, I'll do it." Alta edged past her sideways, back to her, and bent over the tub, adjusting the temperature of the rushing water. Shy liked cold water. Alta used to drive with her to the beach in Mr. Mallon's big old station wagon, though Alta never even took off her shoes on the sand. She would wait with Shy's favorite towel, blue and fuzzy. Sometimes Shy would wave from far out, a speck midway to the horizon. She was most Alta's then, so far from Alta, but not moving toward anyone else, swimming out and out. One time when Alta wrapped the towel around Shy's strong, slim shoulders, she shook against Alta's body from the cold of the water. Alta wrapped her arms around Shy, too, trying to warm her. Shy reached out and put her clammy hands on Alta's sun-baked cheeks. For a moment Alta thought Shy was going to kiss her. Then Shy started to laugh.

"Cold?" she said, looking at her own hands.

"Cold," Alta answered.

"What?" Shy said, bringing Alta back to her bathroom. She noticed Shy's nipples firming up and forced her eyes away.

"There," Alta said, turning the knob so that the water stopped flowing from the bath faucet and, after a moment, shot out of the shower above. "The water is tepid, just as you like it."

"Thanks." Shy still didn't move, but her body was so full, so lush, it seemed to Alta that it quivered. Alta left her standing there and closed the door behind her. She made her way down the hall, enveloped in a silent desire. She ran her fingers across her eyes and sat down in her favorite chair, leaning back the way her father used to when he'd come home from work at the bar, smelling of smoke and spilled whisky. She tried to sit the way he had, looking like he owned the world—his corner of it—or at least that the fight for it was one he might win.

When Shy emerged from the bathroom she was wearing her black dress again, the crepe material sticking to her clean skin. Alta gave her a pocket-shirt to sleep in. Shy went into the bedroom to change and came back out again. Alta secretly admired the way Shy looked in white cotton even more than in her sexy black dress.

"Tired?" Alta asked her. It was after one, though there were plenty of people still out on the sidewalk in front of the house. Shy nodded.

"You can sleep in my bed," Alta said, without making it clear where she herself would sleep.

"Okay." Shy stood there for a few minutes.

"I'm just going to read for a while," Alta said.

"Okay," Shy said again. She went into the bedroom, leaving the door open. "Good night," she called out uncertainly, once she was in bed.

"Good night, Shy," Alta said, trying to sound as if this were normal and they both understood what was happening. Then she lay down on the couch with the latest issue of the *Bay Times*. She read the personals first. She thought it was good to keep up on what people thought they wanted. Then she read the letters to the editor to see what had upset people this week. Desire first, then anger.

But her thoughts kept drifting to Shy: Shy in the bathroom, Shy standing in the T-shirt. Outside, a couple of guys in nun drag skipped by: the Sisters of Perpetual Indulgence. The white of their coifs set off their faces in the half dark of the City night. Alta sometimes thought of how casually we glance over faces we have never seen. Once upon a time we never saw a face we didn't love, or at least know well. But seeing only those you love is different from loving all you see. Living in the City you are constantly drawn to people in fleeting moments full of possibility. Our minds are tribal, unused to all this strangeness. Yet she had trusted strangers, those lovely girls she brought home for a few hours or a night, more than she trusted Shy at this moment. And still, she fell asleep on the couch more easily than she'd fallen asleep in years, straining to hear Shy's breath.

In the morning Alta watched Shy sleep. Shy lay awkwardly on her side, sort of curled around her extended womb. She looked beautiful, peaceful, and Alta wanted to lay her hand against the skin over Shy's womb, where it protruded from the T-shirt, and talk directly to the child as if they were alone. Alta wondered what she could say to the next generation. She wanted words of courage, or comfort, or just the sound of her voice to reach the baby, something it could remember from before it was born.

Alta was in the kitchen making lemonade when Shy woke up. She came and stood groggily in the doorway.

"I had nightmares all night," she said.

"About what?"

"What do you think it means, my mother's baptismal certificate dated in the fifties? She was born fifteen or twenty years before that."

Alta shrugged. "She was baptized then. She must not have been born Catholic."

"She was Protestant!" Shy exclaimed, and though none of this was funny—in fact it was rather sad that Shy knew almost as little about her mother's past as Alta did, and who else would know?—it sounded like a bad joke to hear her say it. When they were in grade school, Protestant was just about the worst thing they could think of someone; Protestants were considered, among their elementary crowd, to be tacky dressers, people who had abandoned the Church's rich history, and with it the aesthetic as well. Encouraged by their teachers, they held the grudge of centuries-old Church politics. Shy recovered herself. "If she never mentioned it, it must not have been important to her. Let's not say anything." Alta didn't agree; a lot that mattered hadn't been said between them, even this visit. Alta didn't want Shy to drop this; somewhere between the time Shy'd left and the time she'd sauntered back into Alta's life, Alta had decided that none of their disguises protected them much. But Alta nodded—who would she have said anything to?—and handed Shy a glass of lemonade.

"I know a friend of your mother's—"

Shy looked at Alta so strangely, Alta stopped speaking. "A friend?" Shy said plaintively.

"Well, yeah. Gerda Koch. I worked for her when I first came to San Francisco. Your mother set it up for me. She's a real character."

"You know Gerda?" Shy said the name as though she'd never said it before, slowly and uncertainly.

"I'd like to take you over there."

"Where?" Shy suddenly seemed wary, like a caged animal.

"Oh, she lives over by the mouth of the Bay. It'd give you a chance to see some of the breathtaking views my city offers."

"Your city?" With visible effort, Shy slid into her saucy, flirtatious mode. She laughed.

"That's right," Alta smiled. "Come on, get dressed."

"Well, *that's* a new order from you, Bossy."

"I just can't wait to take you out on the town."

"What about my mother?" When she said this, Alta realized that Shy was afraid.

"I'll call in sick to work and we'll go by the hospital this afternoon, okay?"

Shy nodded and Alta gently pushed her out of the kitchen, saying, "Get dressed, get dressed," so she wouldn't take Shy in her arms, seeking to comfort and be comforted, and come up empty-handed.

The morning, like all San Francisco mornings, promised spring. In California the seasons come daily: spring, the dewy mornings draped lightly in gray mist; summer, when the sun burns through and rises directly overhead at midday; afternoon autumns, crisp, breezy, when colors show off and the air smells clean into twilight; winter is the night.

Sunday mornings cars line up for blocks to crest the hill at Lombard Street and crawl down the brick-laid roadway whose curves switch and switch back. The tourists gawk and stare, patient with their rituals of observance. What separates residents of the City from those who pass through in maroon rental cars, emerge fresh from towering hotels with glass elevators and flat carpets, is neglect. Residents disdain the tourists who point at the views and the attractions, walk the edges of the water where shops line the street, photograph the intersection of Haight and Ashbury and buy an ice cream cone, come by in busloads to see the gay Mecca of the Castro, safely ensconced behind glass. San Francisco is a lover to her residents, a body they take for granted. They do not look up when she emerges

from the shower naked, do not follow the precise roll of her movements as the uninitiated try to do. They reach out for her when the
mood is upon them and find her always waiting.

Gerda Koch and Miss Pauline lived in a two-story house at the
bottom of Noe Valley. Alta had painted the walls inside, dipping the
roller into a tin full of peach paint. She'd replaced the faulty door-
knobs on the master bedroom and bathroom doors. She had fixed the
leaking sink and the running toilets. She had been in charge of
weeding and mowing the tiny strip of grass out front. Mrs. Koch liked
everything tidy. "Tidy!" she'd shout. "That's how I like it." Her con-
sonants were harsh and guttural, but her face was gleeful.

"Alta!" she said, opening the door wide. She took Alta's hand in
her own crooked one and leaned around to see who was behind her.
Alta had never brought anyone over, even on social visits after she
stopped working there. Mrs. Koch's breath caught.

"Sasha," she murmured.

"Yes," Alta said, stepping back and bringing Shy forward.

"It's nice to meet you," Shy said uncertainly.

Mrs. Koch's stalwart face cleared, as if consciously she willed herself to focus, except she had been extremely focused, staring at Shy.

"I saw you as a little baby, a few months after you were born. You
were like a miracle. I am so happy to see you, Sasha." Mrs. Koch's
voice turned the name to a throaty lullaby, an unexpected announcement of possibilities Alta had not foreseen. "Your mother—" Mrs.
Koch stopped. "I am so sorry about your mother."

"Thank you." Shy seemed overwhelmed, confused.

"Come." Mrs. Koch climbed the stairs with Shy in tow, turning
back to tell Alta about plans to paint the outside of the house in
intricate Victorian colors, plans to plant lemon and fig trees, plans to
put windows in the roof. "Skylights," she announced triumphantly,
as if the word itself presented brilliant poetic possibility.

"Paulie, Alta's here!" she shouted through the bedroom door.
"And Alicia's little girl, Sasha!"

Miss Pauline walked into the living room and took Shy's hand
with all the graciousness of her Southern background and the gentle

firmness that went along with how well she knew herself. "Sasha, I've wanted to meet you for such a long time. Please, have a seat. You, too, Alta." She threw Alta a smile.

"Yes, sit, sit, and we will make tea." Mrs. Koch disappeared into the kitchen, and Miss Pauline followed.

"They know about me," Shy whispered. "How do you know them?"

Mrs. Koch came back in with a tray of teacups, sugar, cream. Miss Pauline followed with cinnamon-dusted sugar cookies on a plate. "We're just waiting for the water to boil."

They sat next to each other on the couch. "Tell me, is there news of your mother?" Mrs. Koch asked, holding out the plate of cookies. Alta and Shy each took one, polite as children.

"I saw her yesterday, and we're on our way to visit again. She . . . can't talk; they don't know how much the stroke affected her mind."

"She looked like she was sleeping." Mrs. Koch seemed to say this to Miss Pauline.

"You've seen her?" Shy sounded surprised.

"Certainly. I came when Alta called, as soon as I heard. I love your mother, Sasha. She brought me to this country when she came with your father. She never let me help her enough, not as I wanted." Mrs. Koch's rough voice became ragged. "Your mother made her choices a long time ago. She's always been headstrong."

"Like her daughter," Alta murmured, smiling at Shy. But Shy was watching Mrs. Koch.

"Did you know her—?" Shy hesitated.

"Mrs. Koch," Alta said, "Shy has never seen a picture of her mother from before she married Mr. Mallon."

Mrs. Koch held up one finger. "Do not move. I'll be right back."

Miss Pauline jumped in smoothly. "When are you due, sweetheart?"

Shy smiled fully for the first time since they'd arrived. "Late October, between the twenty-seventh and the thirtieth."

"We didn't even know you were expecting. It's so odd, because I declare, your mother spoke of you more than anything else."

"She did?"

"Here we go." Mrs. Koch returned, a framed photograph in her hands. In the faded black-and-white, two young women stood together. The older one had the fierce eyes and sturdy structure of Mrs. Koch, and the other might have been a faded duplicate, from the time Alta had last seen her, of Shy, her backyard wonder, her girl-next-door. A miraculously young Mrs. Mallon, far more serious than such a fresh-faced girl should be, in a loose-fitting collared dress that fell to her calves.

It flashed in Alta's mind that maybe they had been lovers, that Mrs. Koch had held in her arms a blond version of Alta's Shy, and that that woman had turned to ash, to wreckage, to Mrs. Mallon. Alta watched Gerda Koch as she held the picture, and she watched the benign and teary eyes of Miss Pauline. What had all these women meant to one another? Was this why Mrs. Mallon had sent me to them? She must have known. Alta thought of the photographs her mother had of her young father. She wondered where Mrs. Mallon's photographs were, and when she had put them away.

"That's my mother?" Shy said. "Where are you?"

"Golden Gate Park, just after we arrived in this country."

"Arrived?" Alta prompted.

"From Austria!"

Shy's expression grew smoother, more blank, as these details were revealed, one by one. Alta couldn't tell what Shy already knew and what she'd never been told before.

"She was a beautiful girl," Miss Pauline said, gazing at the picture.

"She had a lot of secrets, didn't she?" Alta asked.

Mrs. Koch stared around at the walls she kept freshly painted. Alta herself had painted them twice, once peach colored and once a pale mint-green. "Alta, you have what Zahava used to call the ears of a merchant."

Zahava had been Gerda Koch's lover in her Bohemian days in Vienna. They'd lived in an apartment in the university district. Mrs. Koch had told Alta stories of those days, of the parties they'd had, the books they'd argue over, the apartment she and Zahava had made the center of life in their crowd.

"So many have died," Mrs. Koch had told Alta, her firm voice softening with grief, so that Alta had thought she meant recently, in old age. But she had gone on. "War is always a terrible thing, Alta. But the one I lived through . . . you cannot imagine. Even I cannot imagine." Alta had remembered Mrs. Mallon's words, practically the same words.

"What happened to Zahava?" Alta asked.

"She was killed. Murdered at Auschwitz. Zahava was her Hebrew name. It means 'golden one.'"

"Was she?"

"Her heart, Alta, yes. Her coloring was dark, like yours," she said, reaching out and touching Alta's wrist. "She was beautiful, inside and out. A real fighter."

Alta hesitated to ask her next question, though Mrs. Koch had been nothing but open. Alta wondered if Mrs. Koch was Jewish, if Mrs. Mallon had helped her escape from the Nazis. Alta hadn't really known any Jews; she'd grown up surrounded by Catholics. Her mother had her own opinions about anyone who didn't share their faith, and Jews ranked below Protestants. In fact, they were hardly discussed in her house. "Jew" was used mostly as a verb.

"Did Mrs. Mallon know?" Alta finally asked.

"About Zahava?"

"The whole thing."

A strange look had crossed her face. "She was younger than I. A child in those days." She'd risen and pulled down the book of paint samples. "So, Alta, which color for the kitchen, do you think?"

"Ears of a merchant? What did you mean by that?" Alta asked her now.

Miss Pauline tilted her head and caught Alta's puzzled look. "To hear all and say nothing," she said by way of explanation.

"I don't know anything about Mrs. Mallon," Alta said. But she hadn't mentioned the baptismal certificate. She didn't know any facts, it was true. But curiosity is a kind of knowing, a knowing there is something to be known.

"That is the way she wanted it," Mrs. Koch said. She stood up. They could hear the kettle whistling and rattling in the kitchen. "Tea?"

"I'd love some," Shy said, more aggressively than she'd spoken since they'd arrived. Mrs. Koch left for the kitchen. Alta accepted a cup of the strong tea Mrs. Koch always brewed and added to it her spoonfuls of sugar, felt the heat of the water traveling up the handle of her teaspoon, and listened to Shy and her mother's oldest and only known friend exchange trivial conversation about the weather, remodeling, things easy to agree on and already known. Alta saw again that Shy was an experienced accomplice at silence and secrets.

"You'd think a couple of old dykes would be a little less averse to saying what's up," Alta said, handing Shy her helmet. They stood on opposite sides of Alta's bike outside Mrs. Koch and Miss Pauline's house.

"What are you talking about?"

"I just think you learn a kind of commitment to the truth—"

"No, I mean, what do you mean calling them that?"

"Dykes?" Alta looked at Shy, who turned her eyes away.

"Shh!" Then she nodded.

"Hey, the word 'dyke' ain't going to break the city of San Francisco, Shy-girl. Look at them. They're a couple."

"Lots of old ladies live together like that."

"We are everywhere, as the saying goes."

"Seriously, Alta, they're not . . ." Her voice trailed off, as if she was suddenly not at all certain.

"Lovers? Sure they are! I mean, they're old, but they're not dead."

"Have they ever said so to you?"

"That they're not dead?"

Shy gave Alta a look.

"Shy, they don't have to say so. It's obvious."

"Well, it's not obvious to me, and I don't think you should assume that it's important to them just because it's so important to you."

"Excuse me?" Alta exploded. "How could it not be important to them? How can you be lovers for forty years and not have it be important?"

"You're yelling," Shy said sharply, looking toward the house.

"Damn straight, I'm yelling," Alta said more quietly. "Do you want to go back and ask them? Do you want me to?"

She shook her head vigorously. Her pregnancy made her look smug and suburban, and she fit in, even on the empty, tree-lined street, as Alta did not. But Shy's face was young and panic-stricken. This wasn't how Alta wanted things to be between them.

"Come on," Alta said softly, cajolingly. "Let's go to the hospital. We'll see your mother, and then I'll show you her baptismal certificate and we can figure out what to do."

The panic cleared from Shy's face, and she looked cold again and utterly certain. "I appreciate your company for the hospital, and you can show me anything you like, but there's nothing to do, Alta. Things are the way they are. You just have to accept that or you'll never be happy. Really." She looked genuinely worried about Alta, and this was worse; Alta didn't want her pity.

"Why do you think your mother never told any of us that you were pregnant? Did you ask her not to tell me, Shy?"

"Why would I do that?"

"Secrets run in your family, it seems."

Alta thought Shy would get angry, but instead she stared at her and then laughed. "Bingo, Alta."

"What?"

"She didn't tell you because she didn't know. This one was my secret."

"You didn't tell her you were going to have a baby? You're six months pregnant, for crying out loud. When were you planning to tell her, Shy? Were you just going to turn up on her doorstep with the baby? Oh, here's your grandchild, Mom. Or were you never going to turn up at all?"

Shy shielded her eyes from the sun with one hand. "I didn't call her Mom. I mean, I did when I talked about her to other kids, because that's what you all called your mothers. Hey, Mom. But not me. She was never Mom."

"Well, she sure as hell was the one person on earth who would have given her life for you."

"Is that what a mom is?" Dry irony shadowed her whole face, her eyes deep beneath one cocked brow and her lips pressed together.

"If you're damn lucky," Alta said, and pulled her helmet on.

The hospital seemed familiar now, though no warmer. Alta and Shy sat in two chairs by Mrs. Mallon's bedside. She lay there, and they watched her breathe. Alta kept thinking of the photograph, trying to trace the arc between that vivid young woman and this inert older one, her skin so fragile-looking, wrinkled and thin, her eyelids almost translucent, traced with blue veins. Alta had to believe that it was more than years that had laid waste to Alice Mallon. The other bed was empty, and Alta wondered what had happened to the lady who'd been sleeping behind the curtain last time they were there.

"Do you have a hairbrush?" Alta asked Shy.

"You don't have much need of one, do you?" She frowned.

"I thought I'd fix her up a bit."

Shy said nothing, but she dug through her purse and came up with a small plastic comb. Alta stood and carefully touched Mrs. Mallon's hair. It was coarse. She held a section and started gently from the bottom.

"Why don't we start with what you already know about her past?" Alta could feel Mrs. Mallon's breath, faintly warm and sour on her cheek.

"She didn't talk about it," Shy hissed. "Don't upset her, Alta."
Their eyes met, and Shy's were dark and furious. Alta had forgotten
where she'd learned the power of a look.

She turned back to Mrs. Mallon. "Hey, gorgeous," she said. "How
are you feeling?" Alta pressed her hand against Mrs. Mallon's skull to
keep the comb from pulling. "I guess that's a stupid question. How
come people always say that when you're sick?" Alta looked at Shy,
but Shy didn't smile. "Your lovely daughter has graced us with a visit
after all these years."

"What are you doing, Alta?"

"I guess I'd better be the one to congratulate you. You're about to
become a grandmother." Alta stopped, frightened by the coldness
in her own voice. "Mrs. Mallon? Can you understand me?" Alta
arranged the shiny, combed section of Mrs. Mallon's hair on the pillow around her face. "Come here, stand up," Alta said to Shy. Shy
stayed seated. "Shy! Show her. Don't you think you'd better not wait
any longer?" Shy rose, glaring at Alta.

"Look, Mrs. Mallon. Shy's going to have a baby." Alta put her
hand gently on Shy's extended belly. "Isn't that great?"

"I don't think she can hear," Shy said softly.

"But she can know. Don't you think?"

"I don't know." Shy turned her head away.

Alta moved to the other side of the mattress and started in on the
rest of Mrs. Mallon's hair.

"Shy, let me tell you a story. Remember Gina Johnson?" Gina was
a girl in Alta's grade in elementary school.

"So?" Shy asked impatiently.

"And her father, he worked at the office next to Dr. Gilbert's. You
remember her parents?"

"Sure."

"Well, one day I walked into a very gay bar and there was Mr.
Johnson, quite entangled with another man."

Shy's face tightened into a puzzled scowl. "What are you saying?"

"Mr. Johnson is gay."

"He's still married?"

"Yes . . ." Alta watched her closely.

"That's pretty strange, but I bet it was someone who looked like him. That happens to me all the time in Seattle. I see people and think they're someone I know. I even thought I saw you a couple of times . . ." She trailed off, pulling her hand through her hair. "Did you talk to him?"

"No, he avoided me. But I've seen him since then, and it's definitely him."

"What's your point?" Shy leaned back against the chair. She lowered her voice. "You think my mother . . ."

"Was a lesbian? Probably not. But playacting a certain kind of life isn't the same as living it. It's a damned lonely thing. Isn't it, Shy? And I wonder about it. I do." Alta kept working at Mrs. Mallon's hair, watching her gray, unmoving face.

"I could do that if you're getting tired," Shy said after a few minutes.

"All right. Here." Alta handed her the comb, touched her wrist.

"Thanks, Alta," she said.

"It's your comb."

Alta cut the engine in the driveway of Shy's parents' empty house. She ushered Shy up the porch stairs, trying not to look across the drying lawn to her own mother's house.

"Do you have the key?" Alta said. Shy pulled it out of her purse absently.

Alta felt relieved to be inside that miserable house, and not just to be out of the throbbing heat. She looked at her watch. It was already almost five.

Shy sighed deeply. Her black party dress hung limp in the heat. "Okay, Alta, show me what you've found. I'm not saying I think it means anything, but if you want to show me, go ahead." She dropped her hand down, the one closest to Alta. Alta took it in her own. Shy led her up the stairs, and Alta remembered how much she'd trusted her once, how Shy used to show her secret outdoor places and teach her little things about life. Part of Shy's magic had been her age, that she was older than Alta yet she treated Alta as her peer.

Shy hesitated at the top of the stairs. "It's in there," Alta said, pointing to Mr. Mallon's old office. But Shy opened her mother's door. The room was immaculate, as if Mrs. Mallon had known she was leaving and might never be back.

Shy crossed the room, one arm circling her belly. The dresser was heavy wood painted white. On top, in a frame of silver birds, Shy's young face smiled, exuberant, shadows falling across those smooth cheeks, bright eyes. Alta had only one picture of Shy. She hadn't looked at it since she'd left Mrs. Mallon's over five years before, but she knew exactly where it was, in a small box in the back of her closet with some school photographs and a picture of her father at the bar, holding a rag in his hand as if it were some kind of trophy. Shy at almost fifteen, long, skinny white socks pulled up to her knees, her stiff school skirt pleated around her hips. Shy laughing right at the camera. Alta had taken the picture in the Mallons' front yard, and if you knew what to look for—and no one but Alta ever did—you could find out from Shy's eyes just how she felt about the photographer.

There was another photograph on the dresser, of Shy at about eighteen or nineteen, just before she'd left home for good. Shy half smiled from underneath her bangs, her eyes wide. It was a studio shot, one of those packaged deals from Macy's with the fake marbled background. Shy peered more closely without picking up the frame or touching the glass. She seemed to be studying the picture for some clue.

"I stopped cutting my bangs when I left," she almost whispered, looking not at Alta, but at the photograph.

Alta picked it up, as much to break the spell of the room as to look more closely. The bangs and the expression of youthful shock vivid on Shy's face were the only signs it was not a picture of her now.

"I wanted something of the change I'd been through to show on my body." She waited a moment, as if she expected Alta to say something. Alta thought about her work, why she pierced people's bodies. It was not about anger or aggression or any of the adolescent spins the mainstream media put on it. It was about letting something show on your body, having the courage to claim skin, flesh, and life as your own, and shape it. Alta lived in a community that valued scars. She had no piercings herself—didn't want any more holes in her body— but she'd found other ways to own her body, to wear the clothes she wanted even though they were sectioned off in the stores under signs she didn't fit, to walk as she pleased and to look damn good, when she'd always been told, growing up, that she wasn't attractive.

Shy opened the top drawer. The sweetness of hidden sachets seeped up from neat layers of white silks. Shy unearthed one and held it to Alta's face. Alta breathed in the gentle comfort of Mrs. Mallon.

"To me," Shy said softly, "it smells exactly like fear." Alta remembered Old Spice and mothballs, disinfectant and the strong smell of urine. Could scent be the strongest part of childhood? Or only the most lasting? Shy pulled something out of the folds of cloth. Her eyes brightened and she held up a small silver key. "Ah ha, Alta," she said, suddenly sarcastic. "Forget your paper trail. I found the key."

"To what?" Alta tried to ignore her tone.

"No idea." Shy shrugged. "Come on. You wanted to play detective." This time she reached for Alta's hand, but the gesture was devoid of sensuality, caught up in the hunt. Alta felt that old uncertainty about what mattered to Shy, what was important and what was a game.

She let herself be pulled along as Shy searched the house: Mr. Mallon's old office with the twin bed; the kitchen that Shy had cleaned so thoroughly it was lifeless and still again, "just like my mother kept it"; even the bathroom, its medicine cabinet thick with bottles of pills, and unlockable. As silly as it seemed, the key had an old-fashioned air of promise. It must belong to something. But there were no locked doors on the cabinets, no boxes fastened and full of promise. Where Shy found a lock—on an old leather case with a broken zipper, in the open drawer of her father's desk—she pushed the key against an unwelcoming keyhole. They even searched Shy's old room, with its rumpled bed from two nights before. At last they returned to her mother's room, and Shy put the key on the dresser by the pictures.

"Sherlock," she said to Alta, "I'm afraid we've come to a dead end." She pushed her dark hair back and rested her face in her hands, fingertips pressed against her eyes. She looked up again, the sarcasm gone. "God, I hate this."

"Shy . . ." Alta felt out of place standing in the middle of that room.

"Do you realize I'm about to have a child of my own, and I'm still waiting for some sign from my mother, some clue, something . . ." Shy picked up the key and fingered it. "I don't know why we didn't talk, Alta. Why should I have thought to ask her? Ask what? If she had some kind of secret, why wouldn't she have told me? What could have been worse than not knowing?" Her voice tightened across her anger and frustration. "Nothing fits. Nothing works." With her thumb, she flicked the little key into the air. It dropped into the stacks of cushions and disappeared.

Quickly Shy went to the bed and ran her hand under the pillows. For a moment she searched frantically, as if she'd lost it, and then it was in her palm, Alta saw her fingers wrap around it, though from her face Alta could tell it was no comfort at all.

"Why is it important to show up for someone's death?" Shy asked angrily, sitting down on the bed. Alta went and sat beside her.

"You have to show up sometime," Alta said. Shy curled up around her own jutting belly and put her head in Alta's lap. Alta ran her fingers through Shy's hair. It was thick and fine, spread across Alta's thighs. Alta leaned back into a mass of pillows. Shy lay, soft and still, against Alta's legs.

"I saw your mother yesterday."

Alta stopped moving her hands along Shy's scalp. "I'm surprised she didn't put you in a home for unwed mothers."

"You should be grateful you have a normal mother."

"She should be grateful she has a homo daughter."

"Are you happy now?"

"Now that you're here?"

"In your life . . . I don't know."

"I'm pretty happy," Alta said. "San Francisco's a good place for me . . . to be myself."

"It seems like there's no place you wouldn't be yourself."

"You don't understand what it's like."

Shy rolled over on her back and looked up at Alta. "I don't even know why I asked that. What does 'happy' mean, anyway?"

"Getting pretty philosophical there, Shy."

Shy looked from this angle as she used to when they'd watched television together, and without either of them acknowledging it, Alta'd slip her hand under Shy's shirt, brush slowly across her midriff, move inch by inch toward her breasts.

"You've been really generous to me, Alta."

Alta shrugged uncomfortably. Shy picked up a small cushion embroidered with the words HOME SWEET HOME in tiny green and pink stitching.

"I never went to Europe. That's one thing I regret."

"You could still go one day."

"You think?"

"Get one of those baby packs . . ."

"What do you want to see, Alta?"

"That's a funny question."

"I mean of the world."

"Ah, the world. I want to see it change, the world." Alta took a few strands of Shy's hair, so much softer and thicker than her mother's, and braided them. "I want your baby to grow up, and whatever kind of person it is, I want that to be okay. And not just okay." When Alta dropped the end of the braid it fell apart.

"You're kind of sweet under all that toughness."

"Sweet?" Alta growled mockingly.

"Like a kitten," Shy said, pronouncing each t.

"Hey." Alta pulled a fluffy pillow from behind her and threatened to put it down on Shy's face. "I'm a ferocious lion."

Shy laughed, plucking a feather from the pillow and tickling Alta's throat.

"Do you know why I'm not married?" Shy asked. Alta could literally feel her heart thudding. She'd loved Shy all these years; surely *her* feelings for Alta had affected her life. Shy hadn't, after all, married.

"No." Alta shook her head.

Shy pushed her hair back and held Alta's gaze. "I guess you've always known what you wanted. I've done lots of things I wasn't sure of. And I wasn't sure I wanted to marry Erik." She turned and lay on her back. "It seemed separate from the baby, even though he was there. It just seemed like maybe he was the accident. Erik." She laughed, a touch dramatically. "He's so funny. I mean, he's really serious. He works too much, and he doesn't understand me, but he loves me anyway."

"But you don't . . . ?"

"I don't need to marry him. I wanted the baby, and maybe I don't care what people think anymore. Maybe that's not what's important."

"Shy?" Alta took one of Shy's hands and tangled her fingers in it. Shy stayed there, holding on.

"Yeah?"

"I'm glad you know what you want." Alta could feel the deep hum of each breath fluttering to the bottom of her lungs. Alta leaned over Shy. Shy's face moved toward her, and, a moment too soon, Shy closed her eyes. Her lips were soft, and Alta felt Shy's tongue reach for hers. Shy was kissing her back, and that shattered her and put her together again in one instant.

Shy smelled like vanilla, and she tasted faintly of cloves. Alta tasted these things—from her pores, and in the corners of her eyes and the creases of her elbows, her neck—even before she unbuttoned the long row down the front of Shy's dress and rolled her stockings gently off her. Alta lay her back on that heap of blankets and spread her legs, losing her face and dark hair behind the taut heap of her belly.

Alta grazed her teeth along its hard arch and understood, in the back of her mind, the impulse toward cannibalism, the desire to break flesh and taste blood. She teased Shy with a finger down that dark line from her belly button to her swollen lips, the hair matted and musky, trailing up to her ass. She slid her hands under Shy's back, down her spine to the flesh of her cheeks and the beginning of the valley between them. Every once in a while Alta would look up from the depth of her, her short nails digging into Shy slightly as she ran her eyes up Shy's fecund body. And all the time Alta kept thinking, this is Shy, this is Shy.

Alta blew on her clit and a moan stuck in Shy's throat, dry and half silent. Alta opened her eyes. The shadowy room had grown darker as daylight faded. Shy's hand was pressed against her own mouth. In that moment, Alta felt further from Shy than she had since she'd arrived. Shy seemed to be hiding behind her hand and the dusk. Alta jumped up and hit the light switch. The ache of light spread dark circles in front of her vision, but she stayed looking down at Shy until they cleared. Shy kept her eyes shut tight, her head turned away and her hands now grabbing the blanket as if holding back the other side of that moan. Alta reached down with one hand and turned Shy's chin so when Shy opened her eyes she would look into Alta's. With her other hand she continued to touch her. When Shy did open her eyes, Alta saw every bit of shame she'd feared she'd see. Tears crested at the edges of Shy's lower lids, and she looked away from Alta. Alta didn't stop the rhythmic motion of her hand, only let go of Shy's chin and cupped her full, brown-nippled breast and held her gaze. Everything about Shy was cool.

"Oh Shy." Alta shook her head. Sent heat down her arm. When Shy came she grabbed Alta's hand and stuffed the palm against her mouth. And Alta wanted to hold Shy, finally to stop running and lie down with everything she'd feared and wanted for so long. She picked up one of Shy's tears on the tip of her finger.

The phone rang. "Don't get it," Alta said.

"I have to," Shy said, turning away. "It's Erik." She slid to the edge of the bed and slowly launched herself from it, pushing her weight up with her arms. "Wait for me."

Alta looked down at the tear on her forefinger. Shy's teeth had made marks in the skin of Alta's hand, and that was the first message she ever left with Alta that Alta knew she would believe completely, even when Shy was gone.

She could hear Shy downstairs, her voice rocking into the empty house. The laces on Alta's boots had loosened, and now she retied them. She knew one thing: she was done waiting for Shy. She went down to the dining room.

"Shy?"

Shy looked up and her body tensed. She held one finger up. "I'm not happy," she said into the phone. "This is really hard. I can't sit around crying all the time, though . . . What did you do today?" She twisted the phone cord around her hand, just as she did when they were younger.

"Shy," Alta said again, more firmly.

"Erik? Hold on a sec, okay? Okay?" She put her hand over the mouthpiece. "I'm not going to be long, but he likes to talk to me in the evenings."

"I'm leaving. I have to work in the morning."

Now Alta had her attention, for the moment. Shy cleared her throat and spoke into the phone. "Erik? I just need to say goodbye to someone. Can I call you back in a minute?"

"Don't worry about it, Shy." Alta's words came out bitter and hard. Just once, she wanted to be the priority of someone who really knew her, and not just until that person came. Shy didn't say anything. The phone was in her hand, and some guy on the other end, some guy who'd impregnated her, who thought she loved him, probably, and maybe she did, this guy was listening to Alta want one more thing she couldn't have. Alta turned and walked down the stairs and out into the night. It was still velvety warm, though not as suffocatingly hot as in the daytime. She rolled her bike up Shy's driveway and then turned to walk it past her mother's house to the end of the block. She looked ahead down the dark street, at the rundown Lincolns and pickup trucks parked smugly along the curbs, all the different houses faded into uniform silhouettes. The

quiet chilled her, even in the heat; whatever could hide in that stillness seemed scarier than the rowdy dangers of the City.

She had almost passed her old house, pushing the heavy bike
along in the middle of the street. She felt as if she were fleeing Baby-
lon. Then she thought she heard a noise, and she glanced back. Her
mother's face peered from the front window, lit by a candle or small
lamp below. Alta froze.

After a moment she became aware of her heart squeezed and
knocking, and of the salty smell of sex around her. Alta straddled her
bike, kicking the engine alive. The noise sputtered and then shot
through the quiet night. Alta sped around the corner, her hands
shaking, and headed for the bridge.

The next morning before work, Alta dropped by Mrs. Koch's house.
Mrs. Koch was always there in the morning: she called it her time to
putter.

"Where's Sasha?" she said after she had kissed both of Alta's
cheeks.

"She's at home."

"She's a pretty girl, Alta." Mrs. Koch took Alta's arm and gave her
a mischievous grin. "Very dangerous, no?" They reached the top of
the stairs. "Just like Paulie. You don't know, Alta"—she waved her
finger—"the trouble I had with that woman. So. Come into the
kitchen for tea."

They sat at the small breakfast table, just as they had mornings
when Alta worked for Mrs. Koch and Mrs. Koch was giving her
instructions for the day.

"Alta, you're upset. So tell me."

"I'm worried," Alta said. "I'm worried about Shy, and I'm worried
about Mrs. Mallon. It's all this secrecy; it seems wrong."

"Nobody tells anyone everything." This sounded so unlike Mrs.
Koch, Alta wondered if the secret were hers.

"I know that. Mrs. Koch, I'll lie to keep out of trouble as fast as the next guy. But I'm always the same person. I mean, I go everywhere looking the way I do, being who I am."

"That's why I said you were brave." Mrs. Koch topped off Alta's teacup even though Alta had taken only a sip.

"I'm not brave. I don't feel like I have a choice." Alta leaned forward. "If I had stayed over there, I would have died."

Mrs. Koch didn't reply, and Alta had the uncomfortable feeling she'd said something wrong; perhaps because Mrs. Mallon was probably dying, or because Mrs. Koch and Miss Pauline were so much closer to death. Perhaps because Mrs. Koch had lived through a war and had seen more death than Alta could imagine. Then Mrs. Koch met Alta's eyes again.

"It's good the way you live, Alta. That's enough, hmmn?"

"No." Alta put her cup down. "Please, Mrs. Koch. I want to know about Mrs. Mallon, because she meant a lot to me. But I want Shy to know even more. She has to know, so she can make her own choices, and become a mother, and—"

"You know what, Alta?" Mrs. Koch tapped one finger on her teacup. "She will become a mother soon anyway, will she not? The girl is pregnant."

"Are you protecting yourself? Or Miss Pauline? Or did she make you promise not to tell?"

"Tell what, Alta?" She met Alta's gaze.

"If I knew I wouldn't ask."

"If I knew I wouldn't say."

"I hear you knocked up some poor girl, Alta." Harriet winked at her.

Alta shrugged. "Yeah, well, I've got to try every time I have sex. It's Catholic doctrine."

Harriet lay her elbows on the appointment book. "So, tell me about it."

Alta bent down really close to her and put one finger on the schedule page right above where the tops of Harriet's tiny breasts peered from her dress. "I've got an eleven o'clock appointment. I'd better set things up."

"Fine," Harriet sighed, straightening up. "Go on, get to work." She gestured at Alta's little room with her head, the blunt ends of her hair whirling around her shoulders.

All that day at work, Alta was haunted by déjà vu—a recollection not of the external world, but of the mind. She tried to bring herself into the flutter of rainbow flags above storefronts, the laughter of girl-crowds when they passed by, even the gray skies she could see through her window, and the dramatic breaks in them. Amanda, the girl from Renny's party, came in for the belly-button piercing that Shy had distracted Alta from discussing with her. Alta found herself thinking that perhaps she had been mistaken to bring Shy to that party; now even Alta's present life reminded her of Shy. Amanda asked if Stigmata would have a booth at the Queer Street Faire. Alta told her they'd be there, and even signed her up to do a nipple-piercing demonstration, but she didn't go home with Amanda after work, or use the phone number she gave Alta to "call sometime." Instead, she went home to check her messages. Shy hadn't called. Forget her, Alta thought, I should have gone out with Amanda. Well, there were plenty of girls if you knew where to find them.

She called the hospital and spoke to the nurse on duty, who said Dr. Jeffreys had just been by to check on Mrs. Mallon, and that he thought things might take a turn for the better tonight. Alta found herself wishing for a place to pray, the kind of majestic sanctuary their neighborhood church had seemed in her childhood. So she got back on her bike and rode up the winding rise of Market Street and sat looking at the city below, reminding herself that a rich world indeed lay before her for the picking. Still the déjà vu, that familiar discomfort, bothered her. She had thought for so long that her love for Shy was one-sided that she had imagined it could exist in her alone, could carry on uninterrupted even without Shy herself. She had forgotten the little encouragements—the smell of Shy's breath when she leaned forward to whisper a secret; the careless press of Shy's fingers as she tapped Alta's arm, laughing; even the tension in Shy's cheeks when she was upset, which could project across a whole room.

"If you were a man, I would marry you," Shy would tell Alta, until Alta wished she were a man, someone who could have kept Shy from leaving. Alta's rage could burn and bend, but she could not fire love alone. Wooden puppet, she thought of herself, Pinocchio: "I want to be a real boy, Father. I want to be a *real* boy."

Alta used to position herself three people away from Shy in any group, watching Shy's hands move as she talked and nodded, pushed the hair from her face. Now, the unspoken overwhelmed Alta again. Here she was where she had been before, and she hadn't done much differently. Or whatever she had done, the results had been too much the same. The nights Shy had turned toward Alta, her eyes closed and her intentions clear, and her coldness, the equally inexplicable nights she had sneaked away to that cavernous house, left Alta's bed for her own.

Night was supposed to be Alta's time, but it was light she always thought of, whether she was roaming the streets under the solicitous curve of street lamps, or lying wide-eyed and awake, courting sleep. She fired up her bike and found a direction away from Shy and her mother, and the sunken secrets so many people seemed determined to keep that way.

The Stud had never looked so sleazy. The smell accosted Alta as she entered, but she enjoyed it, too—that heady onslaught of sweet and stale spilled liquor and the juice of excited girls, the grind of music against the cool, raunchy silence of the butches waiting and watching.

She pushed her way through, but slowly, enjoying the press of bodies as much as the path that cleared for her as it did not clear for everyone who tried to get through this crowd. Karene, one of the dancers hired by the Stud for these girlz nights, waved at Alta, her

forever legs pumping under a soft-pink baby-doll dress with matching ruffled panties peeking out. Alta winked. Max was spinning out
the sound up in the DJ booth while a couple of girls behind her ran
needles through the soft layers of their skin.

"Alta!" Max's low voice and easy smile greeted Alta. The girls
looked up languidly.

"Hey, Max, how's it going?" Besides being Stigmata's tattoo artist,
Max was a photographer who specialized in shots of tattoos and
piercings, and they'd hung a couple of the pictures at the shop.

"I brought those tattoo removal prints you wanted to check out."
She flicked a couple of switches on the sound system and then spun
her chair around and gestured for Alta to sit. She pointed to a black
portfolio.

"Thanks."

"Thinking of getting something removed?"

"Me? No way. Once I know what I want, I don't change my mind."
Alta took a chair in the corner.

"That's not what I've heard." Max winked at the girls behind her.

"You have to know how long you want something, know what I
mean? If I want a girl for a night, I haven't changed my mind when I
take her home in the morning. No regrets, that's the key."

"Hey, I was just kidding, man. Anyway, there's lots of reasons why
people get tattoos removed. It's not just regret." Max turned back
and started flipping new CDs into the console. The girls were working themselves up into a frenzy of pained ecstasy, tight lines of their
skin stretched over the hard metal of the needle. They were right
over Alta—the DJ booth was pretty close quarters—Alta reached
one hand open toward the disheveled brunette's bared chest. "May I?"

She met Alta's eyes and a flash of electricity charged between
them. "Go right ahead," she said, her lips and eyebrows wavering in
sensuous mockery. "You know what you want."

Alta stood up. The blonde with a half-shaved head had to lean
back against the wall and Alta turned to her, practically pressed to
her skin-tight red velvet pants. "With your permission . . ."

She handed Alta a latex glove.

Alta's hand was already hot, and the rubber molded right to it. Alta ran one finger over the brunette's ridged breasts. The metal picked up the heat right away, and she shivered violently from the subtle pulse of the burn. Alta ran her other hand all the way down her back and pressed her mouth, tongue, and then teeth, to the brunette's long neck. When she reached her ear, Alta whispered, "If you'd like to know more about what I want, let's chat later, shall we?"

The brunette stayed warmly against Alta, waves of desire running between them, and then she pulled back. Her eyes were bright and still mocking. "I'd like that, Alta," she said.

"You know my name, but I don't know yours. I'd say we haven't been properly introduced."

She shrugged. "The unknown are beloved, and the moral are all dead."

"It's easier that way." Alta touched her cap to the blonde and sat back down.

Max had just finished making an announcement over the loudspeaker, and the crowd screamed with joy as the next song rocked, harsh, into the room below. The sounds came muffled to them.

Max unzipped her portfolio in front of them and peered over the photographs with Alta. They were intense images. Some Alta had to study for a while before the gentle tracings of white became visible. This one showed a back, the shadow of the shoulder blade sharper than the faded white echo above it. "A rose dripping blood," Max said. "She had it for fifteen years and it didn't fit anymore."

"What's the process?"

"There are different techniques. You basically destroy the area, make a wound, and then let it heal. Now they can do it with a laser machine that targets the pigmented areas. It hurts like all hell. It shatters the ink into tiny pieces, and the skin absorbs it. It can take five or six sessions. If you're lucky, the body heals."

"Yeah, bodies are forgiving. It's memory that's bad about forgetting."

Max nodded. "The scar is always the least of it."

But the next several pictures showed awful scars. A small rose with tiny green leaves became a hideous pink mark, unevenly swollen, as though worms were burrowing beneath the surface. A mottled square covered an arm where a dove had once been drawn. A spreading scar stretched through the middle of a jungle of flowers, scabbed and pussy.

"They abandoned the removal," Max said. "The wound wasn't healing right."

"Tattoos are a playground for people who know what they want," Alta said, the sour taste of revulsion in her mouth. She had asked Max to show her these pictures for a reason, but now she thought she was far off track. A tattoo removal didn't make much sense for Mrs. Mallon. She wasn't a woman to have had a tattoo, not like Alta's cousins with old boyfriends' names all over their bodies. An East Coast girl once told Alta that lesbians in Buffalo, New York, in the forties and fifties had tattooed blue stars on their wrists. She had been a customer at Stigmata who had gotten the same mark in their honor. Alta tried to picture Mrs. Mallon with that brilliant indigo star, a whole life then repudiated in favor of the suburban humdrum of a marriage to Mr. Mallon. Was this what Mrs. Mallon had made Mrs. Koch promise never to tell?

Max turned the photograph over carefully, revealing the next one. A startling series of close-ups of a middle-aged man's face. The lines of the tattoo removal became fainter in each picture, until they were so tiny and faded they looked like the wrinkles around his eyes. Ghost of a tattoo. "He had this elaborate design on his upper left cheek and temple. He said he couldn't get work anymore. He said the world was different, and it had to do with his age, not just the tattoo. But the tattoo was a liability."

The next picture was an old man. Alta couldn't see the markings.

"Old Jewish guy. It was against his religion to be tattooed. It was one of those numbers from a concentration camp. He said he had it removed for his peace of mind"—she exhaled, an audible sigh—"but he recited the number to me. He knew it by heart." They sat there in silence for a moment, listening to the people dancing below. Alta thought of Zahava; murdered, Mrs. Koch had said. She thought of the way Mrs. Koch talked about Mrs. Mallon bringing her to America. Could Mrs. Koch have been Jewish, like her dark, golden lover Zahava?

Then Max flipped the picture over, and the next one was his arm. Alta knew it was the same man because the edge of his beige sweater was pushed back to his elbow at the edge of the photograph. It was fainter, smoother, but it was Mrs. Mallon's scar almost exactly. "Damn it to hell," Alta said. "Damnit, damnit, damnit."

"Found what you're looking for?"

THREE

On her way out of the Stud later that night, Alta found the brunette from the DJ booth dancing. The needles flashed above a leather halter top and tight skirt. Thigh-high boots clung as close to her legs as Alta could ever hope to.

"I need a good way to get my mind off something. Got any ideas?" Alta asked.

"I guess there must be a lot you could occupy yourself with here."

"That depends on your perspective." Alta kept her eyes hot on the brunette; it wasn't hard.

"Perspective problems sometime mean you need new glasses."

"I don't wear glasses."

"Or to have your eyes checked."

"How's your vision?"

"Twenty-twenty."

"Like all hindsight."

"Oh yeah?" The brunette reached behind the bar and grabbed a maraschino cherry from a silver tub between the lemons and the paper umbrellas. Alta watched her hungrily. "It's the future that's kind of blurry, isn't it?" The brunette dangled the cherry from its red stem above her luscious mouth. Alta opened hers to reply, to say, "I have enough trouble with the past," and the brunette slipped the cherry between Alta's lips, one finger trailing slowly out. The sickly burst of red-sweet filled Alta's mouth.

"That's the thing about what's going to happen." The brunette shrugged. "You just can't guess."

Alta took the brunette home with her.

This world wears genders on the outside. Boys in satin and velvet, boys in gyms. Girls lounging down the street in extra-large overalls, girls in tight denim, girls in corsets and garters. Butches on motorcycles, drag queens on roller skates, women called "sir," sweet boys who blush. Alta could almost breathe the agelessness of the casual heat that traveled between her and the brunette. Her bike drove home on the energy of it.

It was two in the morning when they got to Alta's place, and at four—and no one could describe those hours as boring—the brunette climbed off Alta, shook her mane of hair, and pulled her boots back on.

"Done?" Alta said, leaning on one elbow and raising an eyebrow.

"Greed isn't necessary," the brunette said, smiling against the dryness of her deadpan eyes. "Right now we can consider ourselves lucky and leave it at that."

Alta lay back and looked up at the sky Liza had painted on her ceiling, shady with the light turned low. She'd painted it the last day before she left for Rhode Island. Put newspaper all over the place.

"Now you'll think of me whenever you're in bed," Liza had said.

"Hey, what is this, my sky of tears?"

Liza had had a streak of blue across one cheek. Alta climbed on the bed to be beside her where she stood on a chair and tried to rub it off, but it wouldn't disappear. It occurred to Alta that Liza was waiting for Alta to ask her to stay, that Liza would stay if Alta asked. But if Alta asked her not to go, Alta would start to need her, and when, one day, Liza left, Alta would have forgotten how to let her go.

"I'll take you home," Alta muttered now.

"No need." The brunette zipped up her leather jacket. "I can find my way."

Alta jumped up. "No, I insist."

The brunette turned and grabbed Alta's wrist. "Look, big boy, I'll be fine on my own."

"I thought you promised you'd keep my mind occupied."

"Wrong. This isn't about promises. You know that better than I do." She was at Alta's door.

"Have a good night," Alta said, and the brunette was gone.

Alta shut the door. She stood with her back to the empty room, not wanting to see the familiar lamplight illuminating the still furniture. Alta had said farewell to a string of girls in this apartment: the young ones who lied about their age and watched her every move wide-eyed as though they'd made some kind of a miraculous discovery; the married women who twisted the skin where they'd tanned around the pale thin line where they'd removed their rings, who tried to pretend they weren't just swingers from the suburbs out for a night of real fun; the tough girls, the ones who left faster than they came, brazen girls who showed lots of flesh and no feeling; the androgynes who wanted to be femme but were more scared of lipstick than they were of Alta; the little-boy butches in girl-drag who hadn't found their footing and realized they wanted to *be* Alta; the seductresses with plunging necklines who fell in love for the romance of the night and who were wrecked by morning. But Alta always hated goodbye, hated the rip of girl-presence from her apartment like the tear of a bandage off bare skin. Still, she was wrong, the brunette. It wasn't the uncertainty of the future that held Alta, it was the uncertainty of the past.

Alta tossed and turned until it was late enough to call Shy. The sun came up and bathed the City in pale yellow. A particular peace settled over the empty streets. Usually Alta was only up at this time when she'd stayed up all night.

"Shy?" In the silence that followed, Alta suddenly understood what Shy had meant when she claimed that she had always approached Alta. Alta had only known that she was always waiting for Shy.

"Hello, Alta," Shy said finally.

"How are you, Shyster?"

"Alta, this is a very hard time for me." Alta hated it when she took on that condescending adult voice—especially now that they were both adults.

"I realize that, Shy. Believe it or not, it hasn't been great for me either."

"Well, let's sit here and feel sorry for ourselves."

"Listen, Shy. I think I've figured out something that's really important."

"I don't want to talk about my mother's past."

"Shy, what if we could help her? When I was suffocating from all the lies and denial, she found me a place where I didn't have to hide—"

"You sound like someone on a miniseries."

"Damn you. It wasn't television, it was something very real in my life, and you just didn't happen to be around."

Shy said nothing. Alta could hear her pacing.

"Shy-girl. Meet me. Talk to me. Come on, Shy." Alta closed her eyes.

"All right, lunch," Shy said. "Where?"

Alta kick-started her bike and rode to St. Luke's. It was amazing how familiar the way had become: across the span of the bridge and off along the frontage road to Fourth Street. The next right at Spencer, and she parked in the garage beneath the hospital. The drive gave her time to think. She and Shy were different kinds of liars. Alta's lies were razor sharp—her own distinctions between truth and her version of it remained clear to her. She wanted to see Mrs. Mallon without Shy again. Of course, Shy might have been there, but she wasn't.

The nurses and nuns looked at Alta, their heads frozen and their eyes tracing her movements.

"How's Alice Mallon?" Alta asked Sister Ann, the wrinkled nun she'd met with Shy.

"No news until Dr. Jeffreys comes by," she said. "Only family members are allowed to visit."

"You let me in last time."

She smoothed her skirt. "Well, you were with her daughter."

"Listen." Alta started walking toward Mrs. Mallon's room, and the sister hurried along beside her. "I am a family member, I'm her daughter-in-law and I've known her most of my life."

The nun looked startled, her eyes pale and large between the creases in her small face. "I didn't realize . . . She has a son?"

They reached the door, and Alta saw Mrs. Mallon stretched on her bed.

"No," Alta said, and went into the room. Sister Ann pushed in after her and stood silently as Alta moved a chair to the bedside and sat down. Perhaps the human reality of Mrs. Mallon's fragile gray hair and strained features, her bare arms with tubes running up them, made the nun lose track for a moment of the complex rules governing who can love whom and how.

Alta traced the scar on Mrs. Mallon's wrist. A chill ran over her. She'd prided herself on attention to detail—as a lover, as a body piercer, as a person whose life depended on such awareness. But the smallest things are so easy to become accustomed to without ever questioning them.

"What do you suppose this is?" Alta asked the sister.

"Hmm? I wouldn't know." She stood as if guarding the body.

"Don't you have medical records?"

"It looks like very minor surgery. Perhaps stitches." She peered at Alta with the firm gaze she recognized from the nuns of her childhood. Alta saw the soft layer of her eyelid over her transparent blue eyes. Alta had been raised on their sweet sadomasochism, and it struck her now that nothing had changed much since her childhood. It was as if San Francisco were not a different place, but a different time, and in crossing the bridge she had gone backward.

"Do you think it could have been a tattoo?" Alta said quietly, almost expecting Mrs. Mallon's hand to shift in hers.

"You'd better leave," the nun said, almost apologetically. "She's neurologically shut off. Your presence makes no difference to her."

"When I was in Catholic school nuns spoke more of miracles and less of neurology," Alta said, and then she turned to look at the woman. She was small, with a pinched frailty and Mrs. C.'s thin lips. Her watery blue eyes were not unkind. "Please," Alta added in a more relenting tone, "could you give me a moment alone with her? I've known her since I was seven."

"Well, I suppose so," the nun replied, her mouth still bunched tight. She turned and walked out, leaving the door ajar.

Alta held Mrs. Mallon's hand, traced the veins on its back, the silken skin stretched and wrinkled. Hesitantly, she brushed the white mark on her wrist. Alta tried to imagine a young Mrs. Mallon, but all she could think of was Shy. A strange feeling crept over her. She thought of the swollen scars crisscrossed on Renny's arms, the dark line up Shy's pregnant belly. Was this ghostly patch of skin the mark of a coward hiding something or of a woman surviving any way she could? And why had she chosen this way?

Had Mrs. Mallon confessed her secrets? Their religion, for all its rigidity and oppression, was a forgiving one. But Alta thought people confessed their easy sins—untoward thoughts, shoplifting, even adultery. Easy to recognize, easy to commit. The stuff of their souls they kept to themselves. There is a hierarchy of sins, but the real sins lack neat names, the charm of category. The opposite of every real sin is not a virtue, but another sin, and the truest sinners are always guilty of both. Alta had loved Shy too much and not enough. She had lusted for her soul as she had for her body.

"Mrs. Mallon." Could Alta walk away as Shy had, as perhaps Mrs. Mallon had from what she kept secret? Alta had left her past as best she could, too. She'd left. She'd hurtled forward as fast as she was able. Each girl an island, a moment of respite in the crossing.

"Mrs. Mallon." If Shy's mother lived, Alta would tell her of the place she had given Alta to live out the truth of her life as she could make it; Alta would try to offer Mrs. Mallon the same. She held Mrs. Mallon's still, lukewarm hand and tried to feed into it the flame inside her, as if she could revive life and second chances with heat, and not simply pick up girls and perform piercings.

"Mrs. Mallon," Alta whispered softly, thinking the name meant nothing; perhaps it was a mask, perhaps a haven of safety—the kind of invisibility people had been trying to tempt her with all her life.

"Mrs. Mallon." The name became pure sound, meaningless gibberish, as any word does when you say it again and again with no context.

They'd hung out at the Classic Diner when they were teenagers, but as Alta waited at the scarred, shiny table, the sharp edge of the torn seat-plastic pressing into her jeans, she regretted suggesting the place. It was convenient for Shy, but too uncomfortable for Alta. The waitress pattered with the men at the table behind her, and honeyed the couple on the other side, but she poured Alta's coffee without a word or a smile. Alta had been waiting for half an hour. I could slip out now, she thought, leave a couple of bucks on the table and go. No one would ever connect the sweet pregnant woman, waiting alone, with the tough bulldagger who'd just left. Shy would sit for a while—if she came at all—and maybe ask for a glass of juice, or more likely just tap water with ice, and after Alta didn't show up she'd leave. She'd walk back along the busy road. No one would shout at her or whistle. Erik would call her on the phone and ask her again to come home, and maybe he wouldn't notice she was upset.

Mrs. Mallon's situation churned in Alta's mind. Did Shy know? Was it possible she had known all along and never told Alta? She thought of Shy's stories of Paris, of wealthy grandparents and dashing French cousins, how vague they were, and how fanciful.

Alta looked up from the surface of the table and Shy was in the door, her eyes finding Alta and her bony body with its cargo of baby draped in a dark, flowered dress coming toward Alta. Alta half stood in the booth. Shy's eyes were a smooth bank of grief.

"What's wrong?"

But Alta knew. There are things you know before they are said, even better than after when you have the words to mop up with. Alta hadn't known before Shy walked in, but when she saw Shy it was as if Mrs. Mallon disappeared from the real things around them—the scratched tables and the waitress's dirty looks and Shy's belly. Alta's world had been half floating since her dad died, so the feeling was familiar, but it never got better, it was just that you drove involuntarily into that cold, sharp wind with your eyes open and stinging. Everything Alta had loved had been taken from her one way or another. And the worst thing was how her will to live bucked up strongest then, when it had an adversary. She must have wanted to survive more than just about anything else.

"When?" Alta asked, now as calm as Shy, who seated herself across from Alta without making a move to touch. "I just saw her . . . two, three hours ago."

"She's still alive," Shy said, all the breath gone from her voice. "She had a heart attack about an hour ago. They called me as I was getting ready to come meet you. She's not going to get better." Her voice went ragged and disappeared. Alta stared, her eyes open and almost unblinking at the dirty windows and the thick coffee cups, but the image of that still body convulsing to life came anyway.

Alta knew then that she had let the past lie as much as Shy had, as much, perhaps, as Mrs. Mallon had. Shy had walked back into Alta's life, and Alta had let her. Oh, sure, Alta had kept her at a distance—or tried to with her usual tricks, but keeping one's distance wasn't that clever or unique a feat. They were all so far apart, echoes of their words came mumbled and submerged to each other, and as far as anything made any sense, they ignored it. Alta had studied Mrs. Mallon's scar closely, as if it were a secret passage, one that might burst open and reveal, not flesh and bone, but truth—an accurate story of the past.

"Have you called Erik?" It was the first time Alta had brought him up, but to get at the past Alta had to stand on the present.

Shy shrugged and shook her head. "Not yet. He's going to be upset that I'm not coming back." She signaled the waitress and ordered waffles. Alta got a refill on coffee.

"Not coming back?"

"There's a lot to take care of," she said vaguely.

Alta looked at her closely now, saw the darkness below her eyes, the red rims beneath smudged liner. She reached across the table and took Shy's hand.

"Your mom is a tough lady. She really helped me after you left and my mom kicked me out." Alta traced the curve between Shy's thumb and first finger. She heard the waitress's ditzy laughter as she served the men behind her, and felt a great pity for the faded, scarred world where she'd grown up. She wanted Mrs. Mallon back, but even with her daughter right in front of her, she couldn't say what needed to be said. "She is really wonderful—" Alta began.

"Wonderful?" Shy's voice came hard and high, amazed and bitter. She pulled her hand back, not all the way out of Alta's, but so that Alta had to reach for it. Alta took a deep breath. God, Shy was vivid and alive, her dark skin and adamant cheekbones, her thick hair falling in strands around her face.

"She has her secrets, just like you."

"What are my secrets?"

"I don't know, Shy. They're secrets."

Shy looked at Alta sideways, and Alta was unprepared for the anger in her eyes. The waitress put a plate of waffles in front of Shy and slapped the silver tub of syrup down. "Careful, honey, it's hot." Shy's cold hand was out of Alta's and on her fork. She smiled at the waitress and watched her retreat. Then she leaned toward Alta. "Did you say something to Sister Ann about my mother's scar?" Her eyes danced back and forth.

"Sure—I said that her tattoo—"

"What tattoo?" Shy exploded, and the waitress, who had been headed back in their direction with the plastic pitcher, turned away sharply and sloshed ice water onto the floor.

"Shy, what's going on?" Alta asked severely.

"What big secret do you think my mother had?"

For some reason, Alta hesitated, as if even she had begun to believe that it was the words that made something true. She supposed she did believe that in a way. "I think maybe she was Jewish; that she was in a concentration camp and—"

"You have your own special way of looking at the world, don't you, Alta?" Shy's voice shook with rigid anger. "You're the one with the secrets. Don't you put this on my mother. Don't you dare."

"Well, you know where her baptismal certificate is—dated 1952," Alta threw in. "So you'll be able to give her a Catholic funeral and run off again."

Alta could see the sting of tears in Shy's eyes.

"That's not fair." Shy sat up, proud and awkward in her tight dress. "The past may hold all sorts of crazy secrets, Alta, but my future is looming rather large." They both looked at the arc of her belly. "This is what's important to me." Her voice went soft and gentle, but Alta knew there was iron just below the surface. "Why does her past matter so much to you? Alta?" Her face softened slightly, as if she really wanted to know, though her eyes remained fierce.

Alta pointed a finger at her. "It started mattering to me when you ran away from it," Alta said. "Fair is whatever is easy for you. But you can't just keep running, Shy. Someday you've got to stop."

"You know, Alta," Shy said, for once hushed, her fingers gripping the table, "to you, I ran away, and maybe I did, and maybe I had my reasons. But I went with me, and now this is just my life."

Alta watched the second hand move around the clock on the wall behind Shy's head. "Tell me why you left, Shy."

"I understand you, Alta. You think no one sees things the way they really are, just because no one understood you. You think my mother couldn't be just one more not very happy suburban lady."

"Did you hear me?" Alta grabbed her wrist. "You came to see me, to borrow money, and then you just took off—"

"Yes, I owe you two hundred dollars."

Shy matched Alta's gaze, her hand frozen in Alta's.

"Two hundred dollars." Alta let go of her arm. There was a red mark where she'd held on. "You owe me more than the money, Shy. Keep your damn two hundred dollars. You left, Shy. You never said a word. You never wrote me. You were here in town and you didn't call me. What you owe me, more than anything, is an explanation." Shy looked out the window. Over the top of a scraggly bush, she studied the parking lot. "What were you thinking? Shy? What the hell did you think you were doing? Two hundred dollars. Please."

Shy stabbed a bite of waffle and swirled it around in a puddle of syrup.

"You still think you can pull this, Shy?" Alta shook her head, laughed scornfully. "You think I'm still fifteen years old and believe the sun rises out of your ass?"

Shy took a bite but said nothing.

Alta threw down enough money to cover the bill and brushed by the awful waitress, who didn't bother to call out, as she had to the other customers, "Have a nice day."

Miss Pauline answered the door. "Oh, Alta," she said right away. She put her arms around Alta and Alta buried a sob against Miss Pauline's shoulder. "Mrs. Mallon?"

"She's worse."

"Gerda's upstairs. Come up. I'll make tea."

There was already a new skylight installed in the high ceiling above. Their shadows cut across the bright square of light that fell on the stairs.

"Who is it, Paulie?" Mrs. Koch said, coming out of the next room. "Alta!" She came up and looked into Alta's face. "What is it? Is Alicia worse?"

"She—this morning. A heart attack. She's alive, but not getting better."

Mrs. Koch stared at Alta, her face still and very sad. "Alicia?" Her stocky body trembled and she started to cry. "Paulie?" Alta had never seen Mrs. Koch at a loss.

Miss Pauline took Mrs. Koch's hand and led her to the couch. "Poor Alicia," Miss Pauline said.

"They'll all be gone now."

"Shh, honey." Miss Pauline wrapped her arms around Mrs. Koch, who buried her face. "Alta's here."

"Oh, it's okay."

Miss Pauline sent Alta to turn on the kettle, and when Alta came back with the tea, Alta found Mrs. Koch sitting up dry-eyed again.

"Thank you, Alta."

"Why was she so unhappy, Mrs. Koch?"

"She had a hard life."

"She was Jewish, wasn't she? Like Zahava."

Mrs. Koch looked at Miss Pauline.

"Why did she hide it?" Alta asked.

"Alta, do not try to second-guess Alicia's secrets. Her life is end-ing—" Mrs. Koch bit her lip, recovered, went on. "We must hope that finally she will rest in peace."

"But what about those of us who are left? What about Shy?"

Mrs. Koch shrugged. "So, we make a life."

"Tell me—was she ever really happy?"

"If I could remember far enough back," Mrs. Koch reached, with-out looking, for Miss Pauline's hand, "she was always laughing."

There was a party at Max's that night, and she decided to go, forcing herself to keep on, so that she'd have something left when Mrs. Mal-lon died and Shy was gone. Dressing, she pumped the loud music of hardcore girl-bands out of her stereo, stomped around those shiny floors. She thought of the stories she had told the rush of girls she'd dragged through there—suddenly, it seemed a long time ago.

When Alta got to Max's a dominatrix she'd encountered before was holding court in the living room. Her hair on top was cropped short so that the shaved sides of her head showed from under her leather-girl hat. She wore a little leather jumpsuit painted silver.

"A cow died for this," she kept saying when people complimented her outfit, staring down into her breasts, which offered themselves up from a black lace bra. "They could have done it better synthetically."

A moon-faced butch sat at her feet, licking whipped cream out of one hand and smiling up at her. Alta leaned over the butch bottom and whispered to the dom, "I would have liked to have known you before—after you knew what you wanted, but before you knew how to get it."

"Think there was a time?" she said, laughing with her eyes into Alta's.

"Yes. I do." Alta ran her thumb along the dom's cheek underneath the thin chain that connected her nose piercing to the ring in her ear.

"Alta!" Renny came bouncing into the room with Marcie behind her. Alta left the dom and her butch-toy for Renny and her six-pack.

"A prospect?" Renny whispered as they crowded shoulder to shoulder into the kitchen.

"History," Alta answered.

"Man, you have a lot of history." Renny grinned her wide-fool smile, and her hair flopped in her face.

"Misunderstood history," Alta nodded, flipping the cap off her bottle.

"A toast." Renny raised her bottle to Marcie and then to Alta, and then to the preoccupied room in general. "To misunderstood history."

"I think the whole, entire history of the world has been misunderstood." Marcie played with the rim of her bottle.

"Absolutely, it has," Renny said, guzzling.

Alta leaned back, elbows on the counter. "When I think of all the lies told and the things no one could possibly understand, I find it hard to believe any story can be threaded together out of this mess. We act like the world's getting better—"

"We do?" Marcie said.

"Uh oh." Renny put her bottle down and grabbed Alta's shoulders. "Are you okay?"

"What if Caesar was a cross-dressing woman?" Alta asked, taking a swig of her own beer around Renny's concerned arms. Renny squeezed and let go.

"Cleopatra was a convincing queen," Marcie threw in.

Lilith, their favorite drag queen, minced into the room. "Did someone call?" she batted her enormous eyelashes.

"Is *this* the face that launched a thousand ships?" Renny leaped onto a chair and framed Lilith's gorgeous cheekbones and upswept do with her arms.

"Darling, you'd better believe it," Lilith drawled, pulling out a compact and fixing her lipstick.

"I believe it," Alta said.

"So what about Ancient History, how's that going?" Renny asked. "Or is she gone?"

"Oh no, she's here, all right. Actually, her mother is dying." That sank the mood. Marcie patted the seat beside her, and Alta sat down. "It's so strange," she began, and suddenly she felt as though she were about to cry. "I'm learning about things that are really close to my life that I couldn't even imagine. I don't even know how to say it; it seems sort of unbelievable."

"Something I wouldn't believe?" Renny said.

"Listen, darling, I've seen it all. Twice," Lilith murmured.

"I used to be scared of Mrs. Mallon. She was always quiet and, well, depressed, really, though when I was little, I didn't know that's what was going on. I was in love with her daughter, Shy, the one I call my first girlfriend, though she doesn't. When my mom kicked me out, Mrs. Mallon let me live in her house. I was still scared of her when I came to live there, and then I felt sorry for her, because she wouldn't leave the house, she chain-smoked and stared out the window a lot." Alta sighed. "Then we became friends. I even loved her. She was the first person who accepted me unconditionally. And I thought that was how I accepted her. But you know what?"

Alta looked up and saw Renny and Marcie and Lilith all listening intently. "I didn't really know who she was."

Alta had finished her beer, and Renny held out a fresh bottle,
ever-ready. In the other room, a roar of laughter rose and subsided.

"What do you mean you didn't know who she was?" Marcie asked.

Alta wrenched the top off the bottle and went on. "She has this
scar on her arm, and I think there used to be a tattoo there—you
know, from the concentration camps, World War II. So I'm thinking
she was Jewish, and she survived the camps when she was younger
than me—a teenager—and became a Catholic later on. And she
never told anyone, not even her daughter."

"Ancient History," Rennie said again.

Alta shrugged and tried to smile at her.

"It's strange," Marcie added, "because all the survivors I've known
felt it was really important to talk about."

"Well, I guess we don't hear a lot from the people who decide not
to tell anyone."

Renny asked, "How did you find out?"

"Alta Corral, private eye," Alta said dryly. "I guess when I found
out she was so ill, I just couldn't let her drown in the secrecy she'd
lived in. And there was Shy with all her secrets and I was one of
them, and it seemed that her mother was another. I saw Mrs. Mallon's
baptismal certificate, and she would have been over twenty by the
date. And then she had this scar." Alta pointed to the place on her
arm where Mrs. Mallon's tattoo would have been. "Of course, I'd
seen it before, but I'd never given it any thought. But Max had had
that photo show, and I had a hunch that looks like it might be
right—tattoo removal. She must have done it about the same time
she got baptized, I figure, because it wasn't a laser removal. It was
a bit more primitive—a cutting or a burn. God, I hope she didn't do
it herself."

"Ouch!" Lilith said. "Sounds terrible."

"Yeah, it does," Alta said. Silently, she finished the latest beer. She
hadn't eaten, since she'd worked all evening, and she was starting to
feel the alcohol mixing unpleasantly with sorrow.

"I'm going to use the facilities," she announced. "I'm sorry to be so depressing."

"Hey, man, that's what we're here for."

"Yes, darling, depress us anytime."

"Ladies—" Alta tipped an invisible hat to Marcie and Lilith and made her way to the last door in the corridor.

"So that's what you really want?" The dominatrix came out of a side room behind her and trapped her down at the end of the hall. "One more girl to kneel at your feet and suck your dick?"

It took Alta a minute to recover. "Hey, don't knock it."

The dom put both hands on her hips and seemed to be studying Alta, then dropped to her knees and grabbed Alta's wrists, pinning her from below against the wall. Alta took a step backward to catch herself.

"I use teeth." Her glitter-eyes locked onto Alta. Alta closed her eyes, tried to bring herself into the room with the dom. She looked down at her. The dom's breasts looked divine above the bib of her jumpsuit. Alta lifted one foot up and pressed her boot against the dom's bare shoulder. The dom started to pull Alta with her as she bent backward, her thighs widening over her calves. Her fishnet ass hung out from the high silver edge of her jumpsuit skirt. Then she dropped her hands and lay flat, and Alta knelt over her, one hand finding the ridged crisscross between her legs. She looked at Alta wickedly.

Someone came out of the bathroom, a cute little punk girl with her bangs barretted back from her face with a child's orange barrette.

"Excuse me," she gawked, stepping over the dom's silver stomach. Alta's hand stayed where it was, her finger sliding on all that wet. The dominatrix closed her eyes and the punkette disappeared down the hall. Alta stood up.

"Where are you going?" The dom lifted her head and rested it on her hands, one foot against the opposite wall.

Alta pointed with her thumb.

The dom rolled up. "Let me watch."

Alta looked at her. "Are you crazy? Don't answer. You're crazy." She walked toward the bathroom door.

"Scared?" The dom was leaning against the wall, her hip a curve begging for a hand. Her junior-high logic appealed to Alta.

"Come on," Alta said, gesturing her over. The dom stood in the doorway, her breasts lifted with the motion of her hands overhead, each grasping one side of the frame. Alta did have to go, but she suppressed it.

"You are a pervert," Alta said, turning the sink faucet on and soaping up her hands. The dom said nothing. Alta checked herself in the mirror, chin up, serious. She passed one hand over the dark stubble on her head. Then she walked back to the door, almost pressed against the dom again.

"That all?" The dom raised and lowered her lashes sassily.

"Want more?"

She licked the corner of her mouth, slowly. "No promises," she said, grinning.

"No one's making promises these days," Alta grumbled.

"No one's breaking them."

Lilith was leaving when Alta got back to the kitchen. They blew each other a kiss.

"You've got to love her," Renny said, watching Lilith slink away.

"You're drunk, man." Alta slapped Renny's shoulder gently.

"Getting there. Here, have another—I'm one up on you. Hey, where'd you go?" Renny was straddling a kitchen chair. She pushed her bangs out of her face.

"I got lucky."

"Man, you are lucky!" Renny reached up for a sloppy high five and then pinched Marcie's round ass where it hung over the chair's vinyl. "I'm lucky, too."

"Did you get lucky with history?" Marcie smiled at Alta.

Alta winked at her. "That's right. Listen, we may have been left out of the books, but we were part of all the action." She turned back to Renny. "So I'm going to go." Renny raised her bottle to Alta. Marcie stood up to hug her.

"Come Friday for Shabbat," she said. "Bring Shy."

Friday. Would Mrs. Mallon be alive? The darkly lit rooms behind Alta, with all the noise, drunken laughter, and banter, converged with the bright kitchen.

"It depends on what's going on with Mrs. Mallon," Alta said, pushing back the odd sensation of tears.

"Oh, shit. I'm sorry." Marcie reached up and rubbed Alta's head. "Are you going to be okay? Because we—or rather, I, designated driver—would be happy to chauffeur you home."

"I don't know if Shy would come to Shabbat dinner. She hasn't exactly embraced her hidden heritage."

"How long has she known? Like three days?"

"Twelve hours, now," Alta said, looking at her watch.

"And she's not getting Bat Mitzvahed?"

"It's not that I want her to decide she's Jewish—"

"Though technically, if her mother is Jewish, she is."

"But I don't think Shy believes me."

"Stay and talk to us, Alta," Marcie urged.

"Have another beer."

"Well, let me go tell history we have no future."

Marcie and Renny laughed.

Alta left then. She heard Marcie ask, "Do you think she'll come back?"

"Who knows?" Alta heard Renny say. "She'll do what she has to."

Alta woke up. The phone was ringing, the night before pouring slowly back into her memory. Marcie and Renny had listened to her talk. They'd taken her home and sat up with her. Alta had even dug out the shoebox with Shy's old picture in it. At about 3 a.m. they finally listened to all of Alta's messages and discovered that Shy had not called. Alta got into bed, and Renny and Marcie sat at the foot of it.

"Do you know Shy's having a baby?" Alta asked.

"It sure seems like it," Renny agreed.

"Does she know if it's a boy or a girl?" Marcie asked.

"Maybe it'll be like me," Alta said.

Alta remembered the stories she'd heard at Marcie's Passover dinner last spring, stories about plagues and miracles. "Tell me the part about the children," Alta said to Marcie. "I remember something about children."

"The different kinds of children?"

Alta nodded, her head resting on her pillows.

"Well, the wise child loves *Pesach*—Passover—and asks, 'What are these customs which we celebrate?'" She recited from memory. "He—or she—should be told all there is to know about the holiday and the traditions of our ancestors. It should be explained that they also have meaning as symbols of a great and noble ideal. Freedom for all. The wicked child is scornful and irreverent. He does not feel as though he is part of this whole celebration."

"Oh, so the wicked child is just a he?" Alta teased her.

"He asks his father—or mother—" Marcie went on, ignoring Alta, "in a mocking spirit, what does this service mean to you? as though he were an outsider and had no part in it. He should be scolded and told, 'It is because of what God did for *me*, when I went out of Egypt. For me, not for you! If you had been there, you would not have deserved to go forth.'"

"Pretty harsh."

"Yeah," she agreed, "I always hated that part, but there's something to it."

"Can you imagine?" Alta asked Marcie. "Why would Mrs. Mallon hide something like that?"

"It's really hard for me to say, because everyone I've met who's a survivor of the Holocaust is insistent about not forgetting, keeping the memory alive. Never again: it's the battle cry."

"It really fucked her up."

"Who? Shy, or her mother?"

Her mother's silence was the most powerful legacy Shy had. Alta looked up at Marcie. "Both of them."

At last Alta drifted toward sleep. They tiptoed out, and Renny locked the door behind them with a key she still had from the time she'd crashed at Alta's house when she'd left the girlfriend before Marcie.

Now Alta fumbled out of bed and picked up the phone.

"Shy?"

"Only on first dates. It's Amanda, Alta. Sorry to wake you up. I just wondered if you needed a ride to the Queer Street Faire."

"What time is it?"

"Now? It's ten o'clock."

"Wow. Good thing you called. No, I don't need a ride, I just have to get my bike . . . It's a long, unimportant story. I'd better get going, but I'll see you there."

"Find me back of the main stage. I'll show you where Stigmata's booth is."

"Thanks Amanda, you're a sweetheart."

"Hmm. That sounds sisterly."

"Not at all."

It was hot in the City, almost as hot as across the bay. The mist had burnt off, and heat filled the air so that everyone felt it all the time and walked with every inch of skin wet and aware. Alta thought the heat might keep some people away, but they seemed drawn out to the light, as clunky and delicate as moths circling a candle. Shy wasn't there when Alta arrived with a few minutes to spare before she was scheduled to take charge of the booth. It was crowded, but Alta knew she'd be able to pick Shy out of this crowd of leather and chains, breasts and rainbow-colored hair. Shy had said she wanted to come, promised she would, but that was before their fight, before Mrs. Mallon took a turn for the worse. Still, Alta waited for her in the swirl of bodies, hoped just to see her eyes catch the near-naked boys and glistening girls, the unrelenting colors of the flags, the sharp glare of jewelry unapologetically thrust through nipples and earlobes, noses and eyebrows and belly buttons and clattering tongues. Alta milled through the crowd, greeting people she knew, admiring the girls. Everyone seemed happy to see her; they called her name, prancing and showing off their outfits and attitudes.

Alta made her way back to the main stage. Amanda gave her a big hug. "We're so excited about your demonstration," she said.

"Is that the royal 'we'?"

Amanda laughed. "There's a crowd out there waiting for you, babe. Are you ready?"

"Always." Alta looked down at her, enjoying her butterscotch happiness in the heat of the sun. "Are you?"

She nodded. "Four o'clock, right?"

"Final piercing of the day."

"I'll be there."

At three-thirty, Shy still hadn't shown up. Alta called her from a pay phone, but no one answered. Harriet and Alta pulled the mechanical barber's chair out to the front of the booth. Amanda arrived and positioned herself in the seat. The crowd seemed dense and chaotic.

Alta wondered if the relatively subtle power of metal and flesh would carry across the sweltering heat and distraction of the fair. She focused on Amanda.

"How are you feeling about this?" Alta asked.

Amanda nodded. "Good."

"Are you ready to take your shirt off?"

Amanda lifted it over her head in reply. She had the kind of breasts that moved a lot—they weren't flat against her chest. Her nipples were good-sized, already hard. With a fine felt-tipped pen Alta marked the points of entry and exit for her needles. She handed Amanda a mirror. "How does that look?" The little black dots were well placed, and Amanda agreed. Alta looked up and saw that a crowd had gathered. It wasn't just the half-naked woman; lots of women were baring flesh today. It was the piercing itself. The process is very intense; people identified with the sensations, or what they imagined the sensations would be. Alta saw appreciation in the watching faces.

When Alta turned her attention back to Amanda, there was absolute silence around them. Outdoor silence. Farther off, the fair carried on; there was laughter in the distance and people calling out. But they stood together, and the crowd seemed to know that this was no superhuman feat, but one altogether miraculous, delivered to Alta from the heat of their bodies, the strength of their eyes. She rubbed alcohol over Amanda's dark pink nipples. Amanda met her eyes and smiled. With a steady hand, Alta pressed a small cork to where the needle would emerge, then thrust the sharp metal through. Amanda flinched but didn't move. Alta squeezed her hand. "Halfway there," she whispered. She changed gloves and moved to Amanda's other side. That one went through perfectly. Amanda exhaled sharply.

"How do you feel?"

"Major adrenaline rush." She grinned.

Alta put the end of the ring Amanda had chosen over the needle and pulled the jewelry into the hole. When she'd finished both sides, she took off her gloves and put one hand on Amanda's forehead. Amanda closed her eyes, and they breathed together in a moment of peace. Alta became aware of the crowd again; the spell broke, the onlookers applauded and dispersed. Alta looked around for Shy and found Lara, the girl from the bar long days ago. Lara raised her hand from the elbow and waved, flicking her black hair over her shoulder. She was wearing all white: a PVC halter top and tight PVC shorts that drew attention to her powerful legs in long white go-go boots.

Amanda got her cleaning and care instructions and gave Alta a careful hug. "I have to go show my friends." She grinned. "Thanks, Alta, that was incredible. Give me a call sometime." She wandered off.

"Go on." Harriet winked at Alta. "Max is pulling her van around to pick up the equipment. You're done."

"Enjoy the show?" Alta said to Lara as she approached her, where she'd stayed as Alta had finished up. Lara smiled wide and yet shyly, and when Alta saw her tongue, she pressed Lara back into the dirty plastic panel behind her and kissed her. Lara slid down, her tongue dancing around Alta's.

"You want to go somewhere else to . . . talk?" She said when Alta stepped back.

Alta put one hand on Lara's lower back and started her walking toward the bike. Alta felt her life slide back into place. She didn't need Shy. She would be ready when Shy left. She slipped her hand under Lara's T-shirt and spread it full against Lara's warm skin.

Lara stretched naked on Alta's bed. She had that proprietary languor that overtakes certain women after passionate sex.

"It's been so hot," she said. She reached up and ran her nails gently along Alta's scalp. Alta lay back down, still fully clothed in her leather pants and leather suspenders over a white T-shirt with Stigmata's logo on it. She closed her eyes. "Do that again," she murmured. Lara traced her profile with one soft fingertip and then traced patterns in the Velcro layer of hair on Alta's head. Alta was in a trance when the doorbell rang.

"Go away," she moaned, half-delirious from the tingle of Lara's touch. An urgent knocking, sharp and fast, banged through her daze. She got up and went through the living room toward the front door. In the front hall, the handset had been knocked from the phone, probably when Lara arched backward over it, offering her nipple to Alta's mouth. Alta replaced it, cutting short its staccato atonal alarm.

"Yes, yes," Alta called at the door. She peered through the peep-hole. Shy loomed, in a weird pink maternity shirt and black leggings, oddly distorted by the tiny fish-eye lens. Even so, Alta could tell that she'd been crying. Her eyes were brighter, shiny, the rims tinged red. Alta opened the door partway.

"Oh, Alta, your phone was busy for so long." Her hair fell across her face. Alta imagined the tight way dried tears felt under the eyes, down cheeks and nose. "It's so hot," Shy said. Alta wondered if in licking Shy's cheek she would be able to distinguish between the salt-taste of tears and that of sweat. "Can I have a glass of water?"

Alta let her walk past. Shy stopped in the living room, running her fingers along the edge of the table Alta used as a desk.

"I'm sorry I didn't make it to your demonstration thing."

"Me, too."

"I spent the day sitting with my mom." Her voice rose, full of tears. She sat down on the couch, heavily, her hand reaching behind her as she sat, as if to brace the descent.

Lara appeared in the doorway in one of Alta's T-shirts and a pair of her checkered boxers.

"Shy, this is Lara," Alta said brightly.

"We met at Renny's party," Lara reminded Alta. Her quick tongue and open smile seemed obscene next to Shy's weighted, fragile pres-ence. Shy tried to stand up quickly, but gravity fought against her arched back and seemed to pull her farther into the crevice of the couch. Alta felt terrible, but then she thought of Ryan, how many hours she'd watched out her window, waiting for Shy to come back from a date. Remembered the lights of his truck dying out and the minutes dragging by after that as she watched the darkened cab. And then Shy would crawl in bed with her, smelling of beer and boys, and Alta would still want to run her hands over every inch of her.

"I didn't realize I was interrupting," Shy said, looking at Alta, her cheekbones thin lines of distress and dignity. "I just wanted some water," she added, as if she'd taken the train under the Bay and found Alta's house again only for a glass of water.

"I'll get it." Alta left the room, careful not to brush Lara's arm as she passed. The bathroom door was ajar, and Alta recalled Shy standing naked and unmoving in front of her so vividly she almost thought she could go back to that moment and do something differently. Why couldn't Alta treat Shy with the same casual charm that came so easily when she was with other girls?

From the kitchen Alta could hear Lara's smooth, high laugh beyond the spray of water from the faucet and the crack of the ice as she twisted it from the plastic tray. She brought a glass for Lara, too.

Shy drank her water like a little girl, both hands around the glass, her lips a small O on the rim. When she finished she stood up.

"I'm just going to . . . get my stuff, and I'll head out," Lara said. She disappeared into Alta's bedroom.

"Oh, no, I'm leaving," Shy said loudly as if calling in to Lara, though she looked right at Alta. She turned to the front door and spoke with her back to Alta. "You know where to find me, Alta. I think you always have." She fumbled with the locks.

"Shy . . ."

"Don't call me that. I'm not a little girl." She threw the bolts and opened the door. Outside, she turned back. "Oh, and Alta?"

"Yes?" Alta moved toward her.

"Goodbye." She raised her eyebrows. "Isn't that what you wanted from me?"

"Why don't you stick around, Shy? Why don't you just deal with things the way they are, instead of always running away? Maybe to you, you didn't run away, it's just your life. Well, this is mine. Did you think I'd spend six years sitting around by myself on the off chance that one day you'd reappear on the scene and let me fuck you?"

"You aren't any better than a man, Alta."

Alta stared her down. "I guess that depends on what you're looking for. But no, having sex with me isn't some kind of feminist manifesto. It's just fun. It's hot. It's what you want, what you've always wanted, and if it weren't, you wouldn't be here."

Shy shook her head. "You think that's all you're good for, don't you? You were my best friend. You were the person I could tell everything to—"

"You didn't, though."

"Can you look at it from my point of view for once?"

"Let's see. Your mother is dying and you weren't too damn sure you'd be able to make it to her bedside. Turns out her whole life was a lie, and you never bothered to ask her anything about it—"

"Did you, Alta? If you were so close and she was so open and warm to you, why didn't you chat it up with her?"

Lara came out, dressed again in her faux-leather getup, shoes in hand. "I'm just going." She pointed to the door behind Shy, who stepped aside.

"I'm really sorry," Alta said. Lara shrugged one shoulder, but she didn't smile and her tongue didn't flash. She stepped through the open door and softly closed it behind her.

"I don't know, Shy," Alta said when Lara was gone. "I don't know why we never talked about it. I wish we had."

"Well, you know what they say . . ."

Alta waited for the inevitable quotation or proverb.

"If wishes were horses, beggars would ride. Is that how it goes?" Shy looked at Alta. "I thought we'd be neighbors forever. And when people said, 'Who's Alta?' I could say, 'She's my neighbor.'"

"Do you wish you could be pregnant without showing it?"

Shy looked puzzled. "I never thought about it. But no, I don't think so."

"There are people who think that what you're doing is wrong."

"Having a baby?"

"Well, you aren't married. Wouldn't it be easier on you if it just didn't show?"

She shook her head. "I could always just wear a ring. A wedding ring."

"Ah, there you go," Alta pointed at her. "Lie. That's an option. But you don't. Wear a ring."

Shy shrugged. "It wasn't worth it to me."

"Why?"

"Because I'm not ashamed."

"And you can't call me neighbor anymore."

"Unless I lived here."

"Well, that would be delightful and interesting, but you might still have to come up with some other words."

"Other words?" Shy sat down on the arm of the couch and looked at Alta. She was very sad and very pretty.

"Lover," Alta said. Shy's face stayed smooth and clear. "Best friend. Witness. Convenient ally."

"Ally," she repeated, and smiled.

"Are you okay, Shy?"

"I don't know."

"Where do you want me to take you?"

"I'm going to be an orphan, Alta."

When she said that, Alta remembered what Shy had said that day in fifth grade when her family tree assignment was due. She had her father's half filled in, the Cleveland grandparents and the Scottish and Irish ancestry. Her mother was an orphan, Shy had told Sister Agnes. She didn't eat lunch with Alta that year, having made school friends who, she explained to Alta, she didn't get to see at home. But the information about Shy's orphan mother spread throughout the schoolyard. All their mothers thought Mrs. Mallon was odd, and this became their explanation. It controlled the air of tragedy that quietly surrounded the family.

"What about Paris?" Alta had asked Shy as they walked home after school.

"What about it?" she responded, her voice forbidding.

"I thought . . ." Alta had broken off, running along to keep up with her as she strode ahead. "You said . . ."

"She was born there. The orphanage was in Paris. That's where she grew up, before my father rescued her and brought her to America." They had reached Shy's house.

"Do you want to come over?"

Shy had shaken her head—"I can't today"—and disappeared inside her house.

Alta took Shy outside the City, zipping between lines of still and impatient cars on the freeway and exiting at the highway to the coast, sliding down the side of the mountain with its little houses and great, gray views. Alta saw waves tiny in the distance and the men they could drown, just flecks of confetti, their heads bobbing on the surface. Grass grew in globs in the sands of the hillsides by the road. Those dunes seemed to Alta like the kind of place you only go to— that is, stop the car and get out—on the very first day you're in love, before you even know it, when all you want is a place that seems as new to you and rare as what you're holding between you. Alta never let it get past that stage, but it was from those days, and from times with Shy, that she remembered the feel of sand in wind, and the deep cool layers below the grains that bake hot and sharp in the sun.

"Do you have your bathing suit?" Alta had asked Shy, remembering that she'd said she hardly swam anymore.

"My bathing suit?"

"Don't—do not—tell me you don't have one."

"I actually do have this ugly maternity suit. I just haven't worn it."

"Ever?"

"Mmm," she murmured her assent.

"Do you have it with you?"

"Are you kidding?"

"Well, let's go get you one, Shy. You're going to the beach."

The garish bathing suit with oversized fluorescent flowers stretched out over Shy's stomach; when she stripped to it Alta could see again how her body had really changed.

Shy on the beach was Shy alive among the living, and Alta liked watching her there. Alta sat back on the towel, folded Shy's dress carefully and put it with her own jacket beside where she dug her booted feet into the sand.

Shy stood sideways against the waves. Her father had taught her that; Alta remembered her repeating his philosophy when they'd go to the beach. Stand sideways so the waves can't push you forward or backward. Never turn your back on the ocean. Alta knew all those tricks; they all did who grew up near the coast. Still, Alta preferred to take things head-on, face forward. At least, going over, Alta would know what hit her. Not that she ever went in the water.

Shy waved, her arched back a counterpoint to the convex curve of her belly, the rest of her oddly normal. Alta waved back and leaned one elbow into the towel and the sand below. She smoothed a surface in the sand and drew shapes in it.

And she thought of Mrs. Mallon. The idea that she could die at any moment created a strange vacuum. Shy seemed to be waiting to mourn; Alta was grasping for clues, as if by solving the riddle of Mrs. Mallon's identity she might undo her death sentence. Alta and Shy were the only two people—besides Mrs. Koch and Miss Pauline—who would really care that Mrs. Mallon was gone, and they'd each left her a long time ago. Now it was too late for any reentry, too late for questions and the things they wished they'd said. A real feeling of regret overwhelmed Alta, and she tried to fight it back with the glory of the day, the sky so far up, the sand near sparkling, the clean smell of people and salt water almost as close as taste. All things Mrs. Mallon had seen, once, but would probably never again see or feel.

In the distance, Shy seemed to be vibrating against the wild rise and crash of the waves. She crouched down, still sideways, and let the water bounce off her and spray up. She was a round spot of neon blue creating a geyser. Suddenly, Alta began to worry that she'd gone into labor, that her shaking was a sign of distress. She grabbed their stuff and ran down to the shifting edge of the water, foam surrounding her boots.

"Are you okay? You were shaking."

Shy stood and wiped salty water from her cheeks. "The water feels so good, it reminds me of good times." Alta thought of her mother's old phrase, *Those were good times.* Shy lowered her head. "I was laughing."

Alta nodded and tried to smile at her. "That's allowed."

"Is it?"

Alta shrugged and opened the towel in her hands, her dress and Alta's jacket tucked under one arm. Shy came close and Alta wrapped the towel around her.

"Do you find it hard to believe? That she's dying?"

Alta nodded.

"It always seemed like she was already gone. I never wanted to talk to her on the phone, not really. I never wanted to see her. I felt I had this life in Seattle, and if I could just keep my focus there, I wouldn't be thrown by everything here. But it's so different now. It's almost like she's really gone now. Isn't it?"

"I suppose it is."

"My mother's going to die, Alta, and it doesn't matter if she was born Catholic or what secrets she had. Don't you see? You can't bring her back no matter what you do."

"I know that."

"But you want to, don't you?"

"Don't you?"

She shivered. "I want her to be happy, whatever that means." A light layer of sand was brushed across her cheek. Alta wanted to cause it to come off her face in gentle falls, responding to the subtlest touch of her thumb on the side of Shy's face.

"I want you to be happy, whatever that means."

"You are so corny sometimes," Shy said, but she smiled.

"Hey, Shy-girl, who would have thought?"

"What, that we'd grow up? That I'd be an unwed mother and you'd be . . ." She broke off.

"What?"

"I don't know. Kind of handsome. Kind of tough."

"Kind of?"

Shy looked down and made sweeping plains across the sand with her foot.

"Come on, let's get you dressed." Alta shook out her dress and handed it to her. "And Shy?"

"Yeah?"

"I was always tough."

Back home, Shy wasn't ready to be inside, and she asked Alta to take a walk with her. When they were little they used to walk around and around the block, Shy tromping in the bristly crabgrass that grew in patches along the curb, with Alta beside her on the sidewalk. Alta would tell her stories, made-up tales about Princess Shy in need of rescue. She'd have a boy try to save Shy, Juan or Joey or whoever was following her around for the moment; they'd always fail and Alta would come in and rescue them both. That was generally the plot, but the charge was highly sexual as they walked more and more slowly. Alta would sneak glances at Shy, check her rapid breathing and the intensity of her eyes.

Now they walked together slowly. Pieces of Shy's dark hair had come free of her barrette and lay against her cheek. The bow at the back of her dress fell between the curves of her ass. The strongest part of Alta, the only part that had an inkling of what to do with this woman after six years, wanted to turn her on and make love to her again. But there was more of Alta—to her surprise, much more—that wanted to know the truth: what had happened?

Alta knew that that night or the next she would make love with Shy, and that it would be frightening; scarier this time than all the times before. Alta was starting to know Shy again, know her better, know this new body of hers and the one it grew out of. In order to hold Shy and touch her—even with her fingertips—Alta would have to accept the closing of the space between them, press closer than skin against skin. To make love to someone she knew this well—Alta didn't know how to do it. She would have to learn as she went along.

"The week before you left we went to Tahoe," Alta began.

"Not exactly Tahoe," Shy said. Alta looked at her. "It was near Tahoe."

"We checked into that orangy motel—"

"I checked in." Shy pushed the strands of hair back behind her ears, and they slipped right back onto her face.

"Right." They smiled at each other.

When her dad died Alta was too young—she came unpinned but she didn't know it exactly, not in the same way as now. She and Shy had all this context, tons and tons of past, and it had all come loose. Those days of their childhood no longer seemed to exist on their own, stockpiled somewhere for safekeeping. Mrs. Mallon's past—which was, after all, Shy's past, too, in a way—was lost, and Alta's past with Shy was only memories, and even between the two of them, nothing matched.

"And then what?" Alta pressed her.

"Look, Alta, I can't talk about those boys . . ."

But Alta didn't want to go there either.

"Tell me about the ice," she said, realizing as if for the first time that some things scared Shy even more than sex.

"We ordered an extra cup of ice with every soda we got at the drive-thrus, and it embarrassed you because you were afraid they'd think we couldn't afford two sodas."

"I wasn't afraid. Go on."

"It was hot."

"It was *so* hot."

"It was hotter than today, and the ice felt good."

"And then what?" Alta said.

"I checked in . . ."

"Right . . ."

"And there was ice in the motel room—"

"You made me go get it."

"Oh yeah. I made you get it and then somehow I got naked—"

"You started to take off your clothes while I was at the ice machine."

"Did I? You helped me, though." Shy stopped walking and closed her eyes. "And then you put the ice in your mouth, and your mouth on me."

"What were you thinking? I mean, how did it make you feel?" They stood almost in front of Shy's house, on the side away from Alta's mother's. But Alta didn't care anymore if her mother came out. It was Mrs. C.'s street, but she couldn't pull Alta backward no matter where she found her.

Shy opened her eyes and they were so soft. "I don't want to go back, Alta. I feel so lonely. The truth is, I don't know if I can be a mother. I don't even know what that means."

"I thought you were happy there. I thought you went to Seattle to get away from the things that made you unhappy."

She shook her head, looked down at the sidewalk. "I was pregnant," she said.

All these years, as she'd gone over and over every detail of the weeks before Shy ran away, Alta had never even guessed Shy had been pregnant when she left.

Now Alta said nothing, and Shy spoke as if she were answering questions Alta had not asked.

"I didn't want to tell . . . anyone."

"Even me, Shy? Why not me?"

"You would have hated me, Alta. You wanted me all to yourself."

Alta went over and sat down on the front steps of the Mallons' house. Shy sat down beside her.

"But I knew I didn't have you. I knew about Ryan." His name came out more bitterly than Alta would have liked.

She shook her head, shut her eyes. "It wasn't Ryan."

"What do you mean, it wasn't Ryan?"

"A businessman from Seattle—not a really old one, a younger guy I'd met helping that caterer at one of those conferences."

"Erik?"

"Oh, God, no. This guy was married. I used your money to get to Seattle, and he paid for an abortion." She stopped, took a breath and shrugged. "He helped me out for a few months while I got on my feet."

"Why didn't you just use my money to have the abortion here? Why didn't you let me help you? I mean, really help?"

"You wouldn't have helped me have an abortion."

"That's not true."

"I had to get away, Alta. I was nineteen and my mother didn't want me to ever go. Do you remember how possessive she was?" She stood up and slipped off her shoes. "And what was going on with you scared the hell out of me. When I was younger I could think that you were the . . . the strange one. But nineteen's too old to play that kind of game. I had to stop."

"And now?"

"I don't know what it is about you, Alta. It's not all women. It's just you."

This was where Shy always trapped Alta. Sure, Alta wanted to believe it was only her, who wouldn't? But that let Shy off too easy. The hardest thing was how they couldn't make it right between them—Shy and Alta—they couldn't set straight the misunderstandings and hurt feelings, couldn't put into words everything they should, after all, have said a long time ago. They'd slept together, but they weren't lovers anymore.

"It doesn't have to be all women, Shy. We've been having sex on and off since you were sixteen and I was fourteen. I'm a lesbian, and you're my first lover. So what are you?"

"It's not like that for me."

"That's not how it seemed a few days ago."

"Isn't that enough for you?"

"It's really not, Shy. It's really not."

For a few days they fell into a pattern. Before and after work, Alta would meet Shy at the hospital, and they'd sit with Mrs. Mallon. Her presence affected what they'd talk about, but then Mrs. Mallon's silent presence had always been part of the mix that was Shy and Alta.

The funny thing was, after all those hours of awkward boredom and cafeteria food, of hesitant contact with Mrs. Mallon's papery skin and wiry hair, her halting breath, they missed the moment that slipped her away from them. Mrs. Mallon's death was a phone call from Dr. Jeffreys, an apology from the nurses. Her death was assurances that she had been sleeping peacefully.

"She never slept peacefully," Shy whispered savagely to Alta.

The worst part was that their pattern didn't break apart.

Dazed, and without pause for mourning, they jumped into the business of death: the funeral. They picked out a coffin under used-car-salesman pressure that they honor their dead at an extravagant price. Shy spoke with the church's new priest, and she called Mrs. C. and Mrs. Koch and Miss Pauline. There weren't many people to tell.

Meanwhile, in the nights, they slept side by side, touching peripherally and accidentally, shaping themselves into the contours of their bodies' bent curves, lying awake together in exhausted silence. Sometimes, Alta would think of Mrs. Mallon's closed door, down at the other end of the hall, and wonder what she would do differently if Mrs. Mallon were hiding behind it still.

The evening before the funeral, Shy suggested they walk to the church to say the Rosary for her mother. She and Alta used to walk to school together on the days Mr. Mallon was away. When he was around, Mrs. Mallon had insisted he drive them. Shy had hated this. "She just wants to embarrass me. I'm not a baby," she would complain.

When they walked out the front door on their way to the church, Alta's mother was standing on her steps.

Shy looked at Alta and then went over and hugged Mrs. C.

Mrs. C. put her hand under Shy's chin. "I'm so sorry, dear. If there's anything I can do to help, you let me know."

"Thanks, Mrs. C."

"How's the baby?"

Alta could see Shy's now familiar gesture as she put her hands beneath her extended belly. "It's been moving around a lot. Sometimes it keeps me up at night."

"Well, then, it's a boy, mark my words. Will the father be here tomorrow? I'd love to meet him."

"He can't come."

"Can't come?"

"Well, he didn't know her, and I thought it would be best . . ."

"You get that boy to marry you, Shy. A child needs both a mother and a father. And you deserve a husband, Shy, and a good, normal life."

"Hi," Alta said, stopping a few steps below her. Alta had dressed nicely, in a dark blue gabardine suit Renny and Marcie had gotten for her on her last birthday from one of those elegant men's vintage shops, but Alta felt instantly ashamed under her mother's gaze. Why couldn't her mother see how wrong and ridiculous Alta would look in a dress?

"Hello, Alta." She put one hand over her purse, as if she thought Alta might grab it. "You look just like your father." Alta couldn't tell how her mother felt about this, though she knew for certain that her mother had loved him. But Mrs. C. laughed uncomfortably. "I was just going to see if you needed a ride to church, Shy. I noticed you didn't have a car."

Alta was afraid that Shy would accept, that they'd be stuck driving with her mother.

"Thanks, Mrs. C.," Shy said. "We've decided to walk. I need the fresh air."

"Well, if you're sure. Do let me know what I can do to help you, Shy."

Alta had done everything she could to forget the mother who wanted to comfort and assist. Because when she'd needed that mother she hadn't been there. It would have been easier if she didn't exist, if her mother was only a cruel woman. But she was sometimes kind, and sometimes cruel, and that was worse.

• • •

Alta hadn't set foot in Our Lady of the Assumption—their old, low-lying church, next to and matching their creamy stucco elementary school—since before her mother had kicked her out of the house. Mrs. Koch and Miss Pauline were there, and Mrs. C. was with a couple of the churchwomen and the new priest Alta didn't know. Their few voices echoed even in that small church. Alta wondered if Mrs. Mallon had truly embraced Catholicism in her heart, and what had led her to it. Perhaps she'd converted in order to marry Mr. Mallon. Had he known the secrets of her past? There were moments Alta doubted what she'd pieced together. Perhaps Shy was right—maybe Mrs. Mallon had simply been an unhappy woman. Chronically depressed. The scar could have been a burn, its location a coincidence.

"Hail Mary, full of grace," the small group intoned. *"The Lord is with thee."*

Shy knelt beside Alta, her hands clasped tightly. Sadness mixed with the comfort and strangeness of being there. If the mother is Jewish, the child is considered Jewish, Marcie had told Alta that drunken night after Max's party. But what did a religion or a culture mean if you knew nothing of it? "She was ashamed of her family, ashamed of her past," Shy had said quietly but firmly when Alta had tried yet again to bring it up. "Let's leave it at that."

"Blessed art thou among women, and blessed is the fruit of thy womb, Jesus."

"What are you going to tell your child, Shy?"

She'd shrugged, her laugh turning to a sigh. "I'll tell the baby what my mother told me." The bitterness on her face had made Alta wish she'd left all this alone.

"Holy Mary, Mother of God, pray for us sinners, now and at the hour of our death. Amen."

Mrs. C. sat on the other side of Shy, and Alta watched her go through the motions of praying for Mrs. Mallon. It hit Alta again that Mrs. Mallon was really, truly gone, that there would be no chance to talk to her, not only about her past, but even just to sit across from her, wave away her cigarette smoke with one hand and try to make her laugh. And here were the other two women Alta couldn't afford to lose and couldn't figure out how to keep. If she had everything to do over, what could she change? As she dipped her fingers in the holy water, it came to her that there was only this: she did not know everything that had come before. There were possibilities buried in the secrets, chances to be something you already were but thought impossible. This was the lesson of San Francisco. And it was Mrs. Mallon who had given San Francisco to her.

They left the church in silence. Alta's mother went off with the priest and the other women. Mrs. Koch, Miss Pauline, Shy, and Alta stood in the parking lot that served as playground during the school day. Mrs. Koch took a big handkerchief out of Miss Pauline's purse and blew her nose.

"What would you like to do now, Shy?"

"I don't know."

"Come to our house, both of you," Miss Pauline said. "This is no time to be alone."

"Have you eaten?" Mrs. Koch asked. "You must not forget to look after yourself."

"Alta tried to get me to eat."

"You need some home cooking," Miss Pauline insisted in her quiet drawl. She opened the car door with a key. "Let's go."

Miss Pauline went right into the kitchen to start fixing supper, and Shy joined her. "You stay with Gerda," Miss Pauline whispered to Alta. "She's as sad as I've ever seen her."

Mrs. Koch wouldn't sit down. She wandered around her living room straightening. "I'm running out of projects," she said. "What will I do when this house is finished? It won't need me anymore."

"It won't ever be finished. Like that house where they kept building on rooms, because the woman who owned it had been told that when the house was finished, she would die."

"I'll never die, Alta. I'm destined to outlive everyone I love."

Alta didn't know what to say. She wanted to promise to outlive her, to be there when it was her time to go. But perhaps Mrs. Koch meant the people she had loved for a lifetime. Mrs. Mallon had been the only person who remembered Alta's childhood. Much as Alta had tried to run from it, Mrs. Mallon had allowed her a past beyond the flimsy one she carried in her own memory. Now she was gone, and if Shy disappeared again, Alta would be left with only her mother's anger to prove she'd come from somewhere.

"I'm going to change my clothes so I can clean out the fireplace. Excuse me for a moment, Alta." Mrs. Koch left Alta alone.

Alta could hear Miss Pauline and Shy talking in the kitchen. From the few words she caught, they seemed to be discussing the baby's arrival and the fine points of their cooking.

Alta looked at the framed pictures on the end tables. A much younger Miss Pauline, in her early middle age, marching with a crowd and carrying a placard that said, END RACISM NOW! in black marker. Her mouth was open as if she were chanting or yelling. Alta remembered how strangely elated she had been the first time she'd seen this picture. Beside it stood a snapshot of Mrs. Koch, a cake full of lit candles in front of her and Miss Pauline, her arms wrapped around Mrs. Koch's shoulders, behind her. Alta used to study this picture: how Miss Pauline's chin rested on top of Gerda Koch's head, how assuredly Gerda Koch leaned back against Miss Pauline. There were school pictures of Miss Pauline's niece and nephews, a small oil painting of Mrs. Koch's long-dead terrier.

Mrs. Koch came back in slacks and a button-down shirt.

"You always liked the photographs, Alta."

"Do you have any of Zahava?"

Mrs. Koch knelt in front of the wood-burning stove.

"Here, let me do that."

"Don't get your good clothes dirty!" she insisted. "Just get me a big bag from the kitchen."

Shy was chopping carrots and Miss Pauline was stirring something on the stove. The steamy aroma filled the room.

"What are you doing in my kitchen, Alta? I told you to stay out."

"Orders," Alta said. "One paper bag requested, please."

Miss Pauline opened a cupboard under the sink and handed Alta three bags.

"Thank you kindly." On her way out Alta stopped by where Shy sat at the table and kissed her cheek. Shy looked embarrassed but pleased. "Hang in there," Alta said softly. When Shy looked at her, Alta saw how dark the circles were under her eyes.

By the time they'd finished emptying the flue, dinner was served. Alta and Mrs. Koch made the cooks sit down, and they carried the pot of stew and the tray of hot biscuits to the table. Mrs. Koch and Miss Pauline had never said grace before at their house, but now they all looked at one another without digging into the food. It seemed strange to be sitting together, and equally strange somehow that the four of them had never eaten together before. But strangest of all was that Mrs. Mallon, who'd meant so much to each of them, was not there. It had taken her death to bring them together.

"Thank you for . . . giving us this food, this meal together," Alta said, finally, to Shy and Miss Pauline, and trying to express gratitude in a general way to Whomever—she couldn't exactly call it God anymore—for having contrived to feed them.

After dinner Mrs. Koch made tea. It had been a quiet meal, but not an uncomfortable one. Alta was glad to see Shy eat. But Alta felt listless, dazed, drained of questions and without answers. She wished again that she could have had even one more day with Mrs. Mallon. "Tell me about your childhood," she would ask her: a simple question. She would watch Mrs. Mallon blow smoke, her eyes growing distant as they looked across time. "Alicia," Alta would say. "That's your real name, isn't it? Not Alice Mallon."

"Mrs. Koch," Alta began awkwardly, "tomorrow is the funeral."

"Yes, Alta, tomorrow."

"I won't bother you about it anymore, but I need to know why—"

Shy slammed down her spoon. "Alta, stop it! It wasn't important to my mother. She was ashamed, or she just didn't care. She left it behind, why can't you?" Shy turned to Mrs. Koch. "I'm sorry. Sorry I lost my temper, and Alta's been harassing you. You've been so won-derful tonight—"

Alta expected Mrs. Koch to pick up Shy's compliments, but she just stared at Shy, her eyes bright with tears.

"Sasha," she said, "it was not as you said. Not shame. Not she didn't care."

Shy sat back, her face contorted with confusion. Miss Pauline lifted the pot and refilled everyone's teacups. Mrs. Koch jumped up and disappeared into the bedroom.

"Is she okay?" Alta asked Miss Pauline.

"I expect she will be."

Then she was back, a framed photograph in her hand. She held it up for them. It was old, cracked across one corner, its edges stained. A woman standing against a wall, wearing a loose, collared dress, her dark hair bobbed. She was smiling, barefoot; in her eyes, and her coloring, she looked just like Shy.

"Of course I have a picture of Zahava, Alta. She was the first woman I loved, my first lover. In Vienna, before the war. But I don't need that picture to remember her. Everything about her demanded not to be forgotten from the moment I met her, at a talk on 'Art as Resistance' at the University. Your mother loved her, too," she said to Shy. "That's why she named you after her. Zahava was her Hebrew name. Her given name was Sasha. She was your mother's older sis-ter—your aunt."

Shy's blank expression covered the confused look she'd worn. Alta had seen on it on Mrs. Mallon the day after Shy left: a face for hid-ing. Shy had learned her lessons well.

Gently, Mrs. Koch placed the picture in Shy's hands. Shy passed her fingers over the glass that covered it. Her lips formed the word before the sound came: "Why?"

Mrs. Koch closed her eyes, and her head rocked back and forth. When she opened her eyes, she shook her finger as if she were scold-ing all of them. "I promised her not to tell anyone, ever. It was . . . all that she asked of me, all that I could give her that mattered. It wasn't my nature," Mrs. Koch said fiercely, turning to Alta, "but it wasn't my life. You push and push, Alta, and that's okay." She held a hand up to stop any protestations. "It's good you were born into a different world—not the best world, but a better one. But you do not understand what you push against."

Alta looked from Mrs. Koch standing at the foot of the table, to Shy, her head bent over the photograph in her lap. Alta saw that she'd taught herself to handle anything only in the confines of a very narrow world. Alta looked at Miss Pauline, who sat back in her chair, her arms loosely folded across her chest. Miss Pauline smiled softly at Alta, who found she couldn't smile back. Mrs. Koch came around and stood beside Shy, bent down and, with her arm around Shy's shoulders, put her cheek to Shy's, as she'd done to Mrs. Mallon in the hospital. They looked together at Zahava. "Isn't she lovely?"

Shy nodded, her lips pressed white.

"When you were born, I visited your mother in the hospital. There you were, this dark-haired, dark-eyed child fussing in your mother's arms.

"'Sasha never did like to hide,' Alicia said to me that day.

"She knew I wanted her to name you after your aunt, but I didn't think she would. She was terrified that you'd be punished for something you couldn't help, the way the rest of her family had been. It's hard to make it seem real for you, but we lived through it. It was very real to her, every day of her life. You were her gift to herself, and she felt greedy for having you. She made a rush basket of her secrets and tried to send you to safety on it."

Shy pressed her fingers to her temples. "What about Paris?" she said. Alta noticed the tears on her face.

"I'll tell you what," Miss Pauline said then. "Why don't you all go sit in the living room, where Shy can be more comfortable, and I'll freshen up the tea."

"That's right," Mrs. Koch said, nodding.

Shy stood up with the picture still in her hand. Alta picked up Shy's teacup and her own. They followed Mrs. Koch to the couch, where she and Shy sat. Alta found a place in an armchair at a little distance.

"Right," Mrs. Koch said, tapping the picture as if she were answering the woman in it. "They did come from outside Paris—the Hutners, your mother's family. But that was before Alicia was born. I think her mother, Mrs. Hutner, missed it. She probably talked about it with nostalgia. It's a danger of life, no?"

Alta was relieved to hear Mrs. Koch's familiar humor.

Miss Pauline came back with the teapot steaming. She poured everyone more tea. When she got to Alta, she brushed her fingers across Alta's shorn hair. Alta smiled gratefully. Miss Pauline handed Shy a tissue and sat in the armchair opposite Alta's. Mrs. Koch turned to her.

"Well, Paulie, now what? The promise is broken, and the child is here."

At first Alta thought she must mean Shy's unborn baby, but then she realized that Mrs. Koch meant Shy herself.

"Well, I think you tell her now. If she knows this much, it'd be better if she knew as much as you know."

Alta said, "Why don't you ask her?"

They all looked up at her in surprise—Shy and Miss Pauline and Mrs. Koch. It seemed as though they'd forgotten she was there. Alta smoothed her dark pants with her hands.

"Ach! Alta! What would we do without you? I'm an old woman caught in her age, and my wife is a good woman caught in her kindness, but you—you are a brave woman."

Alta watched Shy's face to see if she'd heard the word "wife." But Shy's face was blank again.

"So, Sasha? What can I do for you, my dear? Would you like to hear an old woman's saddest memories? Would you like to know your mother as I knew her, from a little child? Your mother wanted to protect you, and there were things she didn't want you to know."

Shy sat up straight, her hand resting on top of her belly. "Yes, Mrs. Koch. Please." She looked at Alta, her eyes intense and her chin high. "I want to know."

Mrs. Koch leaned back, holding Miss Pauline's hand on one side and Shy's on the other. "What does one person know of another's childhood?" she began, and Alta remembered something Renny had told her about the couple counseling sessions she went to with Marcie when they were having a hard time. Each one would take a turn talking, and the other had to listen with all her attention, and then say what she had heard. In that way, they passed between them something of the fragile truth caught in and around their words. Alta tried to listen that closely and that well, as if she would be giving her words back to Mrs. Koch as a gift.

What does one person know of another's childhood? Mrs. Koch had not known that she was documenting a life which the forces of history would conspire to make disappear; less still could she have guessed that she would be the last survivor who would carry forward the glimpses and would have the chance to make a history of them, to fill the empty places around which Shy had become who she was. Gerda Koch had met Sasha Hutner's family only once before the events ripped and molded them into and out of her life. She had never seen the happy, golden child her Sasha spoke of; Alicia had been up past her bedtime, sneaking down to hug her sister again and to peer at the strange lady her parents alluded to with terse comments and tightened shoulders.

"Bedtime!" her mother had scolded.

"One. Two . . ." her father had begun to count as the little girl's full mouth quivered.

Sasha had jumped up from the table and swept the child into her arms, Alicia's fair, tear-wet cheek against Sasha's dark neck, peering out from behind the wisps of dark hair that always escaped from the older sister's upswept hair.

Gerda was alone with the parents and the adolescent brother. She asked him a question about school, her words colliding with the mother's offer of bread. The boy never answered; Gerda had assumed his tormented expression was pubescent horror at making conversation. Later she learned that he had recently stopped attending school, because he'd been beaten badly by some of the other boys. *Juden. Juden.*

Sasha came down, laughing. "I sang her the song three times." She turned to Gerda, quickly but firmly touching her hand. "Her favorite song: 'La Mère Michele,' " she said in French. The dinner carried on. The parents were polite. They got on, finally at ease discussing their favorite books. Gerda and Mr. Hutner shared a love of architecture. The boy, David, played the violin, and the mother accompanied him on the piano. David played a wrong note, and his father insisted he begin again, though the mother disagreed:

"It is a performance, Simon—he must learn not to reveal mistakes, but to play on."

"But we heard the mistake. Nothing wrong with a mistake if it is corrected." He glanced at Gerda. "If you'll indulge him."

"It is my luck to hear more!" Gerda assured them, smiling at the boy, who ducked his head.

As the music began again, Gerda turned and saw Alicia, her white nightgown tucked under her toes, seated at the crook of the staircase. The child pressed one finger to her lips, and Gerda winked and turned back to the music.

Sasha's parents wanted her to come home. It was wrong for a single woman to live alone without her family.

"But I'm not alone," Sasha protested.

Two single women! That was almost worse!

Sasha would go home for the Sabbath and return to their apartment Saturday night, usually to a room full of artists and intellectuals, hashing out the merits of Proust versus those of Musil, or playing cards. Gerda did not see the Hutners again until Mrs. Hutner brought Alicia over one Sunday morning. Sasha had returned the night before, very worried. The police had knocked on the Hutners' door Saturday afternoon, and the family had sat very quietly for three worried hours pretending not to be home. The adults had exchanged looks, while David read his book and Sasha whispered stories into Alicia's ear.

"I endanger your life," Sasha told Gerda that night, whispering as she had to her little sister.

"You are my life."

Alicia was frightened, and suspicious of adult attempts to convince her that staying with Sasha and Gerda would be an adventure. Yes, she loved her sister and would have welcomed the treat of a visit, but she knew this was not a vacation. After her mother left, hoarse, fierce sobs shook the child's body, and she ran at her sister as though Sasha were a wall on the other side of which was the life she wanted. She was rude to Gerda, refusing to respond to Gerda's efforts to play marbles with her or brush the hair from her face. At times, in playing with Sasha, Alicia would laugh, or a rush of words would pour from her pouty mouth, and Gerda would catch a glimpse of the bratty wunderkind Sasha had bragged of. Alicia wanted to sleep in the bed with Sasha and resented Gerda's being there. She was happiest on Friday afternoons when they set off through the back streets, for her parents' home on the other side of Vienna, leaving Gerda waving goodbye in the window.

Gerda missed the sophisticated conversations with Sasha, the passionate arguments about a play they'd gone to see or a book they'd read. She gave up, more or less, on "the spoiled brat" as she called her. When Sasha began to go out to her secret meetings, Gerda and Alicia would stay home in silence. Alicia would practice her ballet positions, her spine a rigid line of knots up her back. Gerda would read or sketch. She even managed to capture the childish, haughty line of Alicia's poses in some smudgy charcoal drawings, without ever telling the girl.

Sasha would arrive home to thick silence. Gerda would shove her sketches into an old portfolio, and Alicia would lift her leg up against her ear.

"Has one word been uttered?" Sasha would exclaim, grabbing her own head and making Alicia laugh for the first time all evening.

"Where do you go?" Alicia would say, releasing the leg and bounding over to her sister.

"I am dealing with the real problems we are faced with. How can we pray for peace and live in a battle zone at home?"

"I am getting better at ballet. When things go back to normal, I will be the best in my class." Alicia climbed into Sasha's lap, an oversized child. "I'm already the prettiest. Teacher said it is hard to believe I am not *arier*, Aryan."

"Alicia," Sasha snapped. "You're Jewish, one of God's chosen people. This is what a Jew looks like."

Alicia pointed to Gerda. "She's not a Jew."

"No."

"Not one of God's chosen people?"

"We are all children of God." Sasha leaned her head back against the chair and closed her eyes. Her arms encircled Alicia. Gerda shivered as against a sudden cold.

In the sixth week, Alicia returned to the apartment alone only a couple of hours after she and Sasha had set off for the Sabbath dinner with their family. Gerda heard the key in the lock.

"Sasha?" she called, moving toward the front door. Alicia pushed the door open and stared at Gerda. She brushed past Gerda and sat on the couch, pulling her knees up to her chest and clutching them to her. Gerda looked out into the empty hallway and quickly shut and locked the door. She sat opposite the girl.

"Where's Sasha?"

"She's coming separately."

"What happened?"

Alicia wiped her fingers under her nose, and Gerda suddenly saw that she was terribly upset. Once again, she reminded herself that "the spoiled brat" was only a child, one separated from her parents and thrust into a world whose intentions were not kind. At the same time, fear for Sasha tightened around her chest. Her very breath hurt her.

"They're all gone," Alicia said. "The door to our house was splintered, the china smashed all over the front hall. They'd packed suitcases, and those were torn apart. My mama's nightgown . . ." She was not crying. Gerda had seen her throw fits, cry because she'd been shut away from grownup fun. She'd cried a few days ago because Sasha took away the ballet slippers she'd grown out of, and had not been able to replace them. But now her eyes burned with dryness. She looked up at Gerda. "Sasha sent me back ahead of her. She said I'd be safer without her."

Zahava. Golden one. She'd been right to decide a ten-year-old with Alicia's fair skin and pale hair would be safer without the big sister whose olive complexion and black hair were now grounds for arrest. Alicia began to shake silently. Gerda pulled the afghan off the back of the couch and wrapped it around the girl, and held her shoulders as if anchoring her down, as if her shaking body might gain momentum and propel her up, out the covered windows and into the streets.

They sat together for well over an hour, silent again. They both jolted at the sound of three brisk raps on the door. Alicia's smile bloomed, faltered, and then failed; her eyes widened in terror for a moment, and then her eyebrows settled, her cheeks softened, her mouth stilled. Gerda would see that blank look on her face over and over for the rest of her life.

"Go in the closet," Gerda whispered. "Get behind the clothes."

Alicia jumped up, for once following Gerda's instructions without question. When she heard the closet door close, Gerda approached the front hallway. She put her face in her hands and then lifted her head. "Who is it?" she called casually.

"Gerdela, it's me, Zahava."

Gerda unlocked the door, her fingers awkward in their urgency. Sasha had a box clutched in her hands. Gerda pulled her in and locked the door again, then pulled a chair under the knob. Then she pulled Sasha into her arms, the box digging into their stomachs.

"Is Alicia here?" Sasha asked.

"Yes, yes. I hid her in the closet. Come."

But when she threw the closet door open, not one thing had been moved, and the child was nowhere in sight. Gerda turned. "Alicia," she called. "Where are you?" Nothing. "It's safe now," Gerda said, shuddering at the unavoidable lie in her own words. "It was Sasha, come home to us." From the back of the closet, they heard a whispered scraping. Then a trunk full of old shoes slowly opened and Alicia crawled out. The three looked at each other for a moment, and then Alicia leaned into her sister, resting her golden head on Sasha's chest. Gerda waited for the flood of tears, but they never came.

After that, Sasha and Alicia stayed in the apartment most of the time, except when Sasha left for her secret meetings, which she insisted on attending. Alicia grew quieter and more sulky. Her laughter was occasional and startling. Gerda found herself working hard to please the girl. She'd wait in long lines to bring home a piece of candy or a pastry. At night she'd lie awake listening to Sasha's breathing, feeling the subtle expansion and collapse of her rib cage. The moments between breaths hovered in Gerda's own throat, blocking the passage of air, showing her exactly how long a moment could be when what should have seemed predictable at the other end was suddenly uncertain.

Sasha had brought a few of her family's things from the remains of their home. She'd found her brother's prayer shawl, the one her father had given him on his Bar Mitzvah. She'd brought the Sabbath candleholders and some photographs that had been tossed to the ground and trampled. On Friday evenings, Sasha would bring out the box, and go through the ritual of prayer. Alicia stood beside her, and Gerda sat off to the side, watching these two sisters, the golden one and the dark one, as they gestured the light toward their faces with their hands and sang the blessings. One night a knock at the door interrupted, and the three of them froze. Sasha put out the flames with her thumb and forefinger, and without a sound, she and Alicia cloistered themselves in the closet, behind a fake wall Gerda had built.

Gerda walked to the door, her footsteps echoing loudly against the silence Sasha and Alicia had wrapped around them.

"Who is it?"

"Gerda, it's Peter."

A friend from Gerda's Saturday gatherings that Sasha had insisted go on without her, while she and Alicia hid. Gerda had told her friends that Sasha had gone to join her family. What had surprised her was how easy it was to lie to them, how little they questioned her, these friends with their liberal intellectualism.

"Peter!" Gerda reached for her normally abundant enthusiasm. "What a pleasant surprise."

"I'd forgotten the day, and I was on my way over before I realized it was Friday."

He laughed and she, reluctantly, joined him.

"Perhaps you have company . . ."

"Company? No, of course not."

They spent a strained hour exchanging opinions about Schönberg and Webern while Gerda thought of Sasha and Alicia, unmoving, in that tiny, dark space. Should they be hiding from Peter? He'd always loved Sasha, everyone had. But the world had cracked apart. It was hard to know anything, and Sasha had decided that the less anyone knew, the better. Finally, he left, kissing Gerda on both cheeks. She listened to his footsteps as he bounded down the stairs, each footfall fainter than the last.

When she pulled the fake wall back, she found Sasha and Alicia crouched, their arms around each other. As they climbed out, Sasha shook her almost black hair.

"I kept saying the blessings over and over in my head. Baruch atah, Adonai . . ."

"And you, Alicia? What did you think of?" Gerda asked, reaching her hand out, but somehow not quite touching the girl's arm.

"Nothing," Alicia said. "I made my mind utterly empty."

"That's a kind of prayer, too," Sasha said, brushing her sister's light hair back from her pale face. Alicia just shrugged.

Mrs. Koch lifted her head and Shy was suddenly there, in sharp, hard outline, so that the blush in her cheeks and the bright, deep brown of her eyes and the tears trailing across her smooth face and crumpled mouth were some kind of mural inside a silhouette. Not just to Alta or to Mrs. Koch. They all saw it—Miss Pauline, too, who lifted her tea-warmed hand and braved touching Shy.

"There's more," Shy said.

Mrs. Koch nodded.

"It's better to know everything," Alta said.

"It still won't be enough." Shy got up. "Excuse me for a moment." Alta saw her blink, hard—another familiar movement—and then she ducked down the hall. Alta heard the bathroom door close.

"Alta, you go to her," Mrs. Koch commanded.

"Maybe Miss Pauline—"

"She doesn't know us, Alta," Miss Pauline said. "But she knows you. She loves you. Now go on."

Alta stood, nervous, in front of the door, ashamed suddenly that she had not really tried to get to know Shy again. She'd been so busy protecting herself, she had never really reached out to her Sasha, the grown woman who could be found between the hard secrets of the past and the present rush of illness and death and funeral arrangements.

Alta knocked softly. "Sasha," she said, "let me in."

Alta was surprised when Shy unlocked the door. "I'm okay," she said. She'd smoothed her hair down and wiped the tears away. Her dark hair framed the defined, adult angles of her lovely face starkly. Alta wrapped her arms around Shy, pulling her awkwardly close, feeling Shy's tears begin again between the skin of her cheek and Alta's.

Alta rubbed her hands over and over Shy's shaking shoulders and back. Finally, they clung to one another in the resonant hush of Shy's ragged breath. Finally, the grief flooded from her body. Too soon, she reached up and wiped her hand across her eyes, her body still hunched into Alta's.

"Do you want to go home?" Alta asked—still not sure exactly where that would be.

Shy shook her head. "I'm going to hear it." She separated herself as easily as ever and stepped back to the sink, splashing water on her face and drying it. "Did she think I couldn't take it?"

Alta looked at her, trying to see what she might have missed, just because she had assumed she knew what she'd find. She saw that Shy's olive skin and upright, proud posture came from somewhere, as did her daring playfulness.

"I mean my mother," Shy added.

"I know who you mean." Alta pulled the neckline of Shy's dress straight. "She didn't tell anyone, Shy. You know?"

"I would have known"—Shy shrugged, shivering—"how to help her, how to talk to her. I would have been angry at somebody else."

When they returned to the living room, Shy apologized. Miss Pauline hushed her, and Mrs. Koch put a hand on her cheek and stared into her eyes. "Sasha," she said, "it is right you should know."

"How did it protect me not to know?"

Mrs. Koch released Shy's face, and her hand fell to her lap. "Alicia learned that safety meant hiding, that to know who you were was dangerous, and to be who you were was death. Maybe it was . . . my fault. She wasn't safe with us, so we found a place where we thought she would be protected, a place where some good people were actually willing to shelter a Jewish girl in the midst of all this terror. It seemed the best thing. At the time, it seemed the only thing. Remember, we did not know when it was happening how or when the war might end." Mrs. Koch leaned back into the couch. "More tea, Paulie?" she asked. While Miss Pauline returned to the kitchen, Mrs. Koch began to speak again.

Alicia was sent to a convent sixty miles from Vienna, where a few brave nuns sheltered some Jewish girls among the Catholic boarders. Alicia was very unhappy, at first. How did they know this? Gerda and Zahava visited her four times, at great risk. Each time, Alicia would run, as instructed, to Gerda, and call her *aunt*. Sasha would sit nearby, behind Gerda, in the shadows, to dissociate her Jewish image from the child. Alicia sat limply beside Gerda, grabbing fleeting glances of Sasha with her eyes. With one hand, Gerda would brush the hair from Alicia's face. The girl would shrug her hand away.

"Tell my sister I hate it here," she hissed. "I want to be with her. I don't care about danger."

Zahava placed one finger over her mouth. She slipped a piece of candy from her pocket and handed it to Alicia.

"Alicia told me only one thing, ever, about all the months that followed, when we had no idea where she was." Mrs. Koch put her hands on her own cheeks. This seemed to Alta to be almost a gesture of surprise, shock, even after all these years. "On the boat to America, finally escaping—or so she thought—the country of her nightmares, she told me that she had saved that little piece of candy, some small, hard peppermint. She had saved it for the remaining months at the convent. Since she kept it always in her pocket, it was with her the day the soldiers came to the convent and took her and two other girls away." Mrs. Koch did not look at any of them, but off into a distance that Alta saw was that of time. Her eyes suddenly flooded with fresh tears, and Alta realized that grief was like smell—it hit hard and immediately, without the mediary of memory. "And Zahava," she said, as tears traveled her wrinkled face, "my Sasha never stopped looking for her little sister."

There were gaps, then, in the story, even for Mrs. Koch, rough silences she'd made some sort of peace with. Zahava had been caught a few months later, on one of her missions to find out what had happened to her sister. Mrs. Koch suspected that Zahava had perished at Auschwitz. She had found Alicia at a Displaced Persons encampment after the war. They lived together in stunned grief, in Gerda's apartment, tiptoeing around each other and the things that Sasha had left behind: the candlesticks and the prayer shawl, the box with the photographs. She would not talk about the camps. She simply would not.

"She was so thin, she looked like one of those candlesticks. I wouldn't have recognized her when I first saw her. At that time, I was very empty, very bitter. Alicia had fallen all the way into her silence, and I . . . I let her. I did not know what to say to her. For a while I think we both hoped that Zahava would come back. It was over a year before we found someone who'd seen her die. The man was a neighbor of the Hutners', a butcher named Blatt. Alicia brought him back to the apartment, and he told us that Sasha had been shot saying the words of the Kaddish, the prayer for the dead, over a pit full of the dead bodies of her people. All people were Zahava's people."

Lifting her eyes, Alta noticed they were all crying.

Mrs. Koch shook her head. "Mr. Blatt wanted to marry Alicia. He was three times her age and had lost his whole family—his wife and two little boys. He was trying to get to Israel, and he asked Alicia to go with him. At first she did not say whether she would go. She cooked for him, all the foods her mother had made. Latkes with homemade applesauce, kugel. And we would sit, eating, the three of us together, as if we could fill any of the emptiness, as if we could take our lost ones into our bodies as cinnamon, sour cream."

"Those foods—" Shy said, and then the silence of her tears poured over her words, and her mouth distorted. Alta reached out and touched the surfaces of her, squeezed her shoulders and rubbed wetness from her cheek with her thumb. "What about my father?"

Miss Pauline brought out a box of tissues, and Mrs. Koch blew her nose resolutely.

"Mr. Blatt got his visa to Israel about the same time the official lists of the dead began to come out. One day I came home and found Alicia in the kitchen. She had heated a butter knife over the stove and pressed the flat surface against the tattoo on her forearm. She had to do it more than once before the welt of the burn obscured the numerals. She started to go to church then. Somehow, she remembered the convent as a haven of safety, a place where children were not terrified. It was the last place, too, that she had seen Zahava.

"She met your father in church. He was traveling in Europe, this young, healthy American. He seemed huge and full of the ignorant vitality of life. This was 1950. Her burn had healed to a small whitish scar. Your mother was working as a seamstress, using my last name. There was still a great deal of anti-Semitism. People wanted to forget about the war.

"Everything from the Hutner family home had been taken long ago, by Nazis and neighbors. The only things left were what Zahava had retrieved the day she'd found their house wrecked and her family gone. Alicia stored them away with Gerda's things and did not keep them with her. It was not until last year that she asked to see them, and she made me promise that if anything happened to her, I would come and get them from the house, which I did the day I saw her at the hospital."

Alta remembered Mrs. Koch's bulky purse as they'd left the Mallon house after they'd visited Mrs. Mallon in the hospital. She had wondered if Mrs. Koch was taking a memento, but had not mentioned it. And Mrs. Koch had said to her, "Not to talk about is not the same as not to remember." Alta grabbed a tissue from the box.

"You have the box here," Alta said.

"Yes, Alta, clever one."

"May I . . . Could I see it?" Shy asked.

Mrs. Koch nodded to Miss Pauline, who got up and left the room.

"Sasha," Mrs. Koch said, and a chill coursed through Alta. Shy's eyes searched Mrs. Koch's face. "I'm so sorry. I wanted to tell you, but I had made my promise a long time ago, may Alicia forgive me for breaking my word."

Miss Pauline came back with a black metal lock box, which she held by its silver handle out to Shy. Alta imagined Zahava coming back to Gerda's apartment with this box, salvaged from her family home.

Shy shook her head. Her nostrils flared and her eyes widened at some unseen horror. "I never came back. She wanted me to visit so much, and I just kept saying, not yet, not yet. Some days I hated her. Some days I felt nothing at all." She rubbed her fingers under her eyes, pulling at her face. "I didn't tell her . . ." Her voice cracked.

Mrs. Koch came behind her and held her shoulders, while Miss Pauline reached from one side and Alta from the other. Alta felt the wet drench of tears, her own, Shy's, all of theirs, and the surge of loss that came with the truth Mrs. Koch had to give them. There was no contradicting what Shy said, either. Mrs. Mallon had made her choices, but somehow they were all culpable.

"So my father . . . ?" Shy finally asked. Miss Pauline put the box beside her on the couch.

"Never knew," Mrs. Koch said. "He came back to Europe a year later to study; she got baptized and converted in the meanwhile, swearing me to secrecy. It wasn't my choice to make. I had my safety. I was lost, anyway, to sadness. Years of sadness. And your father loved your mother. He adored her. He didn't understand her, from the beginning, but I think he liked that, too. His family was not altogether pleased, but we did not know that until we got to this country. Your mother told him her family had been killed in the bombing. From this, he allowed for her terror and sorrow, her nightmares—"

"She still had nightmares when I was growing up," Shy said in a rush, as if she'd been waiting for her chance to tell the secrets she'd held for so long.

Mrs. Koch nodded, and Miss Pauline took Shy's hand. Mrs. Koch continued. "She got pregnant, in Vienna, and he married her. She brought me back with them to this country. We made some sort of peace between us; our sorrow brought us together where shared love had not. I did not want to stay in that country, anyway." She wiped her nose carefully on the handkerchief. "Alicia miscarried on the boat coming over. I was with her. She was screaming, in so much pain. Her face turned so white, and all around her eyes, dark, and she kicked and kicked."

Shy rubbed her hands over her belly. Alta remembered her words after their day on the beach: *I don't know if I'm ready to be a mother. I don't know what that means.*

Mrs. Koch leaned back into her chair, and Alta suddenly realized that for all her stockiness, she was very old and not all that big. The back of the chair came up past her shoulders. The skin below her eyes looked puffed with fatigue and sadness. Miss Pauline went over and stood next to her, and Mrs. Koch rested her head against Miss Pauline. Despite all the sorrow, Alta touched again that gladness of knowing that love of the kind these women had for each other existed in the world.

"Open the box, Sasha," Miss Pauline said, and Mrs. Koch nodded intently.

Alta had sat so often with Mrs. Mallon in the days they'd lived together, talking and laughing and sometimes just keeping her company. Now she reproached herself. Why hadn't she asked Mrs. Mallon more about her life? Alta had colluded with Mrs. Mallon's silence, just as Mrs. C. had colluded with Alta's. Mrs. Mallon had instinctively found Alta a place where she could embrace who she was—a butch dyke—but Mrs. Mallon hadn't even given herself that chance. She had never fallen in love with her life. The reason Mrs. Mallon had understood Alta so well was that she too had lived among people who could not allow for the ways she was different from them—who couldn't conceive of another side to the woman who walked their tree-shaded streets, drank lemonade at church socials, and gathered with them to watch the school play.

Shy turned the tiny key in the lock and it clicked open. A quick smile of hope flashed into her eyes and touched her mouth. She reached into the box and lifted out a bundle wrapped in pieces of felt. She unrolled two tall silver candlesticks. "Oh, my God," she whispered, and her jaw tightened as she swallowed back tears.

Mrs. Koch reached toward her. "These are the candlesticks Zahava used to light every Friday night at sundown. Sabbath candles. She used to circle her hands over the flame to bring the light into the new week. And little Alicia would stand beside her and do it, too."

"Marcie could show you," Alta said.

Shy nodded, her eyes meeting Alta's.

There was a long piece of ivory cloth next, fringed on the ends. It unfolded as Shy pulled it out.

"That's a prayer shawl, your grandfather's or your uncle David's."

Shy's silent tears began again.

"Here, look," Mrs. Koch said. She went over and pulled out a small stack of photographs, old black-and-white pictures, yellowed and blurred. A little girl in a flouncy white dress, an oversized bow around her blond head: this was the girl who had hidden herself in Mrs. Mallon. Here she was with her big sister, Sasha, who sat at a wrought-iron table shaded by an overarching tree.

There was an older couple, in brown and gray tones: an elegant blond woman with wavy hair pulled back in a loose bun, tiny earrings hanging from her lobes, in a sailor dress with a double row of buttons down the front. She had Mrs. Mallon's eyes and Shy's mouth. Beside her a man with Shy's pointed nose and dark eyebrows stood in a wide-lapelled suit and vest. He wore a hat with a wide band above the brim.

A small square photograph slipped out from between two others. A delicate web of lines covered its surface, and the arc of a half circle was stamped at one edge. It was a beautiful child with clear, gorgeous eyes. He had a crew cut and looked too small for the heavy jacket and stiff, white-collared shirt. On the back, Mrs. Koch showed them, patches of glue had dried to brown. "The photograph from David's identification card," Mrs. Koch explained.

Another picture of two young women matched the one Mrs. Koch had shown them earlier. Mrs. Koch pointed them out:

"That's me with Sasha." And Shy and Alta both heard the word as a prayer or a whispered chant, the light of incense that promises memory. Alta had thought memory was a form of self-pity, and she'd thought it was a lie, but that day she knew otherwise. These people who had meant something to Mrs. Mallon, meant something to Shy.

There were her grandparents, her aunt, her uncle, and her mother, happy.

"Goodness, it's after midnight and you look awfully tired, Sasha," Miss Pauline said. "Why don't the two of you sleep over in the guest room? That way we can all go over to the funeral together in the morning."

"I think that's a good idea, Shy," Alta said, relaxing for the first time that evening into the comfort of these women and their home together.

Shy nodded to Alta and Miss Pauline and then touched Mrs. Koch's arm. "Gerda?"

"Yes, my dear?"

"Thank you."

Mrs. Koch smiled. "You were a gift to your mother, Sasha. She was so proud of you."

Alta looked out the window. It was dark, but she could see the movement of wind through the great eucalyptus behind the neighboring house. What had Mrs. Mallon found to stare at for all those years? It must have been the people inside her head, the mausoleum of her memory.

Shy and Alta lay side by side in the king-sized guest bed, Shy surrounded by extra pillows so she could lie on her side or tuck one under her lower back.

"Good night, Shy."

"Sasha. I'm Sasha now. Good night, Alta."

Alta listened to the silence in the house for a few minutes, listened to Shy's breath. After a while, Shy sighed deeply, and Alta thought she'd fallen asleep. Then Shy spoke:

"She named me after someone she never even told me existed." Alta reached over the pillows and put one arm around Shy. She felt Shy's cool softness. "Do you ever feel safe, Alta?"

"Safe?" Alta wanted to tell Shy that she could protect her, or perhaps that there was something else besides safety she could offer. But Shy had asked a question, and Alta answered it. "Not really, no. I feel part of something, but I never feel safe."

"I'm not going back." Shy spoke so quietly Alta thought she hadn't heard her at all, and then the words came to Alta in a slow dissolve. She said nothing, and everything Shy could mean lay between them in the giant bed.

The familiar darkness of Our Lady's timber-roofed Spanish interior fell over Alta after the glare of the day heating up outside.

"The grace and peace of God our Father and the Lord Jesus Christ be with you," said Father Michaels, the new priest Shy had pointed out to Alta the night before.

"And also with you." Alta's and Shy's words overlapped.

"There's my aunt," Shy whispered. Alta whipped her head around and saw that Shy meant Patrick Mallon's sister, there with her husband. She looked like Shy's father, only shorter and plumper. The church was nearly empty. Mrs. C. had gotten there before them, and she and a few other church women were moving around accomplishing things. The closed coffin was already on a bier in front of the altar. After a few minutes, Father Michaels moved to the altar and sprinkled the coffin with holy water.

"In the waters of baptism Alice Mallon died with Christ and rose with him to new life. May she now share with him eternal glory."

Shy began to cry again.

"Let us pray," the priest said, and Alta bowed her head.

Alta felt stung by the irony of this funeral and at the same time moved by the rich tradition she felt entangled with and apart from. She wondered to what extent Mrs. Mallon had truly embraced Catholicism, and to what extent she—Alta—had truly escaped it.

"O God, to whom mercy and forgiveness belong, hear our prayers on behalf of your servant Alice Mallon, whom you have called out of this world; and because she put her hope and trust in you, command that she be carried safely home to heaven and come to enjoy your eternal reward . . ."

Alta wondered what regrets Mrs. Mallon had had when Shy left, what she had not said to Alta during those dining table talks they'd shared in the afternoons.

"Amen," everyone said around her.

Shy stood up and walked to the front of the church, her footsteps echoing. Alta flashed back to the day Mrs. Mallon had come to the school assembly to take Shy home. What fear had followed Mrs. Mallon through the rooms and streets of Alta's simple, modern Catholic childhood. How little they had understood her.

Shy's voice was soft, but so clear it carried through the church: "The Lord is my shepherd; there is nothing I shall want. Fresh and green are the pastures where He gives me repose. Near restful waters He leads me, to revive my drooping spirit."

And the reply of the scattered mourners echoed back to her, "Though I walk in the valley of darkness, I fear no evil, for you are with me."

"You have prepared a banquet for me in the sight of my foes. My head is anointed with oil; my cup is overflowing."

"The Lord is my shepherd; there is nothing I shall want."

When Shy returned to the seat beside her, Alta squeezed her hand.

"Could you hear me?" Shy whispered, with more irony than insecurity in her voice.

"Every word." Alta smiled at her.

Alta took communion to keep Shy company, though she hadn't said confession in about four years. *"Because there is one bread, we who are many are one body, for we all partake of one bread."* Mrs. C. played the organ and four pallbearers she'd managed to enlist—two sons of Mrs. Donnogan's, Alta's cousin John, and Mrs. Lucas's nephew—carried Mrs. Mallon out to the waiting hearse.

. . .

By the time they got to the cemetery, it was so hot their mourning stuck to them uncomfortably. The lawns there were green and sloped, the roads curved gently, and Shy looked stark and solitary in her now refashioned and loosened black crepe dress.

"Our sister Alice Mallon has gone to her rest in the peace of Christ," Father Michaels began. "May the Lord now welcome her to the table of God's children in heaven."

It's over, Alta thought. Not just the days when she and Shy had stood on the Mallons' front lawn and launched helium balloons with self-addressed postcards attached for whoever might find them to return to them, not the sweet smell of Mrs. Mallon's hot potato pancakes and the promise of Shy's peaceful grin around a mouthful of sour cream and applesauce, not even the lost chance to wonder and then to be told. Shy was a game Alta had been playing since the day she'd met her. Alta had grown up just to match Shy's pace. She couldn't leave Shy there, in the cemetery, black-clad, pregnant, alone. But she wasn't sure how she could take Shy with her.

"You have died, and your life is hidden with Christ in God . . ."

Alta sneaked looks at her mother, who was standing on the other side of the grave with some of the women from church. "Lord, have mercy," they intoned in response to the priest's intercessions. "Hear our prayer." If Shy stayed, perhaps she could take up again her role as Alta's protector, and they could go to visit Alta's mother together; Alta could ask to look at her photographs. Alta could find out if she could hear something or see something that might make a difference in her own life, even in her relationship to *her* mother. After all, Alta was just doing her best to live in the world and to be able one day to say—as her mother had—"Those were good times," and mean it. If she'd had to find and create that livable world, well, perhaps that journey wasn't as unique as she'd thought.

Shy, standing graveside, still seemed to Alta not to know this. Alta had heard that burying your child is the worst pain there is, because you don't expect ever to have to. But nothing prepares us to bury our parents, either, she thought, to stand surprised and alone, and try to figure out how, since we didn't get here by ourselves, we can carry on that way. Shy looked as separate from everything and everybody around her as Alta imagined she herself did.

"With longing for the coming of God's kingdom, let us pray."

Most of Alta's friends in the City didn't talk to their parents much, if at all. To their families, there was something unbearable in the bodies she and her friends held close, the mouths they kissed, the hands they held walking down the street. If there's no pain worse than burying your own child, why had most of the dykes Alta knew been buried alive? She guessed some choices were more painful yet.

But Alta didn't believe that anymore. She didn't believe they were forgotten; that was too easy. They were separated from the people who'd raised them. But there was something greater than the willed lapse of memory, something more indelible than the expectations built for them with tools and materials not chosen, but given. It was the thing that held them all irrevocably together. All over the world, Alta thought, there are people with secrets, we are their secrets. They sit beside each other on the bus, stand in line at the bank, toast each other at dinner parties and never know that their separate, isolated little secrets are meeting each other at bars and rallies, taking hand to mouth and giving back the sense that we are here and have a right to be. We don't trust them, we shouldn't, yet sometimes there is no other choice. Sometimes, perhaps, we are them.

"Merciful Lord, you know the anguish of the sorrowful, you are attentive to the prayers of the humble."

When no one else would help Alta get unstuck from the tar of her young life, Mrs. Mallon had known how and had done it. While Alta had left Mrs. Mallon in her world of the untold, Mrs. Mallon had found a way to help Alta to a life of openness. Fragile, unbreakable strands of debt and gratitude, anger and retribution had tied them together—Shy, her mother, and Alta. Perhaps Mrs. C., too. With the death of Mrs. Mallon—her body in the wooden coffin before them, the fresh earth marking the hole in the green lawn, waiting—how would the threads hold; where would Shy and Alta swing off to, and where might they land? There was too much they hadn't known, too much they hadn't even asked.

"God of holiness and power, accept our prayers on behalf of your servant Alice Mallon."

Alta found herself lulled by the rich voice of the priest.

"Do not count her deeds against her, for in her heart she desired to do your will. As her faith united her to your people on earth, so may your mercy join her to the angels in heaven."

"Amen," Alta said, joining in with Shy and Mrs. Koch and Miss Pauline, and also with her mother and the other dedicated women who came to the funeral of a woman who'd lived among them for years and whom they'd barely known.

"Go in the peace of Christ," Father Michaels concluded.

"Thanks be to God," the mourners replied.

Shy nodded to Alta, and Alta walked over to her mother and the other women. Mrs. C. looked away as Alta approached. She did not remind the women that Alta was her daughter.

"Thank you for being here, Mother," Alta said quietly. "I know you didn't have to be."

"It's the way I know how to help," Mrs. C. replied. Alta tried to listen beyond her clipped tone. Her mother wanted to help; she believed that. *Do not count her deeds against her.* Alta was sorry to find she felt as trapped as Mrs. Mallon must have been in her coma and even before.

Alta nodded and then gently touched her mother's arm, up by the shoulder. "I think it did help."

"Shall we bring food over to the Mallon place in a little while?" Mrs. C. asked, looking at Alta now.

"Well, Shy's not going to receive guests," Alta said. "We've got to go somewhere else tonight. But thank you, thanks to all of you." The other women stared at Alta, yet would not meet her eyes. But she stayed calm, and they left Shy to her because, finally, Alta was the only one who knew her, and even Mrs. Mallon had never been more than a neighbor these women didn't really know.

Her mother stayed a moment, hesitating, half turned to go. "You're a good friend to Shy," Mrs. C. said, her words coming fast. "And she needs that." Alta nodded, fighting against the tears that pushed up from behind her eyes. Mrs. C. walked quickly away, caught up with her friends. Mrs. Koch and Miss Pauline, who were driving Alta and Shy back to the Mallons', stayed respectfully back a bit. Shy turned as the coffin was lowered, bent down and picked up some wet earth. Alta took her elbow and walked her to the edge. Shy was crying silent tears, loose tears that flew down her cheeks and fell on her hands. She let the dirt go above the deep hole, and every bit of it made a sound and spread across the wood. And then she was sobbing in Alta's arms.

After a few minutes, she looked up and reached out her dirt-smudged hand toward Mrs. Koch, who came forward.

"You're family, too," Shy said, putting another handful of dirt in Mrs. Koch's stiff hand.

"I've buried too many people, Alicia," Mrs. Koch said. "But you will be the last." And she let fall the chunks of earth. They stood looking down as the diggers began filling the hole. Shy slipped one foot and then the other in and out of her black flats.

"Ready?" she said.

"Okay," Alta said, and Shy walked beside her, her hand loosely in Alta's, not as if they were lovers, but as if Shy were a little child and Alta was leading her along. The four of them slowly made their way to the road.

A soft breeze broke through the driving heat. Alta leaned against the hot metal of Mrs. Koch's car and looked back at the green fields dimpled with grave markers. She watched as Mrs. Mallon's grave diggers finished their work and drove off in an electric cart. As they got farther and farther away Alta lost the exact spot where Alicia Mallon lay, though she knew they would find it again, beside Mr. Mallon's marked grave.

They drove off the cemetery grounds in silence. Alta was acutely aware that they were leaving Mrs. Mallon behind in that hallowed earth; it seemed, simply, unfair. This was how she'd felt at her father's funeral. Perhaps we do not have the rites of death perfected, she thought, for it seemed wrong to her, uncomfortable. The remaining brightness of the day, and the way she turned into it and away from the graves frightened her most of all.

In the morning the phone would ring, and Shy would rise out of Alta's bed. Erik would try to convince her to go back to Seattle. Alta had never known what Shy would do. She'd hardly known what Shy had done before, though she'd shaped her life against it.

Mrs. Koch drove them to the Mallons'. The large brown house seemed trapped in shade, its windows somehow emptier without the chance that Mrs. Mallon might peer out one of them. Alta helped Shy climb from the car.

"I hope I did the right thing, Sasha," Mrs. Koch said. "I'm sorry if it was too much so fast."

Shy shook her head. "In this funny way she seems more real to me now than when she was alive."

"I know only two things about this world," Mrs. Koch said, squeezing Shy's hand through the car window. "Everything takes longer than you think, and most things are more complicated than you can imagine."

Shy nodded.

"So give yourself some time," Miss Pauline added. "Every day, just give yourself that day."

Mrs. Koch blew a kiss, and Shy and Alta watched the two women drive down to the end of the block and make a left onto Washington Street without signaling.

"My mother had a friend," Shy said.

"Yeah," Alta agreed. "A good one."

Alta watched Shy pack her clothes and makeup back into the rectangular, old-fashioned suitcase she'd brought. She was staying at Alta's house tonight, and beyond that they hadn't discussed.

"Doesn't Erik want you to come home?" Alta refolded a dress Shy had shoved into the suitcase.

"He likes his routine, and I'm part of it now."

Shy had been part of Alta's routine once, too, as much as eating and sleeping. She'd been part of Alta's every day for the six years she'd been gone, so much so that Alta had not realized she'd created a life that did not, in fact, include Shy.

"I'd miss you, Shy-girl."

Shy looked up from her packing. "I don't think you would," she said calmly.

"I wouldn't know what to do with myself if I weren't missing you."

"You seem to find ways to entertain yourself."

"Don't forget to keep out your clothes for tonight." To Alta's surprise, Shy had asked to go to Marcie's Shabbat dinner with her. They were silent for a while. Alta watched Shy rearrange her clothes to fit in the small suitcase.

When she finally got it closed, she put it by the door and leaned on the wall, facing Alta. "You don't think I should stay, do you?"

Alta hadn't thought that, hadn't known what to think, between the unfolding of Mrs. Mallon's life and death almost at once and Shy's intimations that she might not go back. But as Shy said it, Alta realized that, against everything she'd ever thought she'd feel, she didn't think Shy should stay.

"It's not what you think, Shy. I love you. I'll always love you. But you have been running all your life from something you didn't—couldn't—even understand. If I try to get you to run away to me, I'll forever be wondering when you'll run away from me again. Do you see what I mean?"

Shy noticed a piece of blouse hanging out of her suitcase and opened the whole thing again, spilling clothes onto the floor. She knelt down and began packing again.

"Sasha, listen to me." Alta put her hand on Shy's arm, encircled it with her fingers. Shy looked up. "You are going to figure all of this out. You are going to think about it and think about it and think about it, and one day you'll realize that you think about it in a different way than you did at first, that everything is different.

"I know you are scared about the baby. Your mom was scared all her life, and you still managed to be the sassiest girl I knew. You were brave, Shy, in your own way, and now it's time for you to figure out how to fix things where you are, not by going somewhere else."

"I don't know which part of that last trip to Tahoe scared me more, Alta." Alta flinched internally, surprised at her own surprise that Shy was going to speak of what they'd never talked about. But Shy continued, "Those boys who broke the plants I'd gotten for my mother, or their screaming: dyke, dyke." Shy shut her eyes, and that funny wrinkle appeared above her nose. Then she opened them and looked right at Alta, as if willing herself to face this thing neither of them had spoken of once since the day, six years before, when they'd been attacked. "I thought they were going to . . . hurt us, Alta. But this part of me kept thinking, they're right. I'd let you . . . I'd wanted you to touch me. You made me feel things with my whole body, Alta, even with my eyes squeezed shut and half of me trying to pretend it wasn't happening at all."

Shy leaned her head back against the wall. "I'm tired, Alta. I'm so damn tired."

Alta sat down and put her arms around Shy, in that bedroom where Shy had initiated her not only into the world of sex, but into the human world of love and its counterpart, heartbreak. And then she wanted to say something real to Shy, something beyond the bravado of her fear, something that she'd been realizing as she'd listened to Mrs. Koch's—to Alicia Hutner Mallon's—story. "Shy," she said. "Sasha—" She put her hands on Shy's shoulders and held her away, so she could see her face.

"I never told you this, Sasha, because I was so damn mad at you for leaving me, just when I needed you most. But I don't know what I would have done without you. I know you couldn't do more than you did, but you let me know that I was attractive to somebody, that in some way, I wasn't completely alone in my freakishness. If you hadn't let me touch you . . ."

"I needed you, too, Alta. Different ways, and for different reasons, but I've missed you every one of these days."

"Do you love him, Shy?"

Shy buried her face in Alta's neck. Alta listened to her breathe. After a while, Shy started to talk, her face still half submerged in Alta.

"When I first went to Seattle, I had to start from scratch, make a whole life. Jim—the married man—was sort of a buffer. At least I wasn't alone all the time. But every time I was with him, I kept thinking, someday I'll be married to some guy, and he'll be off having sex with some nineteen-year-old girl." She laughed. "I drive myself crazy the way I think, Alta. I wondered how you were doing. I really did. I pretty much knew how my mother would be doing, and I figured my dad would go on, because that's what he was good at, going on." She lifted her head and half turned. "Will you unzip me?"

Alta pulled the zipper down. The dress opened, exposing a V of Shy's skin. Shy stayed where she was. "I'm sorry I can't be a different person than I am, Alta."

Alta put her hand on Shy's shoulder, by her neck, where the flesh was bare. "Don't ever be sorry about that. What will it get you?"

"I think you are right that I have to go back, at least right now. I'm not very good at just letting things happen. I mean, I always tried to orchestrate everything so my mother wouldn't get upset. Do you remember the things that upset her? It's so strange to think of them now, to try to understand what she was really thinking. She hated the doorbell, even knocking. I used to hover by the door when we were expecting guests, so I could just let them in. She hated church; she really did, at least for as long as I can remember, but she always made me go. She never came down from her room on a Friday night. Do you realize? It's like, I knew that, but I just couldn't even think about it, because it didn't make any sense.

"So I'll go back." Shy shook her head. "I'll go back, and I'll talk to this man I'm having a baby with. I'll tell him the things about me that he doesn't know. Maybe there are things about him I don't know."

Alta raised her eyebrows. "Maybe."

"But I might come back, Alta, come here and raise my baby in the Bay Area. Give her a chance to be—what was it you said? To be whatever."

"Do that wherever you are, Sasha. Do it for her, and find a way to do it for yourself."

Alta took Shy across the bridge, across the sweeping arm of iron and concrete, suspended between their hometown and an island, an island and the place that Alta now called home. The night came toward them, making promises of cooler air, and meanwhile the bike whipped up a breeze around them.

Alta took her to Renny's house. Marcie and Renny embraced them in the hallway, Renny with her grin, her fly-away hair in her face, and Marcie, sweet and sexy and kind. Marcie and Renny held each of them just a split second longer than usual, long enough to let Shy and Alta feel their solid warmth. Renny and Alta looked at each other, able to exchange bewilderment in that look, and an acceptance of that confusion, too.

"How are you doing?" Renny said.

Alta shrugged. "How about you?"

"We're the kings and queens of rhetorical questions," Renny muttered to Alta as they followed Marcie and Shy down the hall.

"In a land of short answers," Alta threw back at her, hanging one arm around her shoulders.

The girl was there. The red-headed girl with the lingering smile, who'd gone with Alta to the Mallons' house the first morning after her mother had called. Most often a nod across the room was enough; it is enough to watch the memory snake down her body—

and hers and hers and hers. But tonight it occurred to Alta that the freckles on her face were a map of stars, and she found her way over to the girl standing in the corner wearing a fuzzy pink dress, a glass of thick, sweet wine in her hand.

"Hey, Alta," she said. "How is everything? Is your friend in the hospital okay?" Suddenly, Alta wanted to hold on to the people who remembered voluntarily, who—like Marcie—told stories thousands of years old, and—like Renny—handed over an open bottle and waited for the message to be delivered or deciphered. How could she thank the girl? Should she fuck her across a kitchen table or low-lying futon frame? Could she put her once again on the back of her motorcycle and take her over the bridge? Alta looked at the soft flesh on her cheeks. Behind her, she saw Shy standing near Marcie.

"You know what?"

The girl looked right into Alta's eyes.

Alta took a deep breath. "I don't know your name."

The girl looked down at the floor and Alta wondered if she'd tease her, or cry, or simply walk away.

"Lucy," she said.

"What?"

"It's Lucy." And she held out her hand until Alta reached for it, took it and felt the softness of her skin.

Then Marcie struck a match and it flared. Alta could almost hear Mrs. Mallon, the odd twists of her accent, her depressed, insightful cadences woven through the sounds of the Hebrew prayer that Marcie recited. She heard Mrs. Mallon's voice as a sort of message across time, the only one she could salvage and deliver, and she did it poorly. But, *Sasha*, Alta heard her say, *Sasha*.

SILENCE EQUALS DEATH, said the placards and pins, the chanting, angry voices in Alta's community. But silence had been the term of survival for Alicia, hidden with her sister's piece of hard candy, first behind the walls of Gerda Koch's apartment and then behind the convent walls, and finally behind the walls of the house next door to where Alta had grown up. Alta had learned to hunt with her eyes, to find girls who would smile back at her on trains and in cafés. They recognized each other because they needed to, and they rewarded that recognition with sex, or friendship, or just a tilt of the head. But, Alta realized now, she'd never looked for or smiled at the Mrs. Mallons of the world. She'd never considered, really, that there were other kinds of silence, many kinds of death.

Shy seemed tired, her face swollen from crying, but she looked strangely alive, her eyes following Marcie's hands. Alta wondered what could come for Shy of a curiosity to learn who her mother had been, to consider who she herself might become, and how. Alta knew she'd want to watch her—she'd always want to watch her—as Shy found her way in the world. But Alta had taken her to the edge of her next journey, as Shy had taken Alta to hers. Marcie cupped her hand behind the candles' tips and touched the flame to each braided wick, which caught and kindled. For the rest of the night, as they ate and talked and joked and sometimes sat in silence, they watched the candles burn.

ACKNOWLEDGMENTS

I am deeply grateful to my agent, Marianne Merola; to my editor, Paul Elie, and the folks at FSG; to the women at Seal Press; to my teachers Dorothy Allison, Magda Bogin, Rebecca Goldstein, Joyce Johnson, and Donna Levin; and to Bob Shacochis for his generosity of spirit.

For their help with the book, warmest thanks to Danielle Blum, Thea Hillman, Xylor Jane, Devi Laskar, Peter Limnios, Kendra Lubalin, Kimberly Madison, Nanou Matteson, Sarah M., Diane Norwood, Melanie Nielson, Ernesto Quintero, Lilia Scott, Felicia Ward, Annette Weathers, Marilyn Weber; to the faculty and students at Columbia's School of the Arts; to the Women's Studies Department at UCSC; and to Heinz von Foerster.

For their recognition of my work, many thanks to the Lambda Literary Foundation, the Publishers' Triangle, Tristan Taormino and Joan Nestle. And for their efforts on behalf of *Shy Girl*, my thanks to the Bluestockings' collective; to Sarah Schulman; and to Gail Leondar-Wright.

And to my dear friends, and to my family of blood and bonding, especially my devoted parents, Larry Stark and Wendy Bartlett, and my wonderful partner, Florence Sullivan—

thank you.

Elizabeth Stark was born in Berkeley, California. She received her BA in Women's Studies from the University of California at Santa Cruz and her MFA from the Graduate Writing Division at Columbia University. She lives in New York City with her partner Florence and their three cats, and she is an Assistant Professor at Hobart and William Smith Colleges in Geneva, New York.

Selected Seal Press Titles

Valencia by Michelle Tea. $13.00, 1-58005-035-2. The fast-paced account of one girl's search for love and high times in the dyke world of San Francisco. By turns poetic and frantic, *Valencia* is an edgy, visceral ride through the queer girl underground of the Mission District.

Alma Rose by Edith Forbes. $12.95, 1-59005-011-5. The engaging story of Pat Lloyd and her encounter with Alma Rose, a charming and vivacious trucker who rumbles off the highway and changes Pat's life forever.

Girls, Visions and Everything by Sarah Schulman. $12.95, 1-58005-022-2. It's summer in New York City and the streets are sizzling. On the Lower East Side, lesbian-at-large Lila Futuransky is looking for adventure, with her keys in her pocket and a copy of *On the Road* in her hand.

Margins by Terri De La Peña. $12.95, 1-58005-039-5. A memorable portrait of the Chicana lesbian as daughter, sister, aunt, friend, writer and lover.

Working Parts by Lucy Jane Bledsoe. $12.00, 1-878067-94-X. An exceptional novel that taps the essence of friendship and the potential unleashed when we face our most intense fears.

Sex and Single Girls: Straight and Queer Women on Sexuality, edited by Lee Damsky. $16.95, 1-58005-038-7. In this empowering and humorous collection of essays, women lay bare pleasure, fear, longing, survival, heartbreak and intimacy—all that comes with exploring their sexuality.

Out of Time by Paula Martinac. $12.95, 1-58005-020-4. A delightful and thoughtful novel about lesbian history and the power of memory, set in the antiques world of New York City.

Bruised Hibiscus by Elizabeth Nunez. $24.95, 1-58005-036-0. A page-turning, hallucinatory novel that tackles the large themes of colonialism, sexism and racism in the 1950s on the island of Trinidad.

Seal Press publishes many books of fiction and nonfiction by women writers. If you are unable to obtain a Seal Press title from a bookstore, please order from us directly by calling 800-754-0271. Visit our website at www.sealpress.com.